THE PORTAL THIEVES

JAMES E WISHER

SAND HILL PUBLISHING

Copyright © 2020 by James Wisher
All rights reserved.
No part of this book may be reproduced in any form or by any electronic or mechanical means, including information storage and retrieval systems, without written permission from the author, except for the use of brief quotations in a book review.
Edited by: Janie Linn Dullard
Cover art by: B-Ro
062320201.0
ISBN: 978-1-945763-77-9

CHAPTER 1

The square sheet of paper-thin mithril glowed white-hot as Otto poured ether into it. Sweat plastered his tattered work shirt to his back and soaked his hair. The glow was so bright he couldn't even see his workshop in the basement of Franken Manor. He squinted and focused on the ether.

The rune was taking shape. A little nudge on the upper-right corner.

Not too much!

He withdrew the twenty-five-thread ethereal construct just in the nick of time. An instant longer and he would have had to start over for the sixth time. The final bend of the rune settled into place and Otto cut off the flow of ether. The blinding light slowly faded and when he could see clearly again, he studied his work.

This piece was the culmination of a winter of toil. After weeks shifting between his master's tower and the armory, more weeks of practice, and too many failures to count, Otto had finally completed the last rune patch. This one would transform the Garenland portal, turning an impressive if useless monument to treachery into the new master portal. Once all the patches had been put in place, Otto would have full control of the continental portal network.

He grinned and wiped his brow. What he wouldn't give to see the look on Valtan's face when he realized what had happened. His power would be used to bring the continent under Garenland's rule despite the other kingdoms' best attempts to destroy them. It would be a delicious reversal, one that would please his master greatly, though not as much as her former mentor's death.

Otto was still far from being strong enough to grant that wish, assuming he ever did grant it. Killing Valtan would also remove a convenient power source for the portals. Once Otto was an Arcane Lord, he could operate the portals himself, but why waste his magic when Valtan was already doing it for him?

That conversation was still a long way off, but even so he dreaded broaching the subject with Lord Karonin. Otto ran a finger along the smooth, cool metal, tracing the shape of the rune he'd engraved. It glowed in his ethereal vision. He needed to go to the palace and let Wolfric know they were ready to move on to the next phase of the plan. Wolfric was supposed to have agents ready to infiltrate the neighboring kingdoms and place the patches on their portals. It was a risky mission, but absolutely essential.

He slid the mithril sheet into a leather binder he'd designed specifically to hold the six patches. He'd take a quick bath and head over to the palace.

Before Otto could collect the holder, the basement door squeaked open and an unfamiliar voice called, "Lord Shenk? It's time."

He frowned and picked up the folder before walking to the foot of the basement stairs. One of the servants stood at the top. Otto had given strict instructions not to be disturbed. If the idiot had interrupted him during the rune forging, he would have ruined three hours' work.

"Time for what?"

"The baby, my lord. Lady Shenk has gone into labor."

And what exactly did they expect Otto to do? Whatever happened was out of his control. The midwife should be with her; it seemed the old crone had practically lived with them for the last two weeks. Not that she troubled Otto, seeing as how she camped out in Annamaria's room most of the time.

Otto climbed the steps and paused beside the beaming young man. He couldn't have been more than a year or two older than Otto, probably a new hire. "Let me make something clear. When I give an order not to be disturbed, assuming the house isn't on fire, you don't disturb me. This is your first and only warning. Another mistake and I'll see you out the door without references."

The servant's smile had curdled as the blood drained out of his face. "Forgive me, Lord Shenk. I assumed—"

"That was your first mistake. Don't assume, obey."

Otto left him to contemplate his future and turned toward the main staircase. It was a short walk down gilded halls to the dining room. When he entered, he found Edwyn pacing, his white silk robe billowing behind him, the handful of heavily laden plates on the table ignored. In his months at the mansion, this might be the first time Otto had seen Edwyn in the same room as a meal that he wasn't eating.

"Are you alright?" Otto asked.

Edwyn started and turned to face him. Rivulets of sweat ran down his many chins. Clearly pacing wasn't something

Edwyn engaged in often. "Fine, my boy, just nervous. Annamaria let out the most bloodcurdling scream a few moments ago. I'm sure she'll be fine, but I can't help worrying for my baby girl."

Otto made an effort to look concerned. Personally, he hoped Annamaria was in a lot of pain. "Did I ever tell you about the noises my sister-in-law made when she was last with child? They'd have curled your hair. She came through it fine."

That the malformed infant had perished was something best left unsaid.

"Yes, yes, very good. I'm sure you'll want to go up and check on her." Edwyn gave him a look of distaste. "After you clean up perhaps."

"My very plan." Otto nodded to his father-in-law and headed to the staircase.

At the top of the steps a shriek ripped the air. Sounded like matters were proceeding. He turned right, down the carpeted hall and away from his screeching wife. His room was on the opposite side of the mansion from Annamaria's, which suited them both very well.

He ducked inside, washed up, and changed his clothes before stepping back into the hall. His preference would have been to simply go straight to the palace, but for appearances' sake he strode back across the mansion to Annamaria's room. Her chambermaid, Mimi, her uniform stained with sweat, stood guard outside the bedroom door. She shrank into herself as he approached.

Poor girl. They'd had a few run-ins when her loyalty to his wife grew inconvenient and Otto feared she believed he didn't like her. The truth was, Otto respected her loyalty, misplaced though it was. He certainly bore her no ill will. If all the people he had to deal with were as obedient as her, his life would be far easier. Instead he had to deal with liars, cheaters, killers, schemers, and old-fashioned idiots.

"Lord Shenk." Mimi's voice quavered. "I don't think she'd want to see you."

"When has she ever? I assume all is well?"

Mimi didn't get a chance to answer before a final scream rent the air followed a moment later by a high-pitched wail. And so the brat was born. How marvelous. At least he could leave.

Before he could escape, the bedroom door opened and the midwife, a crone in black who looked like something out of a child's nightmares, emerged with a tiny bundle tucked into the crook of her arm. Bald, red-faced, and with her eyes closed, the little girl looked healthy enough.

"I gave your wife something for the pain and now she sleeps," the midwife said. "You wish to hold the child? Also, as the father, it is your duty to name her."

Otto had no wish to name or hold Lothair's brat. Let Annamaria pick out a name for her, he couldn't have cared less.

The reply caught in his throat when she thrust the baby into his chest. Otto caught her with his free hand and cradled her neck with his arm.

He grimaced. "Mimi, take her."

The chambermaid hurried over and collected his burden. Relieved to be free of it, Otto turned back to the midwife. "When she wakes up, tell Annamaria any name she likes is fine with me."

"As you wish." Her tone said she didn't approve.

Had her approval mattered to him, he might have been concerned. As it was, he turned and stalked off toward the front door. He had important matters that required his attention.

The only good thing he could see coming from the new addition to the family was that it should keep his wife busy and thus out of his hair. Not that she'd done anything to trouble him since their conversation last fall, but it was only a matter of time before her hate overcame her fear.

The baby should serve as a powerful reminder of what she had to lose. If that didn't keep her in line, nothing would.

CHAPTER 2

Otto handed one of the mithril patches to Wolfric who looked it all over. They were alone in the library. The king had called an early end to court so they could meet away from prying eyes. Even Borden, the captain of the palace guard, wasn't with them.

That also let Wolfric shed the cumbersome robes of state and make do with a simple black tunic and matching trousers. There were times that the crown seemed to fit Wolfric well and others when Otto wondered if he was truly up to the task. Not that there was anyone else to rule the kingdom in his place.

A simple spell confirmed that they were alone. What they were planning was too sensitive for anyone unnecessary, especially nobles with a tendency to drink too much and run their mouths, to know about their plans. The chances of success were small enough as it was.

The silence and smell of books settled Otto's nerves after the encounter with Annamaria's baby. He could still smell the little thing. He suppressed a shudder and focused on the matter at hand. Lord Karonin had told him that the patches would work, but until they were tested, even she couldn't say for sure.

"It seems... thin," Wolfric said at last.

"It is thin. When it's attached, the patch will fuse with the portal, becoming one with it and rewriting its magic."

"And you're certain this will work?"

Otto nearly laughed. Everything he was doing had never been done before, not even by the Arcane Lords themselves. "I'm not certain of anything. But I know that if we can't seize control of the portals, we have no hope of winning the war and this is the best and only way I can think of to manage that. Should it fail, we'll have to try something else."

"Hardly an optimistic assessment of our chances."

Otto took the patch back and slipped it into the leather binder. "I could lie if it would make you feel better. The truth, my friend, is that I'm making most of this up as I go. Did you find agents to handle the infiltration?"

"Five of my best, all loyal to the death and skilled at both stealth and combat. If anyone can reach the enemy portals, they can. Still, I'm surprised you didn't want to send some of your wizards."

"Despite their abilities, even the most experienced of the new recruits was working in a foundry six months ago. They know nothing about espionage, evasion, or anything else useful. They can't even turn invisible yet. Better for everyone if we let professionals handle this mission."

Wolfric nodded, seeming content to trust Otto's assessment. "I ordered the area around our portal cleared as you requested. My agents will meet us there. What do you say we go test your theory instead of debating?"

"Excellent idea." Otto tried to project more confidence than he felt. If the test failed, he'd have to go back to square one.

They left the library and made their way to the main gate. Along the way, a squad of Borden's men fell in around them. After the debacle last fall, Otto had interviewed every member of the royal guard to make certain of their loyalty. He'd been delighted to find that only a handful were less than committed. Those five had been transferred to the First Legion to join the fight against Straken. The men hadn't complained; in fact, some of them had been relieved.

The walk from the palace to the portal was a relatively short one which was why they hadn't bothered with a carriage. The few people on the streets bowed as they passed, but when the group got close to their destination, the streets grew empty and silent. Directly in front of the massive mithril construct stood five men in basic mercenary gear, leathers, a variety of bladed weapons, and packs over their shoulders.

The men all touched fists to hearts when Wolfric arrived. Otto ignored the display and studied the portal. It only took a moment to locate the master rune. It was carved into the metal at the top of the circle. He took the patch for Garenland's portal out of the folio and turned to address the infiltrators.

"Your mission is a simple one, simple but not easy. At the top of the portal lies the master rune." Otto pointed it out just to be sure. "Your task is to place one of these mithril patches over it. If you can do it without being seen, so much the better, but once it's done, only another patch can restore the portal to its original function. Understand?"

"How are we supposed to reach the master rune?" a slim, deeply tan infiltrator asked. "We can't exactly lean a ladder against it and climb up."

That brought a chuckle from the others and Otto offered

an indulgent smile. Let them banter if it helped relieve the stress.

"You won't have to climb up. Once the patch gets close, the ethereal attraction will draw it into place. Watch."

Otto flicked his wrist and sent the square of mithril flying up toward the top of the portal. As soon as it got within a foot of the master rune, sparks shot out ahead of lines of energy that resembled lightning. The ethereal lightning dragged the patch into place. The instant it touched the portal, the patch seemed to melt into it and vanish.

To any non-wizard that would appear to be the end of the process. But in Otto's magical vision, energy swirled and crackled up and down the portal, changing its flow in both directions. Most importantly, nothing seeped out toward Valtan. His power continued to flow smoothly into the portal. As far as the Arcane Lord would know, nothing had changed. He wouldn't be able to sense anything until Otto activated the portal with the master key he'd gotten from Edwyn and then modified into something more than a ritual item. He could have enchanted anything of course, but he liked the idea of using the worthless trinket Valtan gave them.

"Did it work?" Wolfric asked.

"As far as I can tell, the patch did what it was supposed to do. We won't know for sure until all the others are in place and I activate the new master rune. Are there any more questions before I pass out your patches?"

There weren't, so Otto removed the Rolan patch and asked, "Who's going to Rolan?"

The tan comedian raised his hand. "Oskar, my lord. I have the honor of infiltrating Rolan."

Otto handed him the patch. "Now Lux?"

Another hand went up, this time a younger man, barely thirty. "Henry, my lord."

Otto handed him the patch and the spy stowed it in his pack. The young man had an overconfident look about him. Hopefully he'd be up to the task he'd volunteered for.

"Next, Lasil."

The eldest of the bunch raised his hand. He had already started on a beard that showed plenty of gray. "Luca, my lord."

Otto nodded and handed him the patch. This one, at least, gave the impression that he understood the stakes.

"Next, Tharanault."

"Holt, my lord." The fourth volunteer, a man in his mid-thirties with a nervous, twitchy look about him saluted again.

Otto grimaced but handed him the patch. The final soldier, Korgin, wasn't nearly big enough to pass as a Straken citizen which was fine since there was no way anyone would be able to sneak into Marduke. Otto had spoken to him a bit after he was selected for the mission and found the man as confident as he was obnoxious.

Otto handed Korgin his patch and said, "You'll be going north with the army as my assistant. When the others have finished their missions, we'll run an attack on the city walls. That will be your chance to sneak in while they're distracted. I won't lie, you've probably got the most dangerous task of all."

"I'll manage, my lord," he said, accepting the patch.

"You all know your missions," Wolfric said. "Good luck and heaven watch over you."

The men offered another salute and all but one marched off to begin their missions. Otto knew the details of the various journeys they'd have to make by heart and had a rough timeline in his head, assuming everything went smoothly

Otto smiled to himself. When was the last time anything went smoothly?

He just had to trust that everyone else would do their jobs. That might be the hardest part of the whole thing.

CHAPTER 3

Having seen Wolfric safely back to the palace, Otto turned toward home. He wanted to see how the newest recruits were coming along. Despite the snow, they'd been trickling in all winter. He'd thought maybe a few from the other nations might make it through, but so far they'd only seen Garenlanders. He now had ninety combat-worthy wizards who understood basic attack and defense spells. That should be plenty to go toe to toe with whatever reinforcements Straken brought in.

That said, more was always better. Fifteen were in training right now. With any luck, Master Enoch would have them ready to move in time to join the Northern Army when they reached Marduke. After the drubbing Garenland gave Straken last year, no one seriously expected to encounter resistance before the capital.

As he approached the mansion gates, a young man in a black and gold watch uniform came running from the opposite direction. He looked exhausted as he skidded to a stop in front of Otto.

"Lord Shenk?" the watchman asked between gasps.

"That's right. Can I help you with something?" Otto kept his tone cool, but polite. He'd had his fill of watchmen since their late commander decided to poke his nose into Otto's business. The new man, Adelmar something, was supposed to be totally loyal so hopefully they wouldn't have a repeat of that mess.

"Commander Adelmar wanted me to inform you that a wizard has been murdered."

Otto gave him a hard look. "What happened?"

"We're not sure yet, my lord. He was found an hour ago apparently on his way home from his job at a foundry. His throat was cut and his body left in the street. We haven't found any witnesses yet, but the search has just begun. The commander thought that since you were in charge of the wizards in the army, you'd want to know."

"He was correct. Wait right here. There's something I need to take care of then you can show me to the crime scene."

He left the still-huffing-and-puffing watchman to catch his breath and headed through the gates. A pair of explosions sounded as he made his way to the training grounds. On the range, all fifteen wizards were lined up and gathering ether for another round of fireballs with Enoch watching over them.

"Master."

Enoch turned and smiled. "Lord Shenk, I hadn't expected to see you this morning. I heard the good news, congratulations on your firstborn. We'll try and keep the practice sessions short so as not to disturb mother and daughter more than necessary."

Otto didn't especially care how disturbed they were but nodded his thanks. "There's another matter we need to discuss. Someone killed a wizard this morning. I have no idea if it's a personal thing or if wizards are being targeted, but until we know for sure, I want to take extra measures to keep the trainees safe."

"Of course, but what about the wizards out in the city who weren't strong enough to make the cut? They're the ones in the most danger, assuming this is someone targeting wizards."

"A general warning will be issued and the watch will be keeping an eye out for anything strange. Hopefully we can hunt whoever did this down quickly. And while I hate to sound harsh, keeping the wizards that can fight safe is the priority."

"I'll look after them, never fear."

Otto clapped his master on the shoulder and turned back toward the front gate. The watchman had recovered and was waiting for him. "Let's go."

The walk across the city took most of half an hour. Everyone they passed appeared at ease so word of the murder must not have spread. That was good. Not that murder was unheard of in Garen, but with the war and fears of Straken agents, the less people had to think about the better. A panic would help no one but the killer.

A group of three watchmen was standing at the end of an alley between a foundry and sword smithy. They shifted at once to let Otto and his guide through. Further down, a body covered with a blood-stained white sheet sprawled in the dirt. A single figure, a tall, broad-shouldered man that strained the seams of his uniform, stood nearby studying the ground.

"Commander Adelmar," the watchman said. "I brought Lord Shenk."

The commander looked up from whatever had caught his interest and turned toward Otto. His left eye had been destroyed in a fight and a scar ran diagonally across his forehead and down his cheek. Three days of beard covered his square jaw. Wherever Borden found this guy must have been tough. He looked like he could kill a grizzly with just his hands.

"Lord Shenk." Commander Adelmar's voice was as rough as the rest of him. "I didn't mean for my messenger to trouble you, just to give you the news."

"He didn't trouble me in the least. I feel it's my duty to protect the wizards of this city just as much as the other citizens. Any help I can offer is yours. I'll also direct the Crown's agents in the city to look into the matter."

"I certainly won't turn down the help. When can I meet these agents of yours?"

"I'll arrange something. You should know the man in charge of the group at least. He's an interesting character, but totally loyal. What, exactly, do you think happened here?"

"As best we can tell, whoever killed him came up from behind and cut his throat. It was done fast and smooth, poor bastard probably never even knew someone was there before he was dead. Whoever did this, it wasn't his first kill."

"Him?" Otto asked. "You're certain it was a man?"

"Playing the odds. If it wasn't a man, it was a tall, powerful woman. I'm not saying it's impossible, but out of all the murders I've seen, when a woman was responsible, they used poison or they killed someone they knew."

Otto nodded. "I wasn't questioning your judgement. Did you find anything of note here?"

"No. Whoever did this was a professional. No tracks, no witnesses, no nothing beyond the body. My men are talking to everyone in the area, but I doubt they'll find much. I don't suppose there's anything—" Adelmar wiggled his fingers "— magical you can do?"

"I can kill whoever did this in the most painful way you can imagine, but not until they're found. Keep in touch. I'll be in the city for another week or so before joining the Northern Army."

Adelmar offered a half bow and said, "We'll get to the bottom of it, Lord Shenk, have no doubt."

Otto did have doubts, a great many in fact, but there was nothing he could do about them. His skills, considerable as they were, didn't include hunting down assassins. Creating them, sure. But not hunting them down. Hopefully Adelmar was as skilled as he was loyal. But just to be safe, he'd pay a visit to Allen.

If anyone knew what was happening among the city's criminal element, it would be him and Sin.

CHAPTER 4

Allen groaned and rolled over. Sunlight crept under his office door, sending crazy shadows dancing all over the room. What time was it? Too early for sure, but he doubted he'd get any more sleep now. His head throbbed when he sat up. He didn't usually partake of so much of his own merchandise. What the hell had he even been celebrating? Everything was a blur.

"Don't hog the cover." He turned slowly and looked down at a head of dark hair and a pale, perfect shoulder.

"Sin?"

"Did you think you went to bed with someone else?" She shifted to face him. Even first thing in the morning she was stunning, her eyes weren't even bloodshot.

"I don't remember going to bed at all and since you're here, that's a shame. Were we celebrating something in particular?"

"The last independent gang surrendered and joined my guild. We now control all the criminals in Garen. Well, most of them anyway. There will always be a few independents that refuse to join a guild. They're not a big deal."

It all came back to him. Sin had arrived just as he was getting ready to close and shared the good news. He hadn't seen Lord Shenk in months but was happy to have something to report when he eventually showed up.

And he would, Allen had no doubt of that.

"You look anxious," Sin said as she ran her foot along his calf. "Afraid the boss isn't going to like us fooling around?"

Allen barked a humorless laugh. "I can't imagine he'd care. I was just wondering what he's been up to. Lord Shenk doesn't share his plans with me, but I assumed he'd be around to check on our progress at least once during the winter."

"Maybe he trusts you to do what needs doing." Sin's foot moved higher, reminding Allen that he didn't have any clothes on.

There was a knock on the office door and Ulf said, "We have company. I recommend you get ready, quickly."

"Speak of the devil." Allen climbed out of bed and hunted around for his clothes.

Most of them were on his desk, though happily none stank too badly of the booze they'd drowned in last night. Despite the headache, Allen still dressed in record time. When he finished, he turned to find Sin ready as well. She did make skin-tight black leather look good.

"Shall we?" he asked.

She brushed past him and out the door. Allen hurried to join her. When he emerged, Ulf offered him a steaming mug without comment. Some people might consider his flat, silent look indicated disapproval, but Allen got the same look when he emerged alone and not hungover. It was simply Ulf's default expression.

Allen sipped his hangover cure and hurried to join Sin at the table where Lord Shenk already sat. His employer was dressed in blue and gray today, his mithril sword carefully arranged so as not to get tangled in his chair. Lord Shenk hardly spared a glance at Sin which meant he had something serious on his mind. After all, what man wouldn't want to look at Sin?

"I trust your brain is functioning now," Lord Shenk said.

"Yeah, sorry, we had a late night celebrating last night. The last of the gangs is now under our control." Lord Shenk quirked an eyebrow and Allen winced. "I meant they're under your control of course. Um, what brings you by? It's been a while since you checked in."

"I've been busy." That was it. No explanation, no nothing. Well, Allen couldn't be too surprised. "A wizard has been murdered. The watch believes it was done by a professional. Since you now control all the criminals in Garen, I trust finding whoever did this will be a simple matter for you."

Lord Shenk seemed to be in a worse mood than usual today. "Was the victim someone you knew?"

"No, but I dislike the precedent. If someone gets away with killing a wizard, how long before someone else thinks, 'If they could do it why can't I?' Plenty of people still fear and distrust wizards. Getting to the bottom of this matter is your highest priority. Are you familiar with the new watch commander?"

"We haven't met," Allen said.

"I know him by reputation," Sin said. "Adelmar is a known hard case. He wouldn't have been my first choice for a replacement."

"The main thing you need to know about him is that he's absolutely loyal to the Crown. With him in charge, there will be no repeat of any inconvenient investigations like last fall. You'll be working together on this matter." Lord Shenk raised a hand to cut off Allen's objections. "Not directly together, more of an information-sharing arrangement. That's why I spared you, remember, to gather information for the kingdom. He should be along shortly to meet you."

Sin stood. "I believe that's my cue to leave."

"I don't mind," Lord Shenk said. "But if he knows you're working for me, it might make things easier for you should the two of you run into each other when he's carrying out his official duties."

Sin sat back down. "I take your point. Being on good terms with the watch commander might be a prudent thing."

Lord Shenk rose, walked to the door, and opened it. Standing just outside was a burly man in a watch uniform, his arm raised to knock. Allen gave a slight shake of his head. Wizards were strange as well as scary. Whatever the watch commander wanted, it couldn't be any worse than the stuff Lord Shenk had already asked them to do.

Hopefully.

CHAPTER 5

Four days had passed since the first wizard was killed and there'd been no sign of the assassin. On the one hand, Otto was pleased that no more wizards had died, but on the other he was annoyed that this search was distracting him from war preparations.

The Northern Army would be leaving for the border at the end of the month. The plan was a three-pronged invasion that swept across all the primary roads and neutralized every town of any size before moving on to besiege Marduke. Otto hoped to have the portals under his control by early summer at the latest. They couldn't attack the Straken capital until that was done.

He sighed and stretched. The foundries were letting out and he was perched on a flat roof not far from the metal-working district. He'd been watching the area every night since the first killing. The wizards had all been warned about the danger and now traveled in pairs or small groups. They also kept a constant ethereal barrier up as they walked. Most of them were so weak that it would only slow a dagger, not stop one. But more important for Otto, each of the wizards now glowed in the ether, making them easy to track.

As his gaze wandered the streets, he spotted one glow traveling by itself. He focused on that one, extending his sight for a better look. The wizard was a young man barely out of his teens. Otto smiled at the irony of thinking of someone two years his senior as a young man. He swore there were days he felt more like an old man than an eighteen-year-old.

The wizard worked his way down the dark street, completely unaware that Otto was keeping watch over him. As he passed an alley something shifted in the shadows. Only Otto's magical sight allowed him to witness the assassin leaping out, dagger clenched in a reverse grip, to strike down the hapless wizard.

Or at least to try to strike him down. Working magic at a distance, in combat, wasn't easy, but Otto managed to twist the dagger aside enough that it only grazed the young man's right arm.

He yelped and scrambled away.

The assassin wrestled with the uncooperative dagger long enough to allow the wizard to put some distance between them. He turned and hurled fire.

A graceful backflip carried the assassin clear of the blast. By the light of the flames, Otto saw the swell of her chest. No wonder they couldn't find the killer, they'd been looking for a man.

She fled through the streets, running full tilt, leaping any obstacle that got in her way. Otto had no trouble following her to a warehouse ten blocks away. He marked the location, returned his sight to his body, and became one with the ether.

An instant later he appeared outside the warehouse door. Even for a wizard of Otto's power, walking into an almost certain trap required a moment of thought. He could summon the others, but by the time they arrived, the assassin might have fled. This was his chance to end the threat, he couldn't let it go to waste.

He enhanced his night vision as much as possible then wrapped a twelve-thread barrier around his body. That would turn aside anything short of a close-range heavy crossbow bolt. Finally, he enhanced his strength and gathered ether in his hands. The instant the assassin showed herself, she was dead.

While he'd first thought the warehouse looked abandoned, when he tried the door, it opened without a sound. His enhanced vision rendered everything in shades of gray. Not that there was much to see. Some broken boards littered the floor. Mixed in with them was the occasional scrap of steel. He stepped through and sealed the door behind him. She wouldn't escape that way.

Otto walked slowly through the warehouse, every sense alert for movement. She had to be here somewhere. Given the nearly empty space, she should be easy to spot. He scanned the rafters, but nothing lurked there.

Where the hell was she?

He walked deeper into the warehouse. Maybe there was a door in the back. He hadn't noticed one when he looked the building over earlier, but sometimes you missed things when you looked at them through the ether.

But not this time. He walked all the way to the far wall and found no other way out. He'd sensed no magic about the assassin, so she couldn't have teleported away. What was he missing?

Otto looked at the floor. A trapdoor maybe? He sent feelers of ether into the wood. If there were any voids, he'd find them.

Sure enough, five minutes later he located a tunnel. The entrance was so well made, the seam was nearly invisible. His dark vision didn't show enough detail, but now that he knew where it was...

His enhanced fist slammed into the floor and through the wood. He ripped the door free of its hinges and tossed it aside. The entrance was about three feet in diameter and ran at least thirty feet down. The ladder on the side looked older than Otto and he was reluctant to try his luck.

Look before you leap was always a solid idea. He extended his sight down the tunnel. A few seconds later it branched. He went left and found yet more branches twenty yards on.

His sight returned to his body. Searching the maze would take forever on his own, even with magic. For now, at least, he had to accept that she was gone.

Otto left the warehouse and retraced his steps back to where the injured wizard had fallen. As he hoped, Commander Adelmar and a handful of his men were there. Someone had bound the wizard's wound and a pair of watchmen were talking to him.

He motioned Adelmar off to one side. "Any luck?" the watch commander asked.

"A little. First, one reason you're having so much trouble finding the assassin is that the killer is a woman, about six feet tall, and strong. We've got guards at all the gates now, but I doubt they would have given a woman even a passing look, at least as a threat. I lost her in a network of tunnels under an abandoned warehouse. It's a maze down there and I didn't know what I'd run into."

"I didn't think you were afraid of anything," Adelmar said.

Otto smiled. "Everyone's afraid of something, Commander. And even wizards have limits. I haven't accomplished all I have by being stupid. If you want to start searching, I'll speak to Sin about the tunnels. I suspect the thieves might know more about them than we do."

"That wouldn't take much," Adelmar said. "I didn't even know they were there."

"Neither did I. Hopefully we can find her before anyone else gets hurt."

"How many six-foot-tall women can there be in Garen? If there's more than a handful, I'll eat my uniform. Now that we know what to look for, we'll find her, no problem."

Otto hoped he was right, but somehow doubted it would be so simple.

CHAPTER 6

After wrapping up his night of assassin hunting and grabbing a few hours' sleep, Otto made the short walk to the Crow's Nest. The villa hadn't changed since his last visit, same gray paint with gold accents, same dour butler that answered the door, same half-assed collection of decorations in the parlor. At least the old lady that played the part of Lady Crow didn't put in an appearance. After she tried to poison him during his last visit, he found it difficult not to want to melt her brain. He shouldn't take it personally, but he did.

While the butler went to fetch Sin, Otto settled into one of the parlor's overstuffed chairs. The hatchet-faced man in the painting over the fireplace glowered down at him. Otto ignored it and tried to figure out how the assassin had found her way around the city so easily. Like he told Adelmar, the guards probably wouldn't consider a woman a threat. But she still had to have help. Otto had lived in Garen for a year and he knew nothing about the tunnels, there was no way someone from Straken could know about them.

His thoughts were derailed by Sin's arrival. She wore all black as was her habit, but instead of painted-on leather, today she wore a dress slit up to her hip on both sides. While it showed her legs off to great effect, if she was hoping to distract him, she was doomed to failure.

"Lord Shenk, what a nice surprise. I assumed you'd use Allen when you needed information." She sat across from him and crossed her legs, revealing a smooth expanse of pale thigh.

"What do you know about the tunnels under the city?"

She blinked, clearly taken by surprise by the question. "Not a lot. The guild uses them from time to time to move around unseen. They're a maze and not terribly stable. More than one thief has died down there when a tunnel collapsed unexpectedly. Why the interest?"

"Our assassin is using them to evade the watch. She's got skill, but there's no way a local isn't helping her."

"She? The assassin is a woman?"

"Yes, from Straken I assume. Though we won't know for sure until her interrogation. Now, who do you think is helping her?"

"None of my people, I can assure you." She kept her tone even but the whites of her eyes were visible around her irises. She must fear Otto suspected her of betrayal.

"I'm entirely confident of your loyalty, Sin, have no fear on that account. You mentioned a few rogue elements of the underworld that resisted your takeover. One of them would certainly be a prime suspect."

"I'll put some feelers out, see what I can learn."

"Good. Make a list of everyone that has refused to join us. If you can't find answers, I will. Oh, and avoid the tunnels for a while. The watch is going to be searching them."

"I don't know if he'll listen," Sin said. "But I'd advise

Adelmar against going down there. It's really easy to get turned around or run into an ambush."

"I'll pass along your advice. If I didn't fear collapsing half the city, I'd bring down the tunnels myself. I'll stop by in a couple days to see what you've learned." Otto stood and nodded to Sin.

"No need to hurry off." She leaned back and smiled.

Some people didn't know when to quit. It seemed to be her nature, so Otto ignored the offer and showed himself out. He needed to visit the palace library. Hopefully there would be something about the tunnels in the history books. He didn't want to bother Lord Karonin with such a minor matter unless he had no other options.

○

The walk to the palace from the Crow's Nest took only a few minutes. The guards waved Otto through and he went straight to the library. Wolfric had enough on his plate without bothering him with this. In truth, Otto had little hope of finding anything of value. Assuming the tunnels were made recently and by criminals, the odds of them making it into any historical record were slim to none.

When he arrived, two palace guards stood outside the library doors. The men snapped to attention at his approach. The only reason these doors would be guarded was if Wolfric was inside.

"No court today?" Otto asked.

"There were only a handful of petitioners, Lord Shenk, so His Majesty ended the session early."

No doubt Wolfric was thrilled about that. While the king hadn't complained much lately, his distaste for court matters was well known. Lord Karonin once asked Otto if he would like to rule directly instead of letting Wolfric be the figurehead. His answer had been an immediate and emphatic no. He hated dealing with fools even more than Wolfric. Two days on the throne and he'd probably blast every noble in the kingdom.

Otto shuddered at the memory and stepped into the library. The sight of so many books always brought a smile to his face. Outside of the armory, this was the largest collection of books in the kingdom, if not the continent. While the content of the collection might be of less interest, there was still plenty of value.

Wolfric sprawled in one of the couches, a leather-bound volume in his lap. He looked up from his reading and smiled. "This is a surprise. What brings you by?"

"I need some information. I was going to search the stacks, but since you probably know every book in the place, maybe you can speed my hunt. Do you know anything about the tunnels running under the city?"

Wolfric's brow furrowed. "There are tunnels under the city?"

Otto settled in an empty chair across from his friend. "Indeed, a veritable maze of them. I assume Adelmar informed you of the murder the other night?"

Wolfric shook his head. "I haven't spoken to the man and Borden didn't mention anything. Tell me."

Otto gave him the condensed version ending with the assassin escaping him last night. "The watch is busy searching the tunnels and my agents are scouring the underworld. Someone will find her, I'm sure. I'm more worried about the dangers the tunnels present long term, especially whether they extend under the outer wall and into Gold Ward. Should our enemies learn of it, the capital could be in danger."

"Why am I just hearing about this now?" Wolfric tossed his book onto a nearby table. "The situation sounds serious."

"It may be serious and it may be minor. I suspect no one wanted to trouble you with this until they knew for sure. If the tunnels only run under the business district, they shouldn't be a problem and neither should running down the assassin. On the other hand, if the situation is dire, they could tell you when they knew for sure."

"I don't like being babied. Anything that threatens the city should be brought to my attention at once. I'll make that clear to Borden this afternoon. As to books about the tunnels, I've never seen them mentioned in any books I read, and I've read most of them."

Otto nodded, not terribly surprised. "Then I won't waste my time searching."

It appeared that Allen and Sin would have to find his answers. This was Sin's first real test and Otto was keen to see how she managed. If the thief turned out to be nothing but a beautiful distraction, he'd have to reconsider his decision to let her live.

CHAPTER 7

"Lord Shenk came to see you?" Allen asked.

He and Sin were sitting together in the corner of the Sprite's common room. The crowd was modest tonight; only half the seats were filled along with a few serious drinkers at the bar. He'd seen plenty of worse nights and wasn't about to complain. The girls were bouncing back and forth between the tables and Ulf was handling the bar. For a change everything was working the way it was supposed to.

"He did," Sin said. "I admit I was surprised. I assumed everything would run from you to him and back again. Of course, when he showed up at my door, I wasn't about to say he couldn't come in. The business with the assassin seems to have him on edge."

"An assassin that targets wizards would have me on edge as well. Of course, our assurance that we had the underworld wrapped up then this happens makes us look bad. For our continued good health, I think we'd best find out who's helping her and take them down."

"I got that impression as well. Fortunately, there can't be

more than a handful of independent actors that know the tunnels well enough to guide someone around. We should be able to run through them in a couple nights."

Allen nodded. "The tavern closes in two hours; shall we head out then?"

"Yes. How well do you know Lord Shenk?"

Allen stared for a moment, taken aback by the question. "Not very well. He doesn't exactly confide his darkest secrets with me. Why?"

"I've tried to seduce him twice and both times he brushed me off. That's not a reaction I'm used to getting from men."

Allen could certainly understand that. She filled out her tight black leather outfit very well indeed. There was just enough skin showing to hint at what was available, but not so much that she couldn't move freely. Sin was easily the most beautiful woman Allen had ever met, and he'd met his share over the years.

"That look you're giving me now is what I expect." Her smile brought to mind a cat looking at a cornered mouse. "He looks at me with disdain, like I'm beneath him and not in a good way."

Allen shrugged. "The first time you met, you did try to kill him. He may simply see you as a risk not worth taking. And given his luck with beautiful women, I can't really blame Lord Shenk for avoiding another one."

"Troubles on the home front?"

He laughed. "If you think I'm answering that, you're crazy."

They spent the rest of the evening chatting about less dangerous subjects and soon enough closing time arrived. When the last of the guests had gone, Allen, Ulf, and Sin left the Sprite and headed for the rougher parts of the city. Sin took point, walking confidently through the shadowy streets.

Allen was happy to follow along and enjoy the view. Lord Shenk didn't know what he was missing.

The buildings grew shabbier by the stride. A few people were out, leaning against walls, daggers drawn, generally looking intimidating. One shirtless gent with a massively muscled chest was amusing himself by cutting thin lines across his pecs with a sharp knife. From the scarring, it looked to be a favorite hobby.

It was a relief when they walked by and he didn't move. Allen adjusted his sword to allow for an easier draw. Over the years, he'd visited plenty of tough spots to gather information, but there were areas Allen refused to go. Tonight it seemed he was going to pay them a visit.

"I've visited more appealing slaughterhouses," Allen said. "Where are we going?"

"A dive where thieves hang out. Whatever you do, don't draw that sword. If you bare steel, I won't be able to protect you. This is neutral territory. Threats are fine, but violence is forbidden."

"By who? I thought you ran all these places."

"No one runs the Kingfisher but King. He's the only man I've met that scares me even close to as much as Lord Shenk."

"Is he a wizard?"

"Hardly. King used to be a river pirate, ran his own boat. He retired here about ten years ago and opened the Kingfisher. The first three people that started trouble in his place ended up dead and carved into pieces. No one has tried again and everyone obeys the rules."

They rounded a corner and found the first brightly lit building since leaving the Sprite. The Kingfisher stood out from the other places in the neighborhood. It lacked broken windows, no one had tried to set it on fire, and the front door was hung straight. There was no guard at the door. In fact, the toughs that had been littering the landscape for the past few blocks were absent.

Sin went right through the door and Allen hurried to catch up. Inside, the Kingfisher was dark and smoky. A haze from pipeweed and other intoxicants hung in the air. Allen wasn't averse to a drink, but there were a few things he'd prefer not to get hooked on.

A quick look around the common room revealed why there were no toughs outside; they were all inside drinking. Allen had never seen so many people missing pieces of their anatomy in one place. The clientele here made the mercenaries at the Rusty Arms look like members of high society.

The decor certainly screamed ex-pirate. There were ropes hanging from the ceiling, hurricane lanterns fitted with Lux crystals dangling from chains to light the room, and a big ship's wheel over the bar. Standing under the wheel was a man big and broad enough to be from Straken. All he lacked was a beard and a fur-trimmed cloak. If that wasn't King, then Allen didn't know who might be.

Every eye in the place followed Sin as she made her way to the bar. If Allen ever wanted to sneak somewhere, he'd just have Sin go in first. There wouldn't be a soul interested in him.

She leaned on the bar and smiled at the barman. "Long time, King."

"Sin. You're not going to make trouble for me, are you?" King's voice was deep and harsh from too much smoke.

"Of course not. I know the rules as well as anyone. I just need some information." Before he could complain she raised a hand. "Not about any of the locals. There's a Straken assassin running around in our tunnels. If we don't deal with her, the powers that be will."

"The powers that be? You mean your new master, the king's chief advisor?"

"Lord Shenk would certainly be at the top of that list." Sin didn't ask, but Allen couldn't help wondering how King knew about their arrangement with Lord Shenk. He didn't wonder enough to butt into the conversation, though. "She must have a local connection. Whoever it is, is making life difficult for all of us."

"You think it's one of the independents?" King asked.

"Who else?"

"I'll give you one clue, but only because you're so beautiful. Your problem is closer to home. Very close to home."

Sin's frown was the first ugly expression Allen had seen on her. "One of my people, you're certain?"

"You've gotten all you're going to get from me. Unless you want a drink."

"No, thanks King."

Sin motioned them toward the door. As soon as they were outside Allen asked, "Did that mean something to you?"

"Unfortunately. There are only a handful of people I allow into the Crow's Nest. It has to be one of them. One of my most trusted people. When I find out which one it is, I'm going to skin them alive."

Allen swallowed the lump in his throat, suddenly glad he wasn't part of her inner circle.

CHAPTER 8

Sin sat in her room in the Crow's Nest and brooded over the information King had shared. One of her people had betrayed her. It was hard to believe, but King had never lied to her, as far as she knew. It also made a certain amount of sense. Her own circle was the last place she'd look for someone working with a Straken assassin. Now she needed to figure out who did it.

She'd left Allen at his tavern. This was something she needed to handle on her own. As an underworld leader and a woman, any sign of weakness was liable to get her killed. Besides, she needed to prove her value to Lord Shenk lest he decide to replace her himself. Sin allowed herself no illusions about his loyalty to her. She and Allen were useful means to an end, not friends. If it came down to it, Lord Shenk would kill them both without a second thought.

Sitting wasn't helping so she got up and paced. Her room held only a bed and dresser so there was plenty of room to move around. She immediately dismissed the old woman and the butler. They were hired hands who she doubted even knew about the tunnels. No, it had to be one of her long-term associates.

Sin stopped dead in her tracks. Thomas. It had to be him. Since she'd met Allen, she'd been spending all her free time with the handsome tavern keeper, both to get a better handle on her situation and because he was a fun time. Thomas always had a jealous streak, never mind that his job was basically to seduce women for the guild so they could either be robbed or blackmailed. Being ignored by a woman was exactly the sort of thing that would compel him to betray her trust.

Maybe she was wrong, but Sin doubted it. No one else made sense. She turned toward the door. First thing she needed to do was collect a couple of her guys. While she was a fair hand with a dagger, Sin had no illusions about her chances in a one-on-one fight with the bigger and stronger Thomas, and if the assassin was there, forget it.

An hour later, midafternoon on a beautiful spring day, Sin and two of her foot soldiers, Jurgen and Eckhart, both of whom had been with her for years and had proven their loyalty many times, approached Thomas's flat. Her enforcers were armed with swords and bucklers and wore heavy leather armor. Sin had taken time to belt on a brace of throwing knives. If she could help it, Sin wanted to avoid a close-up fight.

"Are you sure Thomas betrayed us, boss?" Jurgen asked.

"Not at all. If I'm wrong, I'll be happy to apologize. If I'm right, I'll cut his heart out. Just make certain you don't let your guard down until we're sure either way."

"We know the drill, boss," Eckhart said. "No need to worry."

Eckhart's overconfidence was what worried her. Thomas was known as a fop among the guild's enforcers, but he was a fair fighter. He'd been making his living as a mercenary when she recruited him. One look at his pretty face and she knew his talent was wasted swinging a sword. But that didn't mean he'd forgotten how.

The curtains of his second-floor flat were pulled shut. That didn't mean anything in itself, but it put her instantly on alert. Eckhart went up the stairs first and Sin brought up the rear. She stayed on the steps out of the way while the guys tried the door. It opened easily. Eckhart looked at her and she nodded.

They went in hard and fast. Sin hurried up behind them.

There was silence from inside and a moment later Jurgen said, "Nobody home, boss."

Sin wasn't surprised, but this was the most likely place to check. Now she needed to figure out what the second most likely place was. Maybe if she looked around, she could get an idea.

The flat looked pretty much as she remembered. Sin preferred to have Thomas visit her at the Crow's Nest, but she'd popped in a few times just for kicks. The living room was clean save for a few spots of dust. She moved into the bedroom. Like the living room, there wasn't much to go on. Even the closet was empty.

Maybe after Lord Shenk's visit Thomas had gotten nervous and found a new love nest. If that was the case, she was in trouble. He hadn't said a word to her about moving. That fact argued that he'd been planning to betray her somehow for a while.

"This is a flop." Sin emerged from the bedroom and moved toward the door. "Wherever he is, it isn't here."

Jurgen and Eckhart took a step toward the door. The moment they did, Sin heard a creak.

She spun just in time to see a long, lean figure slide out of the fireplace. Her entire body was covered in black cloth save for a small slit where a pair of glittering blue eyes stared out.

"Ware behind!" Sin shouted.

They turned and raised their bucklers before charging the slender figure in black.

A pair of curved blades appeared in her hands as if by magic.

The instant those weapons appeared a chunk of lead formed in Sin's stomach. The assassin knew what she was doing.

Sin drew one of her throwing daggers and watched for an opening. If she was smart, she would have run, but leaving her men behind stuck in her craw. Eckhart and Jurgen had been with her for years and she owed it to them to help if she could.

The first blow from the assassin's blades struck Eckhart's buckler. He countered with a swipe of his sword that missed by an inch. The assassin bent out of the way with superhuman flexibility.

Jurgen tried to take advantage of her movement, but the assassin was ready.

As soon as he closed in, she spun away from his blade and stabbed him in the back of the neck. Jurgen went down and didn't move.

Eckhart roared and waded in, trading skill for raw power.

It wasn't a good trade.

The assassin evaded his first powerful strike and countered with a double thrust that took him through the throat and arm pit.

Just like that the battle was over. Sin turned to run and ended up slamming into Thomas's chest. She'd been so focused on the battle, she hadn't heard him come up behind her. He grabbed her right wrist and squeezed until her dagger clattered to the landing.

"Hello, darling," Thomas said. "It's been far too long since you paid me a visit."

CHAPTER 9

Allen had been awake for half an hour and was halfway through his first mug of hangover cure when a single dull thud sounded on the tavern door. He looked at Ulf who shook his head. Considering what usually happened when Ulf answered the door, Allen didn't blame his friend for not wanting to get it. In fact, Allen wasn't all that eager to go himself. Weighing his concerns against his desire not to get zapped by lightning if it was Lord Shenk, Allen reluctantly climbed to his feet.

As a compromise, he collected a dagger from behind the bar before crossing the common room to the door. He opened it a crack and peeked out. No one there. That was both a relief and a surprise. Assuming it wasn't some kid playing a prank, who would just knock and run?

He opened the door the rest of the way and finally noticed the cheap dagger stuck into the wood. It was holding a scrap of parchment. A note delivered with a dagger couldn't be good news. He pulled the blade free and shut the door.

"What is it?" Ulf asked.

Allen shrugged and started reading. As he feared, it wasn't good news. Someone had Sin and wanted him and Lord Shenk to come to the foundry section to negotiate for her life. There was no signature but given that Sin had been searching for whoever betrayed the guild, he had a fair idea who grabbed her. The question was, what did he owe the beautiful thief? Not a great deal, since he'd only tumbled her a few times. They shared an employer and that was basically all. Replacing her wouldn't be that hard.

On the other hand, if they just let her be killed, it wouldn't inspire much loyalty in the other thieves. He sighed. Though he could hardly believe what he was thinking, Allen had to go see if he could save her. It was a stupid idea to even consider, but the payoff might be worthwhile.

"I need to get ready," Allen said. "Take this note to Lord Shenk. If he decides to do nothing, I'm probably dead, so try and be persuasive."

Ulf quickly scanned the letter and asked, "Why are you doing this for her? There are other women in the city."

"I'm hoping to secure her loyalty and that of her followers."

That wasn't the whole truth. The fact was he liked her, probably more than he should, but as Ulf said there were plenty of other women to choose from. What was it about her that made him willing to risk his life? Allen didn't know, but he had made up his mind.

Ulf was long gone when Allen emerged from his office dressed and armed. With any luck, Lord Shenk would be along soon to back him up. With a lot of luck, if he was being honest. Unless he'd badly misjudged their employer, Lord Shenk didn't exactly consider them friends. Allen's main hope was that he considered them valuable enough to rescue.

Allen knocked once on the wooden door, whispered a

silent prayer to any listening angel and set out for the foundry district. It wasn't a long walk. In fact, the place where he was supposed to meet the assassin's helper was only a couple blocks from where he used to meet Crane when he had information to sell.

Those had been the days. No politics, no assassins, and most of all no wizards.

Oh, well. Allen wasn't the sort to brood. He had a new life now and he wasn't eager to lose it. The fact that they wanted to meet implied that there was some hope of a peaceful way out. If they wanted a war, it would have been Sin's head stuck in his door, not a note.

The streets and buildings grew sootier as he made his way through the foundry district. When the rains came, the streets would run black as the collected ash was washed off. The first shower of spring was especially nasty and he was glad the Sprite was far enough away to avoid the worst of the mess.

He passed the alley where he used to meet with Crane and kept going. When he reached the meeting spot all Allen found was an empty building. A sign on the wobbly door warned against going inside and that the building was due to be torn down in a few weeks. As private meeting places went, this one certainly fit the bill.

The ceiling had collapsed, leaving rafters and chunks of broken timber lying on the floor. A small section was clear of debris. Allen bent down and found a small handhold. He lifted the trapdoor and shook his head at the rickety ladder waiting. A flickering light indicated someone was home. Taking a deep breath to steady his nerves, Allen started down.

The ladder creaked when he put his weight on the first rung, but it held. Rung by rung he climbed to the earthen floor.

At the bottom he let out the breath he'd been holding. Dying there would have been a hell of a way to end things.

"Where's the wizard?" a harsh voice asked.

Allen turned and walked down a short passage. Thomas and a tall, blond woman dressed in a skintight black bodysuit stood on either side of Sin, who dangled from chains hammered into a timber that ran the length of the ceiling. While she didn't look comfortable, at least no one had tortured her.

"I said," the woman repeated. "Where is the wizard? Does he want this bitch's blood on his hands?"

"I've passed your message on to Lord Shenk," Allen said. "Whether he'll come or not I can't say. As to having Sin's blood on his hands, I doubt he'd care over much. So, as long as I'm here, shall we discuss your demands?"

"I demand the wizard present himself for execution," the assassin said. "All wizards must die for the lives they took in Straken last year. Your Lord Shenk most of all. His life for hers, that's the deal."

Allen winced. No way was Lord Shenk going to sacrifice himself for Sin. He'd hoped for a peaceful end to the standoff, but now...

No, the only way this could end was with blood.

CHAPTER 10

Otto sat on the hard floor of his bedroom and focused on pulling ether into his body. He'd gained even more power and control over the winter. Forging the mithril patches had pushed him beyond anything he'd imagined. The amount of focus and concentration it took to weave the spells into the silvery metal nearly broke him, but in the end, he'd mastered it and become stronger.

That was all well and good, but he refused to rest on his accomplishments. He could now wield thirty threads for short periods and twenty-five with ease. He felt certain that he was now the second-most-powerful living wizard after Lord Valtan. The problem was the gap that remained between them was still vast. And so every free moment he got, Otto practiced, strengthening his body and refining his control.

He was just about to try and push through and add a thirty-first thread of ether to his effort when someone knocked on the bedroom door. Exhaling and releasing the power he'd gathered, Otto rose and strode over to the door.

Timothy, one of the house pages, stood outside, a scrap of parchment held in his hand. "Message for you, Lord Shenk."

Otto took the scrap and started reading. The note was short and to the point. It seemed the assassin had captured Sin and now wanted him and Allen to come negotiate for her life. Otto didn't negotiate with assassins, certainly not for the life of a thief. But that didn't mean he would simply let someone get away with harming one of his subordinates. That would make him look weak, something Otto couldn't abide.

"The messenger is waiting for a reply, my lord," Timothy said.

Otto had been so engrossed in planning that he forgot the boy was still standing in his doorway. "Tell him I'll deal with it and we'll meet at the Sprite."

"You'll handle it and meet at the Sprite. Understood." Timothy bowed and hurried away.

Otto closed and relocked the door. The time had come to test his powers once again. He settled back on the floor and sent his sight flying. It was a simple matter to home in on the rune he'd placed on Sin's neck. Soon he found himself soaring across the city to the foundry district. Then under it.

In a chamber connected to the tunnel system the assassin used in her escape, he found Sin bound and hanging from a pair of chains. Allen stood facing two others, a tall blond woman that had to be the assassin and Thomas the seducer.

So that was the fool helping Straken's agent. Hopefully they could capture him alive so he could die slowly for betraying Garenland.

Now, how best to handle this? The simplest way was certainly best. He sent a pair of threads into the iron chains that held Sin then shot them into Thomas and the assassin. Both threads fizzled without binding either target.

Otto frowned. That should have worked. He'd woven the magic exactly as he would have done had he used his ring as the iron source. The distance shouldn't have mattered. Was it because he wasn't in physical contact with the iron that the resonance failed? He didn't know and didn't have time to figure it out now.

Thomas drew a knife and stepped toward Sin. Whatever Allen said didn't please her captors.

Plan B then. Otto wove a thick blade of ether to slice through the manacles holding Sin. She thrashed, making it hard for him to cut the steel without slitting her wrists at the same time.

He wasted precious ether to send his voice to the chamber right next to her ear. "Calm down," he whispered.

Sin stiffened. Hopefully Thomas and his partner would think she reacted in fear. Either way, Otto was running out of time. He finished slicing through the manacles just as Thomas moved to within a few inches of her.

She dropped to the floor and before Thomas could move kicked him right between the legs.

The assassin opened her mouth and drew her blades. Otto didn't know what she said, but clearly his agents were in trouble.

He needed a distraction, a quick one.

Otto agitated the ether, conjuring a burst of blinding light.

With a thought he returned his senses to his body and became one with the ether. An instant later he emerged in the cavern, flicked his ring, and bound the assassin. Thomas was lying on the floor in a heap of pain. Otto bound him as well just to be safe then turned to Sin and Allen.

"I see you smoked out the assassin. Well done," he said with only partial sarcasm. They had completed the task, albeit in a less than efficient manner. If Otto had been gone with the army, they would have been in dire straits indeed.

"When I sent Ulf, I didn't know if you'd come," Allen said.

Before Otto could answer, Sin leapt at him, wrapped her arms around his neck, and kissed him full on the lips. When she finally came up for breath she said, "Thank you, Lord Shenk. I thought I was dead for sure."

Otto gently disengaged from the thoroughly distracting woman. "You both seem surprised that I would come help you. I'm not sure what I did or said to make you think that way, but rest assured, I reward loyalty with loyalty. Good agents are hard to find, especially ones that have proven themselves loyal. In all of Garenland you will find no better friend than me."

He turned and looked down at Thomas who, while still curled up in a ball of pain, was now rigid as stone. "You will also find no worse enemy."

"What are you going to do with these two?" Sin asked.

"Hang them of course. Though I think I'll break every bone in Thomas's body first. The assassin, though certainly an enemy of the kingdom, is at least a loyal soldier of Straken. I respect that, even if I can't overlook it."

Sin glared daggers of hate at Thomas. "I was hoping to catch him myself so I could peel off his skin but having all his bones broken is a good second choice. I just wish I could be there to watch."

"I can arrange that if you'd like," Otto said. "Oh, I almost forgot."

He pointed at the assassin and sent a single thread into her brain. A blast of lightning followed, making the backs of her eyes glow.

"There, I don't think she'll be causing any trouble now. Find Adelmar and guide him here. I want to get these two into custody." He smiled at Sin. "Don't worry, Thomas won't be questioned. He'll be heading straight to the palace torture chamber. Enemies of Garenland must learn that there's a steep price to pay for betrayal. I'll order him held until I arrive. I can walk you through the guards if you want to watch or help."

"I can't think of a better way to spend the evening. Thank you, my lord."

"Will you be joining us, Allen?" Otto asked.

"No, I need to get the tavern ready to open." The blood had drained from the man's face.

Otto knew how he felt. Not that long ago, he would have been sick at the prospect of watching Father torture one of his prisoners. Now, it was just another tool in his kit. A weapon to make his enemies fear him. He wondered sometimes if this lack of empathy meant something was wrong with him, but in the end decided that it made him stronger and nothing else mattered.

CHAPTER 11

Otto sat in the royal dining room and sipped tea. He was supposed to meet Wolfric before joining the Northern Army. Two days had passed since the assassin and her accomplice were captured and hung. Otto was happy to be rid of them and to have the issue closed.

There was no grand spectacle; neither of them warranted it. The capital was secure again and that was what mattered.

Sin had seemed to thoroughly enjoy watching her former subordinate thrash and scream. What was the saying about a woman scorned? Otto accepted the necessity of hurting his enemies but doubted he'd ever actually enjoy watching people suffer. Well, maybe Annamaria, he still hated her, nearly as much as she hated him, but at least she had the brat to keep her occupied. He hadn't laid eyes on her in weeks and that was fine.

With the infiltrators all on their way to the various capitals to seize control of their portals, it was time to get the Northern Army moving. The plan was to have Marduke in sight by the time all the patches had been put in place. The timing would be tricky since he had no way of knowing how long it would take for them to complete their missions. Then again, no one ever said taking over an entire continent would be easy.

The dining room door clanged open and Wolfric breezed in, his robe trailing along behind. "Sorry for making you wait, my friend."

Otto chuckled. "The king never apologizes, Wolfric. Besides, the tea here is excellent."

Wolfric dropped into a chair and Otto poured him a cup, passing it over with an ether tentacle. Such little displays of magic never ceased to amuse his friend.

"I understand from Borden that we have you to thank once again for making the capital safe." Wolfric took a sip of his tea. "I never would have believed Straken would send a female assassin. I didn't even know they had female soldiers in their army."

"I'm not sure they do," Otto said. "I'd wager this one was unique or at least rare. Don't worry, the watch has been instructed not to let anyone, man or woman, into the city without a thorough search of them and their belongings. It will slow down entry times, but I think the delay is worth it, at least until the war is over."

"No argument here. When do you head north?"

"This afternoon. I'll be jumping back and forth since I need to monitor the portal as well. I can keep you appraised of our movements and any resistance we face."

"Excellent. I want to finish things this year. The longer it takes, the more the nobles will grumble."

"Once trade is restored and their tax revenue increases, you can be sure they'll be silent again. Did you think any more about how you want to organize the empire once we assume control of the other countries?"

Wolfric closed his eyes and sighed. "Lux and Lasil might work as provinces with the current rulers downgraded to governors, but Straken, Rolan, and Tharanault will never accept Garenland's rule except at the tip of a sword. Occupying forces will be necessary and we should certainly expect some level of rebellion."

"I fear you're right. Distasteful as it might be, some brutality might be needed to bring the locals to heel. Reward those who accept us and punish those that don't. It might take a few generations, but eventually they'll accept reality."

"Maybe not Straken." Wolfric laughed.

"Maybe not, but if necessary, we can cleanse Straken and move our own people in. The country is sparsely populated as it is and only their timber and mines are of any great value."

Wolfric gave him a look. "That's a considerably different position than we were talking about last year. What happened to ruling everyone with a gentle hand, letting them find their own way under our laws?"

"Our earlier plans may have been naive. Having seen the hatred Straken holds for us, I'm not sure they could ever be brought around to living under your rule. I'm not saying we shouldn't give them a chance, but realistically, there's a large part of the population that may need to go."

Wolfric still looked troubled but he nodded anyway. Otto had misgivings of his own, but he would never get the peace he needed to advance his studies if he was constantly running around putting down rebellions. If Straken refused to accept reality, then he would cut them out of the empire.

For the greater good, there might not be any other choice.

CHAPTER 12

THE ROLAN INFILTRATION

It was a two-week ride to the new Rolan border and Oskar enjoyed every moment of the journey. The early spring weather was delightful and he was out of the palace on a secret mission for the king. What could be better?

When Commander Borden had offered him the mission, strictly volunteer of course, Oskar had leapt at the chance.

While he didn't know much about what had happened with the old king and his son, he approved of Wolfric's new direction. Oskar's father always said that when you met a bully, the only way to make him back off was to make it clear that while he might win the fight, he would at least get a bloody nose. If ever there was a bully, it was Straken. And Garenland had certainly bloodied their nose last fall.

He smiled to himself and guided his horse off the road and into the high, dead grass of the plains. New shoots were starting to peek out of the ground, but for now last year's stalks dominated everything for as far as he could see.

And he could see a long way. He felt totally exposed riding in the open like this, but there was really no other choice. The disguise he'd been given would allow him to pass for a Rolan citizen, but not until he reached the other side of the border. If he was caught on this side, the outfit would only serve to make him look more like a spy.

He adjusted the sword at the small of his back. It was kind of pointless since if he needed it, he probably was doomed anyway. But at least he could take a few Rolan dogs down with him.

He was getting close to the section of territory that Rolan seized. Soon enough the patrols were bound to pick up. He needed to avoid being seen since as nice as the horse he'd been assigned was, it couldn't match a Rolan cavalry mount.

Oskar's smile withered when he considered his target. Where Straken was a bully, Rolan was an opportunist. They took advantage of the northern war to steal a slice of Garenland rather than fight fair for the territory. That was a coward's move and if there was one thing Oskar hated more than a bully, it was a coward.

Luck was with him and he made it until dusk without running into another soul. Since there was no cover to speak of, Oskar settled for camping in a swale that would make him at least a little harder to spot. A fire was totally out of the question, so he set a cold camp, ate cold jerky, and washed it down with tepid water. Hopefully it wouldn't be more than a week or two longer to reach Rolan City. Once he arrived, a whole new set of problems would arise, but no sense worrying about that until he had to.

It didn't seem like Oskar had been asleep any time when something sharp poked him in the side. When he opened his eyes he found a small silhouette standing over him. From the height he guessed it was a kid maybe twelve years old. Whatever his age, the spear in his hands looked plenty sharp. Wouldn't take much for him to drive it home either.

"Evening," Oskar said. "Would you mind putting that thing up? You wouldn't want to hurt someone by accident, right?"

The spear never waved from its place six inches from his chest.

"You're not from around here." From the voice he guessed he was dealing with a girl, not a boy.

"That's true. I'm on my way to Rolan City. Are your parents around? A little girl shouldn't be out here on her own."

"I am not a little girl. I'm sixteen years old. And my parents are dead thanks to those cavalry bastards. They died saving me and I mean to make the soldiers pay for killing them."

"I'm going to sit up now, okay?" He inched back a little and eased up. "Say, how did you find me out here in the dark?"

"You've got something magic in your pack. I can see it glowing."

The pack and its precious cargo were as dark as the deepest cave. Only a wizard could see magic like that. "You can use magic?"

Oskar could barely see her nod. "That's why the cavalry men wanted me. Wizards have to go to a special barracks. A prison is more like it. They treat them like animals to be worked, not like people. Mom and Dad tried to keep my powers hidden, but I can't control them very well and I let some sparks slip out. Someone saw and reported us."

He understood her problem now. "Listen, kid, Garenland is only a day's ride east. You'll be safe there. Wizards are free and have full rights as citizens. If you're careful, you should be able to make it across in a couple days."

"I don't want to escape!" Her anger was almost a physical force. "I want revenge."

She finally put her spear up and sniffed. Of all the trials he feared he might face, a crying girl wasn't one he'd remotely considered. His training didn't exactly cover this kind of thing.

"My name's Oskar. What's yours?"

"Corina. You're from Garenland, aren't you?"

He hesitated, but she wasn't apt to believe him if he denied it. "Yes. I'm on a very important mission. Rolan has chosen to become our enemy and if we don't fight them, others in Garenland will be in danger."

"I don't care what you're doing. If it hurts Rolan, I want to help. Besides, without me, you're liable to get lost or caught or killed. What will that do to your precious mission?"

"I'm a professional," Oskar said. "No one's going to find me. Besides, it'll be dangerous. I can't take a kid with me on a mission like this. Cross the border, find a town, live a nice safe life."

"I found you and I'm not a kid. Besides, I don't want a safe life. I want blood. I want to be there when Rolan falls. Most of all, I want to spit on King Villares as he walks to the gallows."

He'd never heard such venom from someone so young. He didn't know how useful she'd be, but Oskar doubted she'd cross the border. If anything, she was likely to follow him which would only increase the risks to both of them. Having a local guide might be useful. Hopefully she could keep him from making any stupid mistakes.

"Alright, on one condition. You do what I say, when I say. Anything else will get us both killed. Deal?"

"Deal. We should get some sleep. The patrols get heavier when we reach the more populated areas." She lay down in the grass beside him, the spear clutched to her like a security blanket.

Oskar shook his head and settled back in. Had his life just gotten easier or harder? He wasn't sure and that worried him.

"We'd attract a lot less attention if you stuck to the road," Corina said.

After a cold breakfast, Oskar and his traveling companion had set out through the long grass. In the light it was clear the girl was pretty, in a waifish sort of way. She'd either been half starved or just had a growth spurt. Her cheeks were hollow, her frame gaunt, and her limbs like sticks. Her long, dark hair was tangled and ragged as were her homespun tunic and leggings. She certainly looked the part of a runaway slave. At the very least she didn't add enough weight to bother his horse.

"I thought you said there would be more patrols," Oskar said.

"There will be, but they'll be less suspicious if they meet us on the road rather than out in the prairie. Your accent might be a problem, though I think you'd just pass as someone that lived on the eastern frontier."

"I can't risk getting stopped and having my bag searched. If they find what I'm carrying, it could be catastrophic."

"It's magic, right?"

"Yeah. Not just that, it's made from valuable material. Even without the magic, it would be worth a great deal of gold. It's exactly the sort of thing a greedy officer might steal in the name of security only to sell later. Anyway, aren't they looking for you too? Surely the local soldiers would have your description."

She laughed, surprisingly bitter from one so young. "Are

you kidding? A scrawny, underfed girl with dark hair describes half the commoners living in Rolan. They also think I'm alone. A father and daughter riding home together wouldn't be something they'd question."

"Do I really look old enough to pass as your father?" Oskar had barely turned thirty. He would have had to get started awfully young to have a sixteen-year-old daughter.

"Older brother then, who cares. The point is, criminals travel the high grass. Honest people take the road."

She had a point, but did he dare risk his mission at the suggestion of a kid? On the other hand, if she was to serve as his local guide, what was the point of bringing her along if he was only going to ignore her?

"Fine." Oskar nudged the horse left toward the distant road. "How far are we from the nearest village?"

"The nearest village is about ten miles southwest, but you'll want to avoid that one."

"Aside from the fact that it's not in the right direction, why?"

"That's where my parents got spotted. Someone's bound to recognize me and the local soldiers will be on alert."

"That's good to know. How about the nearest village that isn't on alert and is on our way to the capital?"

"About thirty miles northwest is the city of Cattal. I went there once with my parents. They've got the second-biggest stockyard in the kingdom. I would have thought you'd want to avoid people."

They reached the road and Oskar urged his mount to a trot. He looked left and right but there was nothing to see beyond grass and dirt. They could have been alone in the world for all the life in the area.

"I do, to a certain extent, but getting into the capital on my own will be far harder than if I'm part of a group. I was hoping to sign up as a caravan guard for a team headed that way. One man in a large gathering will draw way less interest."

"If that's your big plan, then you've got a problem. No one hires caravan guards here. The cavalry patrols protect the roads, deal with bandits or wild beasts. The only people who hire mercenaries are rich folks who are afraid of thieves or rivals. We did a lot of traveling, just my parents and I, and we never saw a wolf, much less a bandit."

Oskar frowned. He was going to have to rethink his whole strategy. But time enough for that when they reached Cattal.

Oskar smelled Cattal before he saw it. The stink of thousands of animals passing through a city didn't go away just because this wasn't prime time for cattle drives. And maybe calling it a city was a bit of a stretch. It was more like a large collection of tents. They were big, heavy leather tents made from numerous cow hides sewn together, but still, it wasn't a city as Oskar knew them.

Given the lack of natural resources, he shouldn't have been surprised. Where was the nearest forest? He didn't know but he hadn't seen a tree in four days.

As he guided the horse between a pair of tents and down an open path that had been worn down to bare dirt by thousands of hooves, Oskar considered their next move. The sun would be setting soon, so finding whatever passed for an inn would be the first order of business. That would also be a good place to do some eavesdropping, maybe get some inspiration about how best to approach Rolan City.

"You know I'm broke, right?" Corina said.

"Relax, dinner and a room are on me. Assuming I can find the local inn."

"Over there." She pointed past him at a long row of tents, the largest of which was lit by glowing lanterns and had a handful of horses tied to a hitching rail out front.

They dismounted and he tied their horse to the rail. Oskar dug his coin pouch out of his satchel and handed it to Corina. "Why don't you handle getting the room and I'll find a table and order dinner?"

She handed the pouch back. "Women don't handle money in Rolan. If anyone saw me with your money pouch, it would lead to a lot of questions we don't want to answer. Just go up to the bar and ask for a tent and two meals. I'll find a table."

Oskar shook his head. How was King Wolfric ever going to rule such a backward people? His mother never would have trusted his father to handle the family's meager savings. Of course, Father was a drunk, so there was that.

Corina was waiting for him beside the tent flap. He went over, lifted the flap, and let her go in first. The common room, if that was the right name for the single-room tent, held fifteen tables, eight of which were occupied. There wasn't a woman visible. The only worker was a lean, hard man behind the bar. His dark mustache was spattered with gray and fine wrinkles surrounded his eyes.

Oskar would have bet his life the bartender was a former cavalry man. Corina went to an empty table in the corner of the tent while he walked up to the bar. There was an iron stove behind the bar with a large covered pot resting on the single burner.

"You're not from around here," the bartender said the moment he arrived.

"No. I grew up near the border. Things are crazy up there

now, so my sister and I are on our way to the capital to look for work. We need a tent for the night and two meals."

"Five silvers for the tent and one for each meal."

Oskar was so relieved not to have to answer any questions that he paid without haggling. The bartender scooped up the coins. Oskar had been provided with coins minted in Rolan for this mission so there should be no trouble there.

"Here." He handed two bowls of thick, brown stew to Oskar. "You're in the third tent down the row."

He returned to Corina and handed her a bowl. There were already spoons on the table, so they dug in. The glop had a mildly spicy, earthy flavor. Pleasant, but anything made with meat really shouldn't have the texture of pudding.

He glanced at Corina. Her eyes were closed and she had a look of absolute bliss on her face.

"You like this stuff?"

"Are you kidding? Spiced goat in brown sauce is my favorite. This isn't as good as my mom's was, but it's still really good. Are you going to eat yours?" She eyed his meal and licked her lips.

He took another bite. He'd eaten worse and one of the first lessons of basic training was that food was fuel. You didn't have to like it, just get it down. "Some bread would be nice."

"There's bread in it. That's why it's so thick."

If she was trying to ruin his appetite, she was doing a good job. Oskar ate as fast as he could, ignoring the taste and just swallowing.

He scraped the bowl clean and tossed it on the table. "Damn it. I forgot to ask about a place to keep the horse. It needs hay and a good rub down."

"Don't worry, there's hay beside the tent we're using and you can rub him down yourself. Everyone has a horse, so the inns include the cost of fodder in the price of a tent." She stood and carried their bowls back to the bartender. A moment later she returned with a pair of clean spoons which she put on the table.

Oskar shook his head. It was a strange system but saved on servers. The worst part was, they were finished but he hadn't overheard anything useful. In fact, he hadn't heard anything at all. Everyone spoke so quietly he couldn't make out anything they said.

Hell with it. He was beat. Time to get some sleep and start fresh in the morning.

They left the big tent, collected their horse and went down to the tent the innkeeper rented them. There was an iron rod and eyelet driven into the ground beside the tent. A short distance from the rod was a pile of hay. While Oskar hobbled and brushed the horse, Corina went inside.

He glared at the tent flap. She could have at least offered to help.

Half an hour later he joined her inside. The tent wasn't huge, maybe twelve by twelve with a single cot. She was sitting on the edge brushing her fingers through her hair. Oskar tossed his tack on the floor.

"You can have the cot," he said. "I'm used to sleeping rough."

"You're not what I expected," Corina said. "We hear stories about Garenland and how all the people are arrogant and corrupt. That you're weak fools who'd rather trade and talk than fight. You seem far nicer than most of the people of Rolan I've met."

"Thanks, I guess. Garenland's a big place. I'm sure if you looked around, you'd find plenty of people like you described. My father used to say it takes all kinds to make a world. See you in the morning."

Oskar gathered the satchel that held his patch and clutched it to him as he fell asleep.

※

Oskar slept well, but lightly. Even though no one had shown the least interest in them last night, he could never forget he was in enemy territory and if they were to find out who he really was the consequences would be dire.

He sat up and stretched, his joints popping as he worked out the kinks. In the dim morning light he could just make out Corina's peaceful, sleeping face. She looked far younger with the tension and anger out of her expression. Poor kid, she'd really been through the wringer. When Garenland ruled Rolan, maybe he could get her a position with Lord Shenk's war wizards.

Much as he would have liked to let her sleep, it was time to get moving. He needed to figure out how they were going to get into Rolan City without drawing attention to themselves. He also needed to find something for breakfast, hopefully something less disgusting than supper.

"Corina, wake up." He gave her shoulder a shake.

She groaned and rolled over. "Five more minutes, Papa."

He winced. That one cut to the bone. "Come on, kid. We've got a busy day."

Another shake got her to open her eyes. She flinched when she saw him. "Oskar? Sorry, I had a dream. I'm awake now."

"I'll be out front. Join me when you're ready." He collected his gear and ducked out into the brisk morning air.

He was far enough south that it felt more like early summer than early spring. Garenland mornings wouldn't get this warm for a month and there was probably still a foot of snow in

Straken. The Northern Army would be marching soon, but they'd take their time reaching the border. That would give the snow a chance to melt down, but hopefully not so much that the ground turned to mud. He'd trained enough to know that marching in the mud was a miserable exercise.

The horse was busy finishing off the hay pile. Oskar saddled him and got his bags situated. A quick peek revealed that the mithril patch was still secure. Not that anyone could have messed with it without him noticing, but why take chances? His main worry was one of the enslaved wizards spotting it the way Corina had. If they hated the government as much as she did, hopefully they'd keep quiet.

He'd barely finished his preparations when Corina stepped out into the sun. Her hair was a mess and she gripped her spear so tight her knuckles were white. Other than that she looked okay.

"What's for breakfast?" she asked.

"You're supposed to be my guide, you tell me. Something crunchy, please, not more glop."

"We'll have to find something in the market." She set out toward the center of the city.

Oskar untied the horse and quickly caught up. All around them people were emerging from their tents. Most ignored them though a few offered a polite nod of greeting. The whole tent-city thing seemed strange, but Oskar hoped to not be here long enough to get used to it.

Ahead of him Corina froze. Oskar stopped beside her. "What is it?"

She ignored him, her gaze focused on a trio of men in brown Rolan uniforms. One of them, the oldest, had tiny gold horses on his shoulders. He must have been some higher-up in the military. All three wore cavalry sabers on their belts.

Corina was focused wholly on the officer. Whatever her problem was, he did not need to draw the attention of the military. He grabbed her arm and tugged. "Relax, kid, you're going to get us into trouble."

She screamed and lunged at the officer, spear leading.

Of all the responses he expected, that wasn't one of them.

The Rolan soldiers were taken totally by surprise.

Corina drove her spear clean through the officer.

The men with him went for their sabers but Oskar was faster. His sword was clear of its scabbard in an instant.

The first soldier fell, his throat spraying blood.

His partner got his saber three-quarters drawn before Oskar ran him through.

He spun but no more enemies presented themselves. Corina was stomping the dead commander's head under her boot over and over again. There wasn't much left now but broken bone and mushy brains. Behind them people shouted and ran. Whatever passed for a city guard would be along soon enough.

So much for sneaking into Rolan City. They'd be lucky to get out of Cattal alive at this point. Traveling with Corina was looking like a worse idea than he'd first thought.

"He's dead, Corina, and we need to go."

She looked down at the ruin she'd made of the dead man's head and gasped. A few staggering steps brought her to Oskar. The moment she reached him she burst into tears.

Heaven help him, not now.

Oskar scooped her up, ran to his horse, and tossed her up into the saddle. He climbed up behind her and snapped the reins.

They thundered down the street, chasing the people that had stepped outside to see what was going on back into their tents. They needed to get as far from the scene of the crime as they could then find somewhere to hide.

His first thought was to leave the city, but there was nowhere to hide on the open plains. If they made for the plains, enemy cavalry would ride them down by noon. No, they needed somewhere out of sight, but where?

"Corina, I need you to pull yourself together and help me. Where can we hide?" Oskar urged his horse to the right down a side street. There was no one around so he reined in, hoping that walking the horse would draw less attention. He prayed the locals hadn't gotten a good look at them.

"I had to kill him," she said. "That was the man that ordered my parents put to death. I couldn't just let him walk by like nothing happened. Could I?"

Oskar wasn't sure what to say. He'd killed a few men during his early career. The first time had left him shaking and weak in the knees, but it got easier. Whether that was actually a good thing or not was another matter. Hopefully she wouldn't throw up on his back.

"Of course you couldn't, though I admit you've put us in a tight spot. A tight spot only you can get us out of. Where do I go?"

"The stockyard. There are new faces coming and going there all the time. If we can blend in with the drovers maybe we can escape. Turn west, it's at the edge of the city."

He blew out a sigh of relief and turned down the next street headed in the right direction. She seemed to have herself under control, for the moment at least. When the danger finally passed, he suspected she'd have a major breakdown. But that was a problem for later.

By some miracle, Oskar and Corina reached their destination without running into any soldiers. That couldn't last, but for now he wasn't complaining. The stockyard consisted of a huge round fenced-in area where cattle could be held until they were sold at auction. There were only a few dozen young cattle milling around today.

Watching over them from a safe distance was a group of half a dozen men in long, leather coats. Broad-brimmed hats shaded their eyes from the morning sun. They looked like they'd been on the trail for a while. Pity there weren't more of them. Hiding in a group of six, all of whom were dressed differently than Oskar and Corina, wasn't going to work.

"Do you have a plan B?" Oskar asked.

"No, this is the only place people from outside the city gather in any number. Maybe we could try a tavern, but the guards will check them for sure. I don't know. Maybe you should just leave me. You can get away while they're questioning me."

Oskar had been debating that very idea since they left the scene of the murder. If he hadn't struck down the commander's guards her idea might have worked, but everyone there had to have seen him kill those two soldiers. Most likely it wouldn't have mattered anyway. The powers that be would still be after him for traveling with a murderer. And if they caught him, they'd find the mithril patch and his mission would be a failure.

That couldn't happen.

"Let's talk to the drovers. At least we won't be so obvious."

Before he could get the horse moving again a shout rang out from behind them. "You there, stop where you are!"

Oskar looked back over his shoulder. Six soldiers in brown uniforms were hurrying toward them on foot.

So much for trying to blend in.

"Yah!" He thumped the horse's ribs and raced away from the approaching soldiers. The problem was he had no idea where to go.

They needed a distraction.

Oskar turned his mount toward the enclosure. "Hang on!"

When they reached the fence, his horse tried to jump, but didn't quite make it. Its hooves clipped the fence and knocked a section of it down.

A little stumble prompted Corina to squeeze him tighter.

Oskar wheeled the horse around. "Hah!"

He drove the frightened cattle toward the opening.

They poured out, trampling everything in their path.

Men and tents fell. Shouts filled the air.

A wall of terrified beef formed between them and the soldiers.

This was their one chance. He couldn't waste it.

They thundered away from the stockyard toward the northern edge of the city. He didn't have a plan beyond getting away from the enemy soldiers.

Corina grabbed his arm. "I see magic."

"Where?" All they needed now was to have a wizard after them too.

"To your left. There's someone standing between two of the tents."

Oskar spotted the ragged figure a moment later. He didn't look like a threat. Whoever it was looked like a bum in a tattered brown robe. The robe's hood cast a shadow across his face preventing Oskar from getting a good look.

The stranger waved them over but made no aggressive

moves. Given how this country treated its wizards, he was inclined to take his chances.

Oskar guided his mount toward the wizard who stepped aside to let them pass. As soon as they were in between the tents, the air shimmered and the gap seemed to disappear.

Oskar dismounted and helped Corina down. "I don't—"

"Shh!" The wizard held a finger to his lips.

Through the haze, Oskar saw a number of soldiers running past. One man looked straight at them for long enough that Oskar reached for his sword. Finally he took off and the street was clear.

"Thanks," Oskar said.

"I didn't step in to save you, whoever you are," the wizard said. "But to save Corina."

"How do you know my name?" Corina asked.

"We were in contact with your parents before their unfortunate passing. You have my most sincere condolences. They were good people who wanted only for you to be free. The plan was to meet here and for the three of you to disappear with us. While we did not act fast enough to save them, I can still offer you safety."

"Exactly who are you and who is 'we'?" Oskar asked.

"Neither of those things is your concern," the wizard said. "I will get you out of the city and out of sight of the guards. After that, you're on your own. Corina and I need to return to the others."

"Oskar saved my life and you're a complete stranger," Corina said. "While I appreciate the rescue, I think I'll stick with my friend."

"Your friend can't protect you. Not like we can." The wizard looked left and right. "The way is clear. We'd best go while the going is good. My horse is down the street. Move slowly and calmly. No matter what happens, make no aggressive moves. My magic can only protect you if you obey these rules."

Oskar hated relying on magic he didn't understand, but he couldn't refuse. There was no way out of this city on their own.

The wizard reached up, grasped the horse's bridle, and led them out into the street. They moved at a steady walk. No one looked at them or even seemed aware of their presence. Oskar knew nothing about magic and so couldn't say if this was something remarkable or minor, and as long as it worked, he didn't care.

Corina's arms were tight around his middle as they rode out in the open. He couldn't blame the girl for being nervous. If anything went wrong, they were dead.

Eight tents from their hiding place, a horse waited outside one of the tavern tents. The wizard untied his mount and swung up into the saddle. His hood slipped back, revealing a weathered face covered with a salt-and-pepper beard. Oskar guessed his age at about fifty, give or take.

The wizard grabbed their bridle again and they took off at the same slow, steady pace. A squad of soldiers ran by, giving Oskar a start, but paying them no attention.

"Why don't they see us?" Corina whispered.

"Beats me," Oskar said. "But I'm not complaining."

For the next two hours they traveled at the same sedate pace, out of the city and across the plains. They kept to the road for a little way but after a mile or so, their guide led them into the plains. When the city was little more than a blur on the horizon the wizard released their bridle.

He blew out a long sigh and sagged in his saddle. "We should be safe for now. The cavalry will be a long time finding our path, if they ever do. I must rest for a time. The magic has left me spent."

They rode into one of the many little gullies that dotted the plains and dismounted. The wizard slumped at once to the ground. Oskar caught a glimpse of his face. The man was as pale as a ghost.

Oskar dug some jerky and a water skin out of his supplies and shared with Corina. It wasn't the breakfast he was hoping for, but it was certainly better than anything he'd have gotten in the city jail.

"Are you hungry?" Oskar asked.

"I have already eaten." The wizard's voice wavered and it sounded like he might pass out at any moment. He turned slowly to look at Corina. "What are your intentions, child?"

"I don't know. Maybe if you told me what was going on I could make a proper decision."

"My name is Miguel and I'm a member of the wizard underground. We help wizards disappear before they can be made slaves by the government. There aren't many of us and we can't save as many people as we'd like to, but we do what we can."

"How did my parents know about you?"

Miguel shook his head. "I couldn't tell you. My superior gave me descriptions of you and your parents and said to meet you in Cattal. My job was to get all three of you to our safe house. From there, the other members would figure out the best place to hide you long term. Since you're from the northeast, most likely they'd have sent you to the southwest. But that's outside my area."

"You should send them to Garenland," Oskar said. If he could get these wizard underground people on his side, it would make it much easier when the army came to take over.

"King Wolfric has granted the wizards their full rights as citizens."

"We know," Miguel said. "The underground has been keeping track of matters in Garenland. My superiors haven't seen fit to share with me how they feel about things."

"Doesn't seem like they tell you much," Corina said.

Miguel shrugged. "I work in the field. The less I know, the less I can reveal if I'm caught. You know my story, Oskar, how about you tell me yours?"

Did he dare risk sharing the truth in the hopes that these people would help him complete his mission? Doing so would go against his orders. Of course, helping Corina went against his orders as well. If he did what he was supposed to and failed, he'd be in worse trouble than if he succeeded.

"I'm a Garenland soldier," Oskar said. "I was tasked with seizing control of the Rolan gate in preparation for taking the capital and eventually the whole country."

Miguel laughed. "What you suggest is impossible. Even we know that the last living Arcane Lord controls the portal network. I don't care how powerful your wizard thinks he is, he's no Lord Valtan."

"Lord Shenk is confident his plan will work. No one explained the process to me and I'm not a wizard so I wouldn't have understood anyway, but I have my orders. My job is to get into Rolan City and attach a mithril patch to the portal there. After that, it's out of my hands."

"Let me see this patch," Miguel said. "It must be the source of the ethereal glow I see coming from your pack."

The moment of truth then. Oskar dug down to the bottom of the satchel and opened the false bottom. The thin, smooth sheet of mithril winked up at him.

"Here." He handed the patch to Miguel.

The wizard looked it over, his eyes getting wider by the moment. Finally, he handed it back and said, "I've never seen the ether woven in such a way. Certainly not by a modern wizard. This 'patch' as you call it, could have been made by an Arcane Lord. How many threads can your Lord Shenk wield?"

Oskar shook his head and put the patch back in its hiding place. "No idea. I doubt even King Wolfric really knows. I think it's in our mutual interests to work together. Living under Garenland's rule would be far better for you and your friends than living like outlaws. Our king respects wizards."

Miguel got a far-off look in his eye. After a moment of contemplation, he said, "This isn't a decision I can make. I will take you to our leaders. I can offer no more than that."

Given his distinct lack of options, Oskar said, "Thank you."

◦

After their little heart to heart in the plains, Miguel hardly said a word to Oskar or Corina as he led them deeper into the prairie. Perhaps he was having second thoughts. Oskar didn't know him well enough to read his expressionless face. Not that he could see it very well since Miguel constantly kept his hood up. It certainly wasn't that cold out, so he had to be doing it to avoid them seeing his face.

Oskar tried to force himself to relax. He'd made his choice, now he had to play it through and see what happened. He looked around, but the scenery certainly wasn't going to distract him. There was nothing but dry, three-foot-tall stalks of grass in every direction.

"I thought there were supposed to be a lot of grain farms in Rolan," Oskar said, more to hear something besides the wind than any desire to know about Rolan's agricultural practices.

"This is grazing land," Corina said. "The big farms are further south near the Rolan River. I'm not sure when they come this way, but sometime this summer, thousands of cattle will be driven into this land and they'll eat everything they can find before being driven somewhere else."

"Were your parents farmers?"

"No, cattle traders. They'd buy from the big ranchers and drive the herd to smaller towns to resell them. We weren't rich, but we never lacked for food. I basically grew up in the cook wagon."

"Sounds nice," Oskar said.

Corina looked at him with tears in her eyes. "It was."

"Sorry. I didn't mean to upset you."

"You didn't." Her smile was more melancholy than happy. "I like remembering the good times."

"We're here," Miguel said.

"Here" was a spot in the middle of nowhere. Oskar didn't know what sort of game the wizard was playing but...

Miguel raised his hand and the air shimmered like heat waves in the middle of summer. When it stopped, a longhouse made of sod was visible. A young man and an equally young woman, maybe in their midtwenties and dressed in cloaks a bit less tattered than Miguel's, emerged, looked them all over, and settled on their gazes on Miguel.

"Either you're one short or have one too many," the woman said.

"Things happened. A lot of things. Are they free?" Miguel asked.

"Yes. We've been expecting you for days," the man said.

"Like I said, things happened." Miguel dismounted. "You can leave your horse here. We have a small stable in the back."

Oskar dismounted and helped Corina down. He grabbed

his satchel and slung it over his shoulder. No way was he leaving the patch here where anyone could get their hands on it.

Miguel led the way past his friends or whatever they were and into the longhouse. It was cool and dark inside the sod building. The only light came from a sputtering Lux crystal hanging from the ceiling. Inside there was a table and six chairs, three of which were occupied by the oldest, wrinkliest people Oskar had ever seen. They were dressed in the brown cloaks that seemed to be in fashion with the magical underground. It made these three look like half-filled burlap sacks.

"You have brought us an unexpected guest," one of them said. Oskar would have guessed a woman if he was pressed, but her voice was so gravelly he couldn't be sure. "Clearly your mission didn't go as expected. Tell us everything."

Miguel obliged, providing details that Oskar hadn't known about his meetings with Corina's parents. When he got to the part where they were killed, Corina let out a little whimper. When Miguel finished his story, three pairs of shining eyes focused on Oskar.

"Our people in Garenland have heard about your new king," the female elder said. "They speak approvingly about what he's done for our people. They do not speak of this plan to take control of the portal network."

"That's good as it's a secret mission. Should word escape, my fellow agents would be in grave danger. I risked a great deal sharing this information with you because I believe it's in our interests to work together to force those who have made wizards slaves out of power."

"You think your king would be better for wizards?" one of the other elders asked. Oskar couldn't even begin to guess at the sex of the one that spoke, so desiccated was the voice. "In our experience, once someone gets power, they tend to revert to bad habits."

"Perhaps, but King Wolfric already has power in Garenland and he has given wizards there the same rights as every other citizen. He even made one of them his chief advisor."

"Show us the artifact this advisor has made," the woman said. "Maybe that will convince us of your chances."

Oskar removed the patch and handed it to her. All three elders stared at the patch in silence.

At last the woman said, "When Miguel described the item's power, we suspected it was taken from one of Lord Karonin's storage facilities. The power that hides this place comes from such a storehouse. There were many items of power there, though this was one of the few we could figure out how to use. But this is new magic. I wouldn't have believed that someone exists in this day capable of such magic if I hadn't seen it with my own eyes."

Oskar took the patch back. "So will you help me?"

She looked to the man on her left and he nodded. The man on the right nodded next. "It seems we are in agreement. Miguel will help you enter Rolan City. We will also send a message to the other leaders to be on the lookout for your allies. I can't guarantee they will be willing to help as well, but they might."

Oskar offered a bow of thanks. Hopefully he hadn't just led the others into a trap. But if he had, he probably wouldn't live to rue the mistake.

Rolan City was what Oskar thought of when he thought of a city. Unlike the collection of tents that was Cattal, the capital had actual wooden buildings. The streets were still dirt but at least the castle was made of stone. As he walked around beside Miguel and Corina, ignored by everyone around them, he couldn't help thinking that the Garenland army wasn't going to have much trouble conquering the city.

Beside him, Corina was staring around at everything, like she'd never seen real houses before. And maybe she hadn't, assuming her parents never brought her here. He hadn't really wanted to bring her along, but she insisted. After everything that had happened, he kind of felt like she deserved to see the mission through. Maybe when all this madness was over, he'd bring her to Garen, now that was a real city.

In the lead, Miguel was glaring around at everything like he'd have preferred to burn the place down. He'd hardly spoken a word on the ride here. Clearly, he didn't approve of the elders sending him along to lend a hand. At least he hadn't complained. As long as he did the job and kept quiet, Oskar wouldn't complain either.

A fifteen-minute walk from the edge of the city brought them to the portal. It was an exact replica of the one back home save for the position of the runes.

Corina gasped and murmured, "By the angels."

Miguel glared back at them. His magic only blocked sight. Anyone paying attention would hear them talk.

Oskar dug out the patch and searched for the master rune. Doing this in broad daylight where anyone might see the square of mithril appear out of nowhere was dumb, but Miguel insisted they complete the task as quickly as possible and Oskar agreed wholeheartedly.

At least the crowd gathered near the portal was smaller than the one that often passed near the portal at home. Plus, everyone seemed focused on their business rather than on what was happening around them.

There it was. The master rune was the only one in the same position here as on the Garenland portal. He drew back and got ready to throw.

"Over there!" someone shouted.

Oskar snapped around. A group of watchmen had gathered and one of them was pointing right at Oskar and his companions.

"What's going on?" he asked.

"We need to go." Miguel started walking, forcing Oskar and Corina to follow.

"We're not finished," Oskar said.

Miguel picked up the pace, ignoring Oskar's complaint. He looked back and found the watch hurrying after them.

"Get ready to run," Miguel said.

Corina grabbed Oskar, her nails digging into his arm.

"Now!" Light exploded amidst the watchman.

They ran.

People screamed.

The scene was chaos.

Somehow Oskar managed not to lose track of Miguel. Ten blocks from the portal they finally stopped. Oskar gasped for breath and the others were doubled over clutching their sides. At least they'd lost their pursuers.

"What was that? One of them could see us," Oskar said.

"Not us, but the magic I was using to hide us. It was bad luck we ran into a watch wizard. There can't be more than half a dozen of them."

"Watch wizard?" Oskar hid the patch again. "I thought all wizards, outside of the underground, were slaves in Rolan."

"They are, but some, after proving their loyalty over many years, serve with the watch, helping catch rogue wizards in exchange for extra benefits. They're the worst sort of traitors." The hate in Miguel's voice sent a shiver up Oskar's spine. He wouldn't want to be a watch wizard and run into their guide alone in a dark alley.

"What now?" Corina asked.

"We'll have to approach at night," Oskar said. "No magic. In the meantime, we need somewhere to hide until dark."

"There's a place we use sometimes," Miguel said. "Not exactly friends of wizards, but certainly not friends of the kingdom. They'll let us hide out for a while."

There wasn't much in the way of nightlife in Rolan City. Not that Oskar had been out much back home, but he got the impression that at least parts of Garen were busy at night. But whatever. The fewer people around to see him sneaking toward the portal the better. Miguel was with him, but somehow he'd convinced Corina to remain behind at their hideout.

He smiled to himself. Hideout was a perfect name since they were staying with the local thieves guild. Considering they were all criminals, it wasn't much of a stretch. However, for such a rough crew they'd been very welcoming. When Oskar took Miguel aside to find out why, the wizard said that some of the underground wizards had helped the guild master out of a rough spot a few years back. The guild remembered its friends. Plus they didn't want to get on the wrong side of a bunch of wizards with nothing to lose.

Oskar froze between a pair of dark, empty buildings across from the courtyard that surrounded the portal. Four guards, including the watch wizard from earlier, were keeping watch. Half a dozen lanterns filled the area with light. There was no way he was going to be able to sneak over there without getting spotted.

He pulled a little further back into the shadows. "How could they have known we'd be back?"

"Maybe they were just hoping," Miguel said. "Do you want to retreat and try again tomorrow?"

"No, the longer we wait, the better the odds that we get caught or one of our hosts gets greedy and tries to steal the patch. I don't suppose you can magic us up a distraction?"

Miguel's expression was partially hidden by shadows, but even so Oskar could see he was pained. "I could turn invisible and run when the wizard spots me. I don't know if it will draw away all of them..."

"Don't worry. If you can get rid of the wizard and at least one guard, I can handle the rest."

"If the elders hadn't ordered me to help you..." Miguel muttered. "Get ready."

Oskar silently drew his sword. Even if he killed the guards, what he did to the portal would remain a secret.

Miguel vanished and darted out of their hiding place. He'd barely covered twenty yards when the watch wizard shouted, "There!"

The wizard and two of the guards ran out of the courtyard, presumably after Miguel who was still invisible. The remaining guards were watching their rapidly disappearing comrades, their backs to Oskar.

He'd never get a better chance than this.

Oskar sprinted out.

The first guard turned to face him just in time to get his throat cut.

The second guard was a fraction faster.

He got his saber drawn in time to block Oskar's first strike.

Oskar spun away from the guard's riposte and stabbed him in the thigh.

The guard staggered and bent over clutching his leg.

Oskar finished him with a slash to the back of the neck.

Their clash hadn't taken long or made much noise, but that was no reason to linger. He dug the patch out and threw it up toward the master rune. A brief flash like lightning nearly blinded him. When he could see again, the patch had fused with the portal and was gone.

With his mission complete, Oskar ran after Miguel. The wizard had taken a big risk to help him out. Oskar would hate to see the man get killed.

○

Oskar needed only seconds to find Miguel and the guards chasing him. Three blocks from the portal, in a blind alley, the watch wizard and his companions had him cornered and bound. Oskar peeked around the edge of one of the buildings.

The watch wizard was holding back while the two guards advanced with their weapons drawn. Oskar assumed that the enemy wizard was doing something to restrain Miguel's magic. Therefore if the wizard was eliminated, Miguel should be able to handle the guards.

His reasoning took less than a second and the instant he made his decision, Oskar charged full force down the alley.

The watch wizard didn't even have a chance to turn around before Oskar's sword ran him through. It was a good blow, right to the heart.

A moment later lightning danced over the bodies of the guards and they collapsed. Miguel straightened and brushed off his pants. "Took your time."

Oskar grinned and bent to check the guards.

"They're dead. There was no way I could spare them once they saw my face. If my description got around, it would make my work for the underground impossible. We should get back before anyone else shows up."

That was a plan Oskar could embrace. They hurried out of the alley at a quick walk, just two guys eager to get home. Heaven must have been watching over them as they made it without meeting another soul.

The hideout was in the basement of a miller that didn't ask questions or mill much grain. There was an outside access door upon which Miguel knocked a specific rhythm. The door opened a crack and a pair of narrow eyes glared out. As soon as the thief was satisfied that it was them, he opened the door just enough to let them enter. Once they were inside, Oskar noticed the loaded hand crossbow in the thief's grasp.

Dangerous friends. Sometimes that was the best sort to have.

As soon as he moved beyond the entryway, Corina came running up. "Are you both okay?"

"Yes, and the mission is a success." Oskar smiled but Corina still looked worried. "What?"

"You've got blood on your face."

He reached up and brushed his cheek. His hand came back

with a red smear. "I'd best wash up. Don't worry, though, it's not mine."

"Now what?" Miguel asked.

Oskar shrugged. "My orders are to wait until our forces emerge from the portal. If I can provide them with valuable information, that's great. But my mission is over. I appreciate you both helping me. Rest assured, my superiors will hear how valuable both the wizard underground and the thieves guild has been."

"We'd just as soon you didn't mention us at all." The doorman spoke from behind Oskar. He hadn't heard the thief sneak up behind him.

"If that's your preference, I'm happy to oblige." At least he was happy to oblige until he gave his report. Once he was safely back in Garenland, he'd have to tell everything that happened. One thing he really didn't want was another private questioning from Lord Shenk.

Oskar shivered. Anything would be better than that.

CHAPTER 13

THE LUX INFILTRATION

Henry made his way to the caravan yard to join up with the merchants headed to Lux. Lord Shenk had arranged for him to join a Franken caravan as an extra guard. He felt strange wearing mercenary garb instead of his usual uniform. Henry had served in the palace guard for five years, two of those directly under Commander Borden. His loyalty had finally paid off with an important mission.

Though he couldn't deny that getting assigned to the Lux infiltration was a disappointment. The tiny country barely had an army to speak of. How hard could it be to sneak up to the portal and attach the patch? The other guys would probably all have great adventure stories to share when they got back. What was he going to have? A tale of riding on a hard wagon bench for days before sneaking out at night to attach the patch.

Oh well. As long as he succeeded, there was sure to be a reward and maybe even a promotion.

Henry hitched his pack higher up on his back. When he thought about the mithril patch nestled deep in a hidden compartment in the bottom, it made the pack feel ten times heavier. That thin piece of metal was worth more than his pay for a lifetime of service. And having been interviewed by Lord Shenk, he got the distinct impression that it was worth more than his life.

Six wagons were gathered in the yard near Northgate. Despite everything that had happened, Garenland was still on reasonable terms with Lux. The only thing that had changed as far as trade was concerned, was that they had to pay a toll to enter now. Not that Henry was any expert. He'd been schooled just enough not to sound like a complete idiot if questioned by the Lux military.

"Hey! Hurry up!" A fit, middle-aged man dressed in green and brown waved at him. "You're the last one. We need to get a move on."

"Coming, sir." Henry double-timed it to the waiting merchant. "Reporting for duty, sir."

"You must have been in the military," the merchant said. "That's good. In my experience military men are disciplined and can follow orders. And hopefully fight. The bandits are largely cleaned up, but largely doesn't mean completely. I'm Jack, the caravan master for this trip, but you can keep calling me sir. You were hired on Lord Shenk's recommendation and I'll expect you to live up to that."

"I'll do my best, sir."

"Good." Jack pointed at one of the wagons where a hunched-over old man sat loosely holding the reins. "That's your ride. Grumbler's been on this run more times than you've got teeth in your head. Follow his lead and you'll do fine."

Henry nodded and made his way to his assigned wagon. Riding with a man named Grumbler didn't sound like it was going to be pleasant. When he reached the wagon, Henry slung his pack in the back, nestling it in an open space behind the tarp-covered load. He didn't actually know what they were hauling to Lux. For the purposes of his real mission, it didn't matter, but he was curious.

Using the wagon wheel as a ladder, he climbed up beside Grumbler. "Morning. I'm Henry and it looks like we'll be traveling together."

The old man muttered something and stuck out his hand. Henry shook, took off his sword belt, and dropped it onto the bench with the sheath beside him.

Grumbler muttered something else that Henry couldn't understand. "I'm sorry, sir, but I can't hear you. What did you say?"

"Let's go!" Jack shouted. He was mounted on a roan mare at the head of the group.

Grumbler threw the wagon brake forward and shook the reins. The wagon lurched, forcing Henry to brace himself using the footboard. Once they were out of the gate and underway, the ride smoothed out a little, but he didn't dare relax. One pothole and he'd end up sitting on the side of the road.

"So what are we hauling?" Henry asked.

Grumbler muttered something, coughed, cleared his throat, and spat something black and tarry in the grass on the side of the road. "We're hauling silica. They need the damn stuff to make their fancy crystals. Hell if I know what they do with it, maybe feed it to their wizards."

They were the first words Henry had been able to understand though he felt little more enlightened than before he asked. Minerals and ore were way outside his area of expertise.

"Do you expect trouble on this run?" Henry asked.

"Nah. I only ever been attacked once and that was years ago. Now if we were headed south or east, that would be something else. But the Lux run is the easiest any caravan can make."

That was exactly what Henry figured. Sounded like he was more likely to die of boredom than anything on this trip.

ᛟ

Henry was right, the trip to Lux was a cake run. They had to pay a tax at the border to a group of rather embarrassed border guards, but beyond that they didn't encounter another armed force. Even the roads weren't horrible. They weren't smooth by any means and his ass was going to be delighted not to have to ride in a wagon for a few days, but other than that, the trip couldn't have been more tedious.

Still, it was worth the boredom to see Crystal City. The capital of Lux was easily the most beautiful city in the world. Certainly it put Garen to shame. Every building was decorated with crystals. Most were made of brick and topped with slate roofs. The streets were paved with cobblestones and so smooth the wagon hardly bounced.

As they rode through the streets, Henry couldn't stop staring. This had to be as close to heaven on earth as a man could find. Even the people were all well dressed and clean. There were no urchins running under the wagons trying to get run over.

"Quite a sight, ain't it?" Grumbler asked, breaking the spell.

"It certainly is. Where are we taking our load?"

"Workshops near the docks. They keep the wizards right next door to the fishermen. All the things that might offend their delicate senses all in one spot out of sight." Grumbler turned his head like he wanted to spit then thought better of it. "It's pretty here, but rotten at the same time if you take my meaning."

Henry wasn't sure he did, but he just nodded and went back to enjoying the view. About ten minutes from the main gate they reached the city center where the portal sat. It was surrounded by a wide, flat area where wagons were gathered to travel to the other kingdoms. There were only a handful waiting, but since their main export was magical crystals, they probably didn't take up much room.

His gaze shifted to the portal itself. A quick scan of the markings located the master rune exactly where Lord Shenk said it would be. It was early afternoon now, but soon enough night would come and he could complete his mission. Maybe his next task would be a little more challenging.

They left the portal and soon the cry of gulls filled the air along with the pungent aroma of fish guts and saltwater. Henry had never smelled the ocean and wasn't eager to do so again. Grumbler turned left at the end of the street and drove parallel to the docks for a ways until they reached a collection of six warehouses.

A single man in sailcloth trousers and a leather vest waved as they approached. Jack dismounted to talk with him while Grumbler reined in.

"Who's that?" Henry asked.

Grumbler cleared his throat and spat. "Warehouse boss. He handles supplies and keeps the wizard under control. Jack and him go way back. That's how he got the job running this caravan. All about who you know."

Grumbler spat again to show what he thought about that system. Henry didn't care one way or another. The system worked the way it worked. The merchants and the nobles would always have the advantage over ordinary people, that's just the way it was. Worrying about it accomplished nothing.

Better to show how useful you could be to the most powerful person you could find and ride them as high as possible. At least that had always been his plan. This mission was his chance to move to the next level and he wouldn't let anything get in his way.

"Looks like the ass grabbing is done," Grumbler said. "Now we can unload. When we're done, we usually celebrate at a tavern not too far off. You coming?"

"Wouldn't miss it," Henry said.

Grumbler slapped his shoulder. "That's the spirit. We get some guards that think they're too good to drink with the rest of us. They don't usually last long."

Little did Grumbler know just how short Henry's time with the caravan was going to be. Still, he had hours to kill before nightfall, no reason not to spend it with the rest of the caravan. One drink was all he'd take. Henry would need a clear head for what was coming.

✧

Grumbler laughed and slapped Henry on the shoulder. They were seated on a bench in the center of a crowded common room. It was mostly drovers and guards from different caravans filling the place. No merchants from Straken were around thank goodness. Heaven only knew what would happen if a dozen Garenlanders ran into a group from Straken. Who was he kidding? Even if blades weren't drawn, fists at least would fly.

Not that a fight was completely out of the question. The old man was on his sixth ale and the alcohol had loosened his tongue. Worse, at least in Henry's opinion, it put him and the other drovers in the mood to sing. If ever there was a reason to start a tavern brawl, the drovers' sorry excuses for singing voices had to be just under insulting someone's sister.

By some miracle, no one in the crowded tavern objected to the noise. The fact that the caravan members were leaving behind a fair chunk of their pay no doubt helped. Either that or the other patrons were so drunk the caterwauling sounded good to them.

Henry sipped his ale and shook his head. No one could be that drunk.

He stood and shouldered his pack. The sun had long since set and it was time for him to get to work.

"Where you goin'?" Grumbler slurred. "We're not leaving until noon. No need for an early quit."

"I need some fresh air," Henry said. "Don't worry, I won't be long." He didn't add, *hopefully*.

"I'll come with you." Grumbler tried to stand and failed.

"I'll be fine." Henry dropped three silver coins on the table. "Next round's on me."

This brought a cheer from the table and a belch from Grumbler. With his new friends bought off by booze, Henry made his way to the door. Outside he took a deep breath of cool night air. They were close enough to the water a faint whiff of fish still lingered, but it was much better than stale ale, vomit, and unwashed men. He pitied the poor serving girls.

He shrugged. None of that was his concern. It was time to do what he came here to do. Henry strolled along the sidewalk, just a first-time visitor enjoying the sights. And what sights they were. If the city was nice in daylight, it was stunning at night, lit by scores of crystals. It felt like a city out of a storybook.

As he got closer to the portal, what he couldn't figure out was why there were no people out on such a fine evening. He'd considered waiting until later if it was crowded, but this was perfect. There wasn't a soul in sight.

The portal gleamed in the moonlight as he approached. The gathering area around it was empty. Henry grinned and unslung his pack. As he started untying it someone shouted. "Hey! You there, stop."

He froze. He'd done nothing illegal and had no desire to leave a body on the ground.

"Turn slowly to face me," the same voice said.

Henry complied, careful to keep his hand away from the hilt of his sword.

It was well that he did. Four watchmen stood ten paces away, three of them armed with loaded crossbows. They wore blue and silver uniforms with a crystal on the chest. No armor, but each had a heavy truncheon hanging from his belt. There was no way he could fight his way out of this.

"Is there a problem, sir?" Henry asked.

"Aside from a string of three murders in the last week, not a thing," said the squad leader, at least Henry assumed that's what he was from the chevrons on his sleeve. "We've orders to bring in any suspicious characters. Since you're the only person we've seen stupid enough to be out when a killer's on the loose, I'd say that makes you suspicious. Now, unbuckle that sword, and drop your bag. You're coming down to watch headquarters."

Henry obeyed. All three crossbowmen looked nervous. He couldn't complete his mission with a quarrel in his chest.

"I assure you I'm not a killer. I just arrived this morning in a caravan from Garenland. My companions are in a tavern just up the road. They'll tell you."

"Maybe you are and maybe you aren't," the spokesman said. "That's for the watch commander to decide. Put your hands behind your back."

Henry soon found himself manacled and marching across the city surrounded by armed men who were still watching him for any excuse to shoot. He should have known things were going too smoothly.

The rest of the city was as quiet as the area around the portal. When they at last reached a two-story stone building with heavy doors and bars on the windows, Henry was guided inside and through a crowded open floor where a dozen watchmen were seated at desks shuffling papers. If there was a killer on the loose, this didn't seem like the best use of their time, but he wasn't about to point that out.

They led him past the desks and beyond a door to a room lined with iron-barred doors. Henry had visited the watch in Garen twice in the course of his duties and so was familiar with the cells. These were only partially occupied, one by a drunk, judging by the smell, and the other by a scantily dressed woman. He couldn't guess what she'd done since as far as he knew, prostitution was legal in Lux.

They shoved Henry into the first empty cell and removed his manacles.

"How long am I going to be stuck here?" he asked. "My caravan is leaving at noon tomorrow."

"You'll stay here until the commander says you can leave." And with that pronouncement, the squad leader and his men marched out, leaving him alone with his fellow detainees.

With nothing better to do, he lay down on the narrow cot

that was the cell's only piece of furniture and closed his eyes. What happened next was out of his hands.

◯

Having been trained to sleep lightly, Henry was awake and sitting up at the first hint of approaching footsteps. He was stiff and sore from sleeping on the thin, too-short cot, but otherwise had no complaints about his treatment. Assuming you didn't get upset about being arrested for taking a stroll that was.

A moment later a weathered man in a watchman's blue and silver uniform appeared in front of his cell door. He had a close-trimmed white beard and didn't look like he'd slept any better than Henry.

"You're the man my watch brought in last night?" he asked.

"Yes, sir."

"Well, you'll be glad to know that you're no longer a murder suspect. While you were in our cell, another person was killed halfway across the city. A ten-year-old girl this time. She slipped outside for just a minute. I swear when I get my hands on the son of a bitch... Anyway, I'm sure you don't care about my problems." The commander produced a key and unlocked the door. "You're free to go with the watch's apologies. It's early yet, so you should have no trouble making your caravan. You'll find your kit outside."

Henry nodded and held out his hand. "No hard feelings and I hope you catch your killer."

"As do I." The commander shook his hand and led him out of the holding area.

Henry's pack and sword were lying together just outside the door and he paused to collect them. He still had a mission to complete, but with watchmen out patrolling all night for the killer, it was going to make his task all the harder. He wanted a challenging assignment, but now he was regretting wishing for one.

Oh well. For now, he just wanted to get out of watch headquarters and check over his gear. Having his pack out of his control left a queasy feeling in the pit of his stomach.

The moment he left, Henry found a nearby bench and sat down. He pawed through the contents of his pack. His rations were untouched as was his spare dagger. Even his money pouch looked full. Now for the big question. At the bottom was a flap that hid a shallow compartment.

As soon as he touched the cloth, he knew something was wrong. Henry tore the flap open and stared into the empty space. The mithril patch was gone.

No, no, no! This couldn't be happening. If he failed, King Wolfric would kick him out of the palace guard and heaven only knew what Lord Shenk might do. He shuddered just thinking about the possibilities.

One of the watchmen must have taken it. The only time his pack was out of his possession was when he was in a cell. Did one of the men that brought him take it or was the thief someone that worked at their headquarters? Henry ran his fingers through his hair. What was he supposed to do?

There was only one option. He'd have to speak to the commander and see if he knew anything. Maybe one of his subordinates had a reputation for sticky fingers. He tied the pack back up and marched straight across the street to watch headquarters.

Back inside he went directly to the nearest occupied table and said, "I need to speak with your commander."

A pig of a man with three chins looked up at him with

small, hard eyes. "What makes you think the commander would want to talk to you?"

"I was arrested by mistake last night. After I left, I thought of something he'll want to hear. Or do you not want to find whoever's killing your fellow citizens?"

The watchman grunted and pushed himself up. "Wait right here."

He lumbered off deeper into the building. At the speed he moved, Henry was going to be here until noon. A few of the other watchmen on duty glanced his way, but most of them seemed to have better things to occupy their minds. Lucky them. Henry couldn't stop imagining the low fire he was going to roast over if he didn't recover the patch.

After what seemed like hours but was probably only fifteen minutes, the watch commander arrived with Three-Chins. "I hadn't thought to see you again so soon," he said.

"I hoped not to see you ever again," Henry said. "Unfortunately, when I went through my bag, I found something missing, a rare and valuable good luck charm that has been in my family for generations." What a pile of crap that was, but hopefully he'd buy it. "I always carry it with me, but when I checked the pocket where it rests, it was gone."

The commander stiffened. "Are you accusing one of my men of stealing?"

"I'm saying that when I was taken into custody, the item was where it belonged and when I got outside this morning it was gone. Now, assuming none of your prisoners had access to my belongings, I'm forced to assume that someone here took it hoping for some easy coin."

"Come with me."

Henry followed the commander to the rear of the main room and through a door. Beyond it was a large room with shelves full of odds and ends. A single man, tall and thin as a stork, bustled about, dusting, adjusting, and otherwise fiddling with the items.

"Collins," the commander said. "Where is Grayson? His shift doesn't end for an hour."

"I came in early and he asked me to finish his shift. I owed him for a bottle of whiskey, so I said sure. He left in a hurry. I hope everything's okay at home."

The watch commander ran a hand down his face. "I see. Thanks, Collins."

They stepped back outside and Henry asked, "Where does this Grayson live?"

"I don't know what you're thinking. Actually, I have a pretty good idea what you're thinking. You can forget it. No one takes the law into their own hands in my city. I'll send a team over to recover your property. Better than that, I'll go myself. What, exactly, did you lose?"

Henry really didn't want to say, but he had no choice. "A thin square of mithril marked with good luck runes. It's been in my family for centuries. Please understand, if I can't get it back, my family will never let me live it down."

"Mithril, eh. Even a small piece would be worth a fortune. Not that that's any excuse for one of my watchmen stealing. Rest assured we'll have Grayson in custody and your property recovered by the end of the day. Name's Kordwin by the way."

"Henry." They shook hands. "I'm counting on you, Commander."

Henry waited on the same park bench across from watch headquarters. Sure enough, twenty minutes later Commander Kordwin and a squad of six men emerged and turned north. He fell in a little way behind them. Maybe he couldn't help take down the thief, but damned if he was going to sit around and do nothing. An extra pair of eyes never hurt anything.

The streets of Crystal City were a good deal more active during the day than they were at night. The people tended to dress in light colors, the women in dresses and the men in tunics and trousers. There wasn't enough difference between these people and the ones back home to say so. If Henry closed his eyes, he could have been on a street in Garen on his way to an early supper at his favorite tavern.

As he walked, he made a point not to smile or make eye contact. It would be hard to think of these people as his enemy if he came to think of them as just regular folks living their lives. He shook his head and quick-stepped to catch up with the rapidly marching watch patrol. He had a mission and he needed to focus.

When they left the center of the city behind, the buildings grew less and less fancy. They were still far nicer than the slums of Garen, but they lacked the crystals and ornamentation of the richer parts of the city. The watch patrol stopped outside a three-story brick building. Commander Kordwin gave orders to his people and the watchmen spread out to surround the building. Henry was relieved to see they were professionals. Hopefully they would soon recover the patch.

He smiled to himself at the irony of the city watch retrieving an item that would allow Garenland to take control of their portal. Henry doubted the commander would be pleased if he ever found out.

With his men in position, Kordwin went inside with one other watchman. Henry waited, arms crossed and foot tapping. How long could it take to arrest one rogue watchman? After a long ten minutes, Kordwin emerged from the building, alone. He looked right at Henry and crooked a finger.

"Nobody home?" Henry asked.

"No. Grayson was long gone and in a hurry too. There were plenty of stolen items in his flat, enough to see him in prison for twenty years. Unfortunately, your item wasn't among them. He must have known we'd be coming. I'm sorry. I promise we'll search all the pawn shops. Something made of mithril will be hard to miss."

"Let me help. Please. I can't go back without it so I'm stuck here until another caravan south shows up. You've got a murderer to catch. If we work together, maybe we can help each other."

Kordwin scowled, clearly not thrilled with the idea of a stranger poking his nose into watch business. At last he said, "You have a point. I can make you a temporary officer of the watch. It'll give you the right to ask questions and even arrest someone should you catch them committing a crime. Understand, should you misuse this authority, you'll face the same penalty any of my men would."

"I accept your terms. I only want to retrieve my good luck charm, Commander, not cause you trouble."

"Fair enough." Kordwin snapped his fingers and pointed at one of the watchmen that had gathered a few feet away. "Give me your badge."

The watchman removed a round brass shield the size of

Henry's palm from under his heavy cloak and handed it to Kordwin.

"Here. As long as you carry this, you'll have all the authority of a watchman. Grayson is a small man, five and a half feet tall and thin as a rail. He has dark hair and a long, thin mustache. I swear, if I didn't have a lunatic killing the daughters of the richest families in the city..." He handed the shield to Henry. "Don't make me regret giving it to you."

"Where can I find the nearest pawn shop?" Henry asked.

Kordwin was already headed back toward headquarters and he ignored Henry's question. Wonderful, looked like he really was on his own.

He shrugged and started walking. As a palace guard, he knew enough about basic investigation to know he needed to have a look around the neighborhood. While it was unlikely Grayson would be dumb enough to sell the patch at the shop nearest his flat, you could never discount the stupidity of someone that would steal from the watch evidence room. Though from the sounds of it, he'd been doing it for a while with no one the wiser.

Henry would have bet his new badge that the skinny little man dusting the shelves when they arrived was in on the scam. Either that or he was a "hear no evil, see no evil" sort of guy. He'd known a few of them in the guard. The sort that would never admit one of their fellows was capable of doing something wrong. They acted like an accusation against one of them was an accusation against all of them.

If worst came to worst, Henry could always beat the information out of Collins. He'd prefer not to since that might see him back in the watch cells again.

Six blocks of walking later, he came to the first pawn shop. It sat on the bottom floor of a three-story building. A sign with a scale on it hung over the scarred wooden door. Henry ducked inside and found a single room filled with laden shelves. If he had to search it all, he'd be here forever.

He angled across the room and found a young woman about seventeen sitting on a stool behind the counter. She looked at him with bored eyes and asked, "Buying or selling?"

Henry flashed the shield. "I'm hunting a thief. A watchman named Grayson stole something very valuable from watch headquarters. The item was made of thin mithril and marked with runes. Has anyone been in to sell something like that?"

"Grayson's a thief?" Her eyes nearly bugged out of her head. It seemed Henry finally had her attention.

"That's right. Since this is the nearest pawn shop to his flat, I'm visiting you first. So how about it?"

"No, we couldn't afford to buy something that valuable. He always seemed so nice. Grayson even helped me out of a tough spot with an over-eager guy a year ago. I can't believe he's a crook."

"For what it's worth, you can be a nice guy and a thief. If he didn't sell the item here, where do you think he could have gone?"

"Crystal Hill for sure. That's the only place with enough money to buy anything made of mithril. There's a place called the Treasure Vault. They buy and sell all kinds of stuff. If what you're looking for is anywhere, it's there."

"Thanks, I appreciate your help." Henry touched the side of his head in salute and left the shop.

Crystal Hill. He didn't know where that was, but he'd find out soon enough.

Finding Crystal Hill took all of five minutes. Henry couldn't stop staring at the houses. Some of them actually had crystal turrets at the tops of the roofs. Every street corner had an iron post with a clear crystal topping it. It was basically the Lux version of Gold Ward, where all the rich and powerful lived. At the northernmost point was the Crystal Palace where the queen held court. He had no intention of getting anywhere near there.

The Treasure Vault sat off the main street down a narrow alley. Not exactly prime real estate, but he suspected the locals didn't want to advertise that even they occasionally had need of a pawn broker. Not that Henry especially cared about the nobility's sensibilities. With any luck, he'd get what he needed and be on his way to less rarefied air in short order.

The pawn shop's front door was made of thick, heavy oak. It looked like it would easily withstand a battering ram. He knocked and a moment later a gate opened at eye level. A pair of dark, beady eyes glared out.

"What?"

Not terribly friendly. Henry held up his shield. "I need to speak to the owner."

"You aren't from this district," the man behind the door said. "I know every watchman in Crystal Hill and you're not one of them."

"You're right. I'm hunting for a thief and I was told that if he wanted to sell a rare and valuable item, this was the place to do it. Now you being a forthright and honest citizen, I'm sure you'll want to help. After all, it would be a shame if I found any other stolen items in your store. We might even have to shut you down."

The doorman grumbled and slammed the viewing window.

Two locks clunked and the door swung open. The man behind the door stood a little over four feet high and had a melon-sized hump on his back. Off to one side was a stool he'd used to see out the gate. The two of them barely fit in the entryway.

As soon as Henry was inside, the hunchback slammed the door and threw the locks. "Follow me. The owner's inside."

He opened the second door and led Henry into a large open room filled with glass cases. All manner of finery gleamed in the light of glowing crystals dangling from the ceiling. At a table on the far left-hand wall a rotund woman dressed in ten yards of red silk sat examining a diamond as big as Henry's thumb knuckle.

"Boss. Watchman here to see you."

She set her gem down and smiled, revealing a mouth full of yellow, smoke-stained teeth. "What a handsome visitor. Please join me."

Henry sat across from the woman. She was wearing enough perfume to make a skunk flee and underneath it was a faint hint of something rotten. The sooner he could get this done the better.

"I'm Madam Sun. What can I do for the watch today?"

"An item was stolen from watch headquarters by a man named Grayson. It was a square of mithril and quite valuable. According to everyone I've spoken to this is the only place he could sell it. Has anyone come in with an item like that?"

"I'm afraid not, darling. We don't have a scrap of mithril in stock. Pity, many of the nobles will pay top coin for anything made of the stuff. Your informant got one thing wrong. This might be the only business where he could sell it, but there are plenty of private buyers that would be happy to take such an item off his hands."

Henry cursed his luck. He couldn't go house to house

asking after Grayson; the high and mighty wouldn't stand for it. How was he going to find the patch now?

"If it's any help to you," Madam Sun said. "I can tell you the family most interested in collecting mithril items. The matron of the house is quite well known for wearing multiple mithril pieces out and about. Your thief is bound to know them."

"That would be a great help, thank you."

She raised a knobby, twisted finger. "You'll have to do something for me first."

Henry frowned. "Besides not arresting you for refusing to provide material information to a watchman?"

She flashed her yellow smile. "Just a little thing, darling. A quick kiss for a poor, lonely woman."

Madam Sun puckered up.

Maybe he could kill her and convince the hunchback to talk. Kissing those unnaturally red lips was apt to give him some sort of disease. He didn't have time for this.

Screwing up his courage, Henry kissed her as quickly as he could. His next stop would be for a whiskey to kill any germs. "The name."

"Melinda Horemots and family. She's the biggest mithril collector in the city. If your thief doesn't try to sell to her, I don't know where else you might search."

Henry stood. "Thank you. Good day, madam."

She licked her lips and waved. "Come again when you can stay longer."

He hurried out and found the hunchback waiting to let him out. The little man hobbled over to the door and opened it.

Henry paused before stepping outside. "Where can I find the Horemots' estate?"

"Mithril Street of course." The hunchback pointed north toward the palace.

Henry nodded his thanks and hurried off. Hopefully he could beat Grayson there.

○

Mithril Street was only a block from the royal palace. There were three giant mansions on it and only one had a gate with a sign over it that was made of silvery metal. If they were rich enough to use mithril for their sign, Henry couldn't begin to imagine how much wealth the family must possess. Enough to pay a good price for the patch certainly.

Henry paused to look the place over. The six guards on duty at the front gate looked him over in turn. While it was unlikely he'd get an audience, maybe the guards could give him some information. He crossed the street and pulled his shield.

"I'm looking for a thief with mithril to sell. Madam Sun suggested he might pay you a visit." Henry described Grayson. "Have you seen him?"

"We've had no visitors today, watchman," one of the guards said. "With all the murders, we've been extra careful about who we let in. Perhaps instead of chasing thieves, you should be looking for the killer."

"Commander Kordwin is looking into that case himself. Just because one crime spree is going on, it doesn't mean that we can simply ignore all other crimes in the city. To do so would be chaos. Should you see Grayson, please hold him and alert your local watchman. Thank you for your time."

Henry touched his forehead with his index finger and walked away. He doubted the guards would have told him if Grayson had shown up. Sharing their master's secrets was a good way to find yourself out of work. His main hope was that Grayson hadn't made it this far yet. With any luck he could catch the thief on his way here. But first he needed to find a good vantage point.

Mithril Street was nothing but residences. What he needed was a high position where he could see everyone coming and going. Henry studied the skyline and spotted a four-story building that overlooked the area. With a silent prayer that the owner would be the sort that liked to help the watch, he hurried towards it.

The four-story building turned out to be apartments. The front door was unlocked so Henry ducked inside. A middle-aged man sat behind a desk in the lobby. He looked up from the book he was reading and quirked a shaggy eyebrow.

"Can I help you?" he asked.

Henry flashed his shield and said, "I'm hunting a thief. I need to use the balcony on your fourth floor as a lookout position."

"This is your lucky day, watchman," he said. "Our last tenant just got married and moved into her husband's house. I trust you'll put a good word in for me with the government."

"Absolutely." Henry had no intention of doing anything of the sort but if it made the landlord happy, he was willing to play along. "Is the door locked?"

"Yep." The landlord opened one of the drawers of the desk and tossed Henry a key. "There you go. Just make sure you lock up when you leave and return the key to me."

Henry nodded his thanks and hurried up a nearby staircase. At the fourth-floor landing he found a locked door which the key fit. Beyond it was a foyer. It seemed the entire floor was a single apartment. The place was fully furnished, only the dove-gray walls were blank. He tried to imagine how much it must cost to rent a flat this size and failed. It would have made a comfortable home to a family of eight with room for guests.

A quick search brought him to a window overlooking Mithril Street. He had a perfect view of the mansion's front gate. Henry dragged the smallest chair he could find over to the window and settled in to wait.

***

Henry had been waiting all day, staring out the window, and seeing nothing but the guard change two hours ago. As the sun slowly set, he was beginning to think he'd chosen the wrong place to watch. Unfortunately, he didn't have any other ideas about where to look for the thief. It wasn't like he could just give up and go home. He had a mission to complete.

As the crystals came to life, shedding a white glow over everything, he finally saw movement. In fact, he saw two people approaching the mansion. A short, thin weasel of a man approached the front gate. He had a small package under his arm, a package just big enough to hold the mithril patch. Though Henry couldn't make out any details at this distance, that had to be Grayson. The question was, who was the second person sneaking in over the back fence?

He leapt to his feet. Hadn't Commander Kordwin said that the murderer stalking the streets at night targeted the daughters of wealthy families? With everyone staying inside now, if whoever it was wanted to keep killing, he would have no choice but to go to his victims.

Henry rushed out of the flat and ran down the steps, completely forgetting to lock the door behind him. As he ran past the front desk, he tossed the key to the landlord. "Summon the watch. The murderer's at the Horemots' manor."

He was out the door before the man could even speak.

It was a short run from the apartment building to the mansion and when he arrived Grayson was still trying to convince the guards to let him in. Henry tackled the thief to the ground and rolled him on his stomach, putting a knee in his lower back.

"I don't know how much the last shift told you," Henry said, showing the guards the shield the watch commander had given him. "But this is the thief I've been looking for. There's also someone sneaking across the rear lawn. I didn't get a good look, but with a killer on the loose I think you'd best find out who it is."

The guards looked at each other, turned, and ran for the house.

"I don't know you," Grayson said. "I thought I knew everybody in the watch."

"I'm a new hire. I'm also the guy you stole from. I'll be taking back the mithril patch. If you struggle or give me any trouble at all I'll cut your throat and leave you to bleed out in the dirt. Understand?"

"Yeah, sure. You must be new. Watchmen don't talk to prisoners like that."

Henry took the small package from Grayson and opened it. Just as he hoped, the mithril patch was inside and appeared undamaged. He wiped his brow and slipped it back into his pack where it belonged. What he needed now was a length of rope or something he could use to tie Grayson up.

He shook his head. Why was he acting like he was actually a watchman? What he should do was bash the idiot over the head and make a dash for the portal. He looked at the mansion where a killer even now might be stalking the halls. He owed these people nothing, but leaving defenseless people at the mercy of a murderer didn't sit well with him.

"Dammit." Henry dug out his spare tunic and cut the left arm off. It wasn't exactly ideal, but it should hold Grayson until the other watchmen arrived.

With the thief bound and his property recovered, Henry ran for the mansion. He told himself capturing the killer would help with his cover while he waited for the Garenland army to arrive. Maybe he'd eventually even believe the lie.

The guards had left the front door open, so he rushed in without pausing. The entry area was empty.

Henry cocked his head and listened. There had to be some people in here somewhere and wherever they were was where the killer would be headed.

There was a crash from upstairs.

He raced up a curving staircase and down a carpeted hall towards where he thought the sound had come from.

He passed three doors before coming to one that was open partway. He pushed it the rest of the way open and found the figure in black, a curved dagger in one hand, and a young woman in a nightgown in the other.

The murderer put the dagger to her throat and said, "Step away or I'll kill her."

The girl whimpered and tears ran down her face.

Henry shook his head. "You're going to kill her anyway. The only way you're getting out of here alive is if you surrender. Harm the young lady in any way and I'll cut you down where you stand."

"You're bluffing. Unbuckle your sword and and let me walk out of here and I'll let her go. I promise."

"I'm supposed to take the word of a killer?"

"It's not like you have a lot of options."

The monster had a point and Henry had an idea. "Fine."

He dropped his pack and unbuckled his sword, lowering it slowly to the ground so his hand was close to the open pack.

"On second thought, I think I'll kill you both right now." The killer raised his dagger.

The instant he did, Henry pulled out the mithril square and threw it as hard as he could. The thin, sharp edge stuck in the killer's throat, shredding flesh and sending blood spraying everywhere.

He fell slowly backwards, releasing his hostage as he did.

She ran over and wrapped her arms around Henry, crying into his chest. Moments later the thud of footsteps came from behind him.

Commander Kordwin appeared in the doorway a moment later, his sword drawn. He had a dozen guys behind him.

Kordwin looked from the killer to Henry. "You got him and the thief. Quite a day's work. Are you trying to make me look bad?"

"Just dumb luck. I'm glad I could be of service." Henry offered the commander his shield back. "Now that I've recovered my property, I suppose you'll want this back."

"Not unless you want to give it up. You've certainly proved your worth to me. Garenlander or not, you're welcome to stay a member of the watch."

"Since I probably missed my caravan, I'll take you up on that offer, at least until the next one arrives."

"Jenna!" A gray-haired matron pushed her way through the press of watchmen.

The girl in Henry's arms abandoned him at once and ran to her. They embraced while he recovered the mithril patch, pausing to clean it on the killer's shirt.

"It's been a long day, Commander," Henry said. "I think I'll call it a night. Should I swing by watch headquarters in the morning?"

"Yes, I'll have something for you. And welcome to the team." Kordwin held out his hand and Henry shook it.

This was perfect. What better place for a spy to hide than in the city watch? He cut off a grin and made his way out of the mansion. There was one more thing he had to do.

The walk to the city center was a short one. Tonight, at least, he didn't end up getting arrested. When he reached the portal, he found the gathering area empty and not a soul in sight.

Perfect.

With a flick of his wrist, Henry sent the patch spinning toward the master rune. Lightning crackled and drew it into place, perfectly fusing the patch with the portal. His mission complete, he headed toward the tavern where he'd been drinking with the others from his caravan. Hopefully they either had rooms or could direct him to a cheap inn.

When he pushed through the tavern's front door, he was shocked to find Grumbler sitting at the same table they'd occupied the night before. Henry had assumed the caravan would be well on their way south by now.

Henry took a seat across from his driver. "This is a surprise."

"Jack said since you were recommended by Lord Shenk we'd give you an extra day. Where the hell have you been?"

"I got arrested."

"What?"

"Apparently there's been some killings and when I went out for a walk last night the watch nabbed me. The real killer was caught today so they let me go."

"You must have the worst luck of anyone I've ever met."

"Yeah. On the plus side, I found a job here. So while I appreciate you all waiting for me, I won't be heading back to Garenland." Henry clapped Grumbler on the back. "Sorry."

Grumbler shrugged. "I was just happy for the extra day off. Jack won't be so pleased. That makes me happy too. Well, good luck to you, kid."

"You too. Maybe I'll see you around on your next run."

"If you do, drinks are on you."

Henry grinned. "Deal."

CHAPTER 14

THE LASIL INFILTRATION

Luca eyed the flat-bottom riverboat resting on a sandbar beside the river. It didn't look entirely seaworthy. In fact, the timbers the riverboat was made of appeared to be still green. That couldn't be of course, no one would sail down the river with a boat that new.

He'd set out for the river immediately after receiving the mithril patch from Lord Shenk and His Majesty. The danger and importance of his mission had been made perfectly clear. Garenland's future rested on his and his comrades' shoulders.

Four burly, bare-chested men were busy loading heavy crates into the boat. Half a dozen others were unloading a wagon further up the beach near an empty boat identical to the one they were using. No one had told Luca what sort of merchandise the ship was carrying and he didn't especially care. As long as it wasn't something that would attract the attention of the border guards.

The last thing he needed was attention. His mission was one that required subtlety and stealth. Slipping in to Lasil's capital wasn't going to be easy. Everything he'd read indicated that it was one of the most heavily fortified places on the continent.

Its nickname was Vault City and not just because it was home to the largest bank, possibly in the world. Their soldiers were supposed to be topnotch as well. Henry had been bitching ever since he learned he was getting the easy run into Lux, but Luca would have happily traded places with him.

Only the young and stupid sought out nearly impossible challenges. When you'd served as long as Luca, you learned the value of taking the easy road sometimes. Despite that, he'd gotten what he considered the hardest mission. That was the price of being a veteran.

"Welcome, welcome." A short, jittery man with a goatee and bright red tunic hurried over waving his hands. "You must be the security expert Lord Shenk told me was coming along for this trip to study our security protocols."

"That's right." Luca didn't know why Lord Shenk decided that his cover should be a security expert rather than just a simple guard, and he wasn't about to ask. If that was the part he was supposed to play, then play it he would. "I'm sure everything you're doing is fine, but it never hurts to have an outsider take a look. I might see something you missed."

"Yes, yes, absolutely. You'll see. Everything's exactly as it should be. No items going missing on my boat, rest assured. We'll be loaded and ready to go in a few minutes. Please, make yourself comfortable until then."

The little man hurried off without even mentioning his name. What he said about items going missing was interesting. Maybe Lord Shenk had a secondary purpose for sending him on this mission. He'd have to keep his eyes peeled for thieves as well.

A few minutes turned into over half an hour, but finally

they were ready to go. A dozen crates were secured under a heavy, oiled canvas. The stevedores turned out to also be oarsmen. They sat at a pair of benches with long oars beside them. The nervous merchant stood in the rear at a tiller. The idea that the jittery little man was in charge of navigating them safely down the river didn't fill Luca with confidence.

Luca settled himself at the front of the boat. When everyone was ready, the workers from up the beach trotted down and pushed them out into the current. The oarsmen unshipped their oars and pulled hard to draw them into the center of the river. The merchant's hands were steady on the tiller as he guided them through the smooth water.

Heartened by the crew's competent handling of the boat, Luca allowed himself to believe they'd make it to Lasil in one piece rather than as drowned corpses.

His confidence lasted until an hour after lunch when the first whitewater appeared ahead of them. The handful of boulders jutting out of the water looked awfully threatening.

"Look sharp on the oars!" the merchant shouted.

The boat bucked as they hit the first riffle.

The merchant jerked the tiller and barked, "Hard left!"

The oarsmen on that side pulled while the ones on the opposite side lifted their oars out of the water altogether.

Luca gripped the side of the boat so tight that the wood scraped his palms.

He'd barely gotten set when he was thrown the opposite way.

"Dig hard, boys! Hard!"

Luca's stomach twisted and his heart raced. He'd faced many foes in battle without batting an eye, but this was madness. How did you fight a river?

Two more sharp lurches had his head over the side and his lunch going to feed the fish.

And then it was over and they were in smooth water. Luca pried his hands free of the railing and checked them for splinters.

"Your first time through rapids?" The merchant had tied off the tiller and made his way to the front of the boat.

"Yeah. You could tell?"

The little man smiled, his jitters seeming to have remained behind on the riverbank. "I had a hunch. I've made this trip with landsmen before. Don't worry, there are only a handful of rapids like that one."

Luca shook his head. If he had to live through that five more times, he was likely to be dead before he could complete his mission. "Why would you risk the river if you could just travel by portal? I mean I understand it now, but it sounds like you've been doing this for a while."

"If you're selling in northern Lasil, it's actually faster to bring the goods into the river post and distribute them from there. The central mountains make traveling from the capital with a wagonload of merchandise sketchy at best."

The merchant would certainly know about sketchy travel. "What's the river post?"

"Oh, that's a trading post right beside the river. We call it the river post. Anyway, I've never lost a cargo so you can relax and enjoy the ride. We'll get there intact, never fear."

Easier said than done. "We weren't properly introduced earlier. I'm Luca."

"Of course, forgive me. I'm Donovan, Captain Donovan when we're on the boat, but I won't hold you to anything so formal." Donovan shook Luca's hand vigorously. "Didn't mean to be rude earlier. I'm nervous when I'm on land. There's some water around here somewhere if you want to rinse your mouth."

Donovan hurried back to the tiller and adjusted their course. The captain at least seemed to know what he was doing. Feeling a little better than he did earlier, Luca tried to relax.

Donovan called out, "Oars ready!"

Luca looked over his shoulder. Another stretch of rough water was fast approaching.

Clearly, relaxing wouldn't be in the cards anytime soon.

○

Luca had never spent much time traveling. He was born in Garen, joined the watch then transferred to the palace guard. He'd certainly never seen a backwoods trading post. He doubted anyone had seen a trading post like this one.

The river post featured a twelve-foot stockade of sharpened stakes on three sides and a river on the fourth. The buildings were built of odd-sized planks and timber and the smell filling the air would curl your nose hairs.

Donovan guided the boat to a dock and they quickly tied up. They made the journey in less than two weeks. Luca didn't know if that was good or not, but he was delighted to get out of the bloody boat. If he never had to get in another one for the rest of his life it would suit him fine.

Luca collected his pack and stepped out onto the pier. His legs wobbled but he soon enough regained his balance. He'd need a few hours to recover before sneaking into the interior. Climbing mountains would be a snap compared to the boat ride.

"Told you I'd get you here in one piece." Donovan clapped

him on the back. "I trust you'll give Lord Shenk a good report?"

"Of course," Luca said, finally remembering his cover. "So what happens now? I assume Lasil runs the trading post."

"Nope, we run it. Garenland merchants, that is. We're only about a mile over the border. They run patrols through the area to make sure we don't get any ideas, but other than that, this is a little slice of home. We'll stay the night and ride north in the morning."

"Ride? What about your boat?"

"It'll get knocked apart and used to repair the buildings or build new ones. They come downstream good but going back not so much. Trust me, a horse is a better option."

That at least explained the ramshackle nature of the river post. The whole thing must have been built out of scrapped boats. "I won't be returning with you directly. I need to check out the trading post as well."

"I see. That makes sense I suppose. The Frankens paid for most of this so it's only natural they'd want you to make sure everything's shipshape. You should at least wait until the next boat arrives. Riding north alone can be sketchy."

"I appreciate the advice."

They shook and Donovan went back to oversee the unloading of his cargo. Luca shouldered his pack and walked into the trading post.

The largest building had a crude sign out front with a frothing mug carved in it. That had to be the local tavern. Luca angled that way and slipped through the open door. The interior was every bit as rough as the building itself. The floor was dirt, the tables barrels, and the chairs old shipping crates. There was no bar, but three open barrels sat at the rear of the building. Each one was half full of the foulest-smelling ale and wine he'd ever encountered.

He walked right back out of the tavern. If there wasn't a well, he'd take his chances with river water. It couldn't be any nastier than the booze.

To his great relief, Luca discovered that the smaller huts were available for anyone visiting to use. They weren't much, but they were clean and had a cot, which was all he needed. He'd get a few hours' sleep and sneak out late tonight. It was a long hike to Vault City and the sooner he got going, the sooner he'd arrive.

○

Three days out from the river post, Luca reached the mountains. He assumed they had a name, but he hadn't bothered to learn it. Tall, jagged, and still capped with snow, the peaks were a formidable barrier. Only three passes allowed entry to the more populated southern half of Lasil. The mountains were one of the reasons Lasil had never been invaded.

Since there was no way he could sneak through the heavily guarded passes, Luca would have to find a path over on his own. He shook his head, hiked his heavily laden pack a little higher on his shoulders, and set out.

His initial approach was easy enough. The foothills were clear of snow and not too steep. Signs of deer and other wildlife abounded. If he got short of preserved food, hunting shouldn't be an issue. At least that was what he thought until he reached the higher slopes. The trees began to peter out and a brisk wind made him shiver. It blew down from the peaks, across the snow, picking up a bitter chill along the way.

Luca hoped to avoid the highest parts of the mountains.

There had to be some narrow passes high enough up that no one considered them a danger, but low enough that they were open this time of year. Finding them wouldn't be easy, but then again if this had been an easy mission, the king would have given it to someone else.

He reached the snow line an hour after noon. Almost immediately he cut a set of tracks. They looked human, but too small to be an adult. What on earth would a kid be doing out here? He hadn't seen anything resembling civilization in a day and a half.

With no better ideas, Luca set out after the kid.

The first snowflakes started falling half an hour later. Luca glanced up at the leaden sky. Hopefully it wouldn't be too heavy a storm. Either way he needed to find shelter soon. He glanced back the way he'd come and immediately dismissed it. He'd passed nothing for hours that would serve.

A long, mournful howl cut short his musing. Was that a wolf? Luca was no expert on the local wildlife, but this didn't seem like the sort of area a pack of wolves would live. There was nothing visible for as far as he could see across the snow. A sick feeling twisted his stomach as he picked up the pace.

That howl had come from the same direction the kid's footprints were headed. As he quick-marched through ankle-deep snow, Luca wondered why he was even bothering to check on the kid. It was really none of his concern.

His concern or not, he didn't change course. Maybe it was his training or his nature, but protecting people was something he had to do, especially those who couldn't protect themselves. Lasil might be an enemy of Garenland, but this child had done nothing to harm his nation.

The howls grew louder and more frequent as he continued along the kid's path. At least the snow wasn't picking up.

Flakes fell at a slow, steady pace, just enough to be annoying, but not a real hinderance.

Luca crested a small rise and found a pair of humanoid figures covered in fur looming over a boy perhaps thirteen armed with a crooked spear woefully inadequate to fend off those two creatures. Behind the boy cowered a small animal with tight, curly black fur.

The boy bared his teeth and poked at the two monsters.

One of them batted the spear aside, sending the boy staggering to his right.

He scrambled back into position, seeming undaunted by his failure. The monster's howls held a different tenor this time, almost like laughter. The creatures were taunting the boy, enjoying his fear and helplessness.

Luca had originally thought they were mindless beasts, but now he wasn't so sure. If they were intelligent, he'd have to be more careful how he attacked them. Judging by their size and the breadth of their shoulders, they would be powerful opponents.

One of the creatures surged forward, knocking the boy to the ground.

So much for being careful.

Luca roared and charged, trying to draw their attention away from the boy.

Fortunately or unfortunately, depending on your point of view, he succeeded. Both monsters spun to face him, giving Luca his first close look at his opponents. They looked like wolves that had been stretched and broadened into men. Thick fur covered their bodies and they wore no other clothes. Their hands ended in long, sharp talons that looked like they could tear a man into pieces easily. Their arms were long enough to counter the reach advantage of his sword.

Luca attacked with a high, passing slash at the right-hand monster's throat.

It dodged back, far too fast for such a huge creature.

The second monster moved to intercept him, forcing Luca to duck under its claws. The wind of the strike parted his hair. Had that blow struck home, he would be missing his head right now.

His riposte sliced a red line in the monster's arm.

It snarled and pulled back.

Unfortunately, this was only to make room for its partner to pick up the attack.

The ferocity of the creature's assault forced Luca back. It was all he could do to evade the slashing claws that wanted to spill his guts in the snow.

His only hope of ending this battle was to take a gamble.

A big one.

Luca stepped back and wavered like he'd lost his balance.

His opponent took the bait and charged.

Luca planted his back foot, ducked, and thrust, letting the wolf creature impale itself on his sword.

As its partner died, the second monster howled, this time in seeming despair. There was certainly no question about the fury in its snarl when it bared its fangs at Luca and crouched, ready to charge.

As its muscles bunched, the boy stabbed it in the leg.

The beast turned, ready to strike him down.

That was all the opening Luca needed.

He charged and leapt, hacking at its neck with all the force he could muster.

His sword bit deep, slicing halfway through the monster's neck.

It collapsed, twitching a couple times as it bled out.

Luca cleaned his sword on the dead monster's fur and sheathed it. "Are you okay?"

The boy straightened and puffed out his chest. "Sure I am. It'll take more than a couple wolflings to bother me."

So saying, the boy collapsed face first into the snow. Four long, bloody lines had been scratched in his back. If Luca didn't get those bound quickly, he'd probably bleed to death.

As he stepped toward the unconscious boy, the snow began to pick up.

○

The annoying flakes of snow had turned into a full-fledged storm. Wind-driven snow screamed across the entrance to the shelter he'd constructed. It wasn't much of a shelter. Luca had found a fallen tree and arranged the branches into a wall that he covered with snow to create a crude lean-to. Much as he hated the survival instruction all palace guards received—Who even needed survival instructions when you spent all your time in a castle or the city? —the knowledge had certainly come in handy.

Though it had taken most of his meager stash of medical supplies, Luca had bound the boy's wounds and for the moment he appeared to be resting comfortably. The beast he'd been so intent on protecting lay curled up in a fuzzy ball beside him.

At first Luca had thought the animal was a sheep, but even a yearling ram didn't have spiral horns. This one did, tiny ones that curled around once before ending in blunt tips. Whatever it was, it had followed him calmly enough as he carried the boy through the storm.

Now it was a waiting game. With any luck, the storm would

break by morning. When it did, he'd have to figure out what to do with his unconscious companion. Leaving the injured kid on his own wasn't an option. Hopefully he'd be from a relatively nearby village and Luca could just escort him home and be on his way.

As he was gnawing on his second strip of jerky, the kid sat bolt upright, gasping like a drowning man coming to the surface.

"Easy, kid, you're safe now."

The boy looked at him. "You killed the wolflings. Thank you. No warrior from our village could defeat two of them on his own."

"You helped, remember?"

He puffed up with pride. Luca hoped he didn't collapse again. "I'm going to be a warrior one day. Uni! Is he okay?"

"If you mean that little bundle of fluff, he's right beside you. Got a name? I can't keep calling you kid."

"I'm Jorge." He petted the little animal as if to assure himself that it was unharmed. "Uni will be the sire for the next generation of mountain sheep. If he escaped, it would have meant big trouble for our village."

"Is that what brought you out to this desolate spot all alone?" Luca handed him a strip of jerky.

Jorge nodded. "I was on guard when Uni escaped. It's my responsibility to bring him back. Father always says a shepherd protects his flock."

"I suppose he does at that. Why don't you get some rest? We're not going anywhere until this storm passes."

Jorge gnawed on his jerky. The boy didn't seem overly nervous about being trapped in a small space with a complete stranger. Granted Luca had just saved his life, but still, a little caution wouldn't be a bad thing. From what he could see, Jorge had an unhealthy lack of fear.

If Jorge wasn't going to sleep, Luca figured he might as well try and get some information. "Are there more of those monsters around?"

"A few. No one really knows how many there are. They mostly keep to the mountains and hunt wild goats. They only bother us when they get desperate. Not that they aren't happy to kill and eat anyone dumb enough to go alone into the hills."

"Like us?" Luca asked.

Jorge smiled and stuffed the last of his jerky into his mouth. "A man's got to do what a man's got to do. Say, what are you doing out here anyway? You're not from our village."

"I'm looking for a way across the mountains." Luca looked around as though he were about to share a big secret. "I was hired to find a way to avoid the soldiers in the passes so they can't collect any taxes."

Jorge's expression soured. "We all hate the soldiers. They charge northerners like us taxes on our wool and mutton just like we were foreigners. They do it because the merchants don't want us selling our goods directly to their customers. They're too scared we might make a coin that could have been theirs."

It seemed Luca had found some potential allies. That was good. He could use all the help he could get. Outside it was getting dark and the snow showed no sign of letting up. Hopefully they didn't end up buried in the snow.

Sometime during the night, the storm stopped. As soon as they woke, Luca and Jorge set out with Uni trotting along beside them like a puppy. Luca didn't have great experience with animals, but he was pretty sure sheep didn't act like that as a general rule. Though all signs of their tracks were gone, Jorge took the lead without any hesitation.

An hour of trudging through the cold and white brought them within sight of a small collection of round huts. Smoke rose from them, coloring the air gray. Off to one side of the village a pen had been constructed and a collection of sheep that looked like bigger versions of Uni wandered around and pawed at the snow.

Half a dozen men armed with spears stood a little way off to one side of the pen. Jorge loosed a shrill whistle and waved both hands. The men waved back as the boy ran toward them with his furry friend in tow. Luca held back until one of the men, the biggest and burliest, beckoned him down.

Reasonably confident that he wouldn't get run through the instant he arrived, Luca marched down to the gathering. The man that waved him over thrust out a hand. "My boy says you saved him from a pair of wolflings. I don't know how I can ever thank you enough for that. He's a good boy, but overconfident."

Luca shook and managed not to wince at the man's grip; it was strong enough to bend iron. "It was pure chance that we ran into each other and I was happy to lend a hand. As for thanking me, if you can point me in the direction of the nearest unguarded passage, I'm happy to call it even."

"And why would you be looking for an unguarded pass?"

"My employers are looking for a way to avoid the taxes for entry. My name's Luca and I'm from Garenland. Our merchants have been getting crushed since we were kicked out of the Portal Compact. Anything we can do to save a coin helps."

"We've done business with Garenland merchants for years. Always got a fair price for our goods, which is more than I can say for our countrymen." Jorge's father spat to one side. "I've got no use for those bastards in the passes below. If I can stick my thumb in their eye, I'm happy to do it. I can show you our pass. It's too small for anything but a single-file line, but you're welcome to use it."

"Thank you. Are you certain you won't get into any trouble for helping me?" Luca didn't really care if they got into trouble but figured asking would be in character.

"Who's going to know? Come on. It's a long walk so we'd best get started."

It was indeed a long walk, but at least they didn't run into any wolflings. That was a trade Luca was willing to make any day. Jorge's father turned out to not be much of a conversationalist. That also suited Luca. While he was playing his part, he wasn't all that good of an actor. Silent trudging through the snow was much safer than making small talk.

Seven hours after leaving the village they stopped at a narrow path that bent around a steep peak. Barely wide enough for a single person to pass and covered with snow, the path looked like a good place to kill yourself.

"When you reach the far side of the mountains, the path levels out and gets wider. If you hurry, you should be able to make it before dark. Good luck." With a wave Luca's guide hurried back the way he'd come.

"That was... abrupt." Luca shrugged and started working his way down the narrow path.

There didn't seem to be any ice yet at least and hand grips

were plentiful on the rough stone wall. The passage looked tricky but doable. Luca picked up his pace. The last thing he wanted was to be stuck out on a narrow path for the night.

Vault City certainly lived up to its name. Luca eyed the massive walls, easily sixty feet tall and half that thick. In the time he'd been watching from his hiding place in a grove of spruce off the main road, he'd counted sixty different guards patrolling the walls. To be safe, he'd assume there were a hundred altogether, minimum. There was a single gate that had a heavy guard as well and every wagon or mule entering was thoroughly searched. No way was he getting in by hiding in some poor merchant's goods.

After completing the mountain passage, he'd hoped the worst of his task was behind him. That had clearly been wishful thinking. If anything, getting inside was going to be harder than crossing the mountains.

The gate was definitely a no-go. Since the city was built practically on the ocean, maybe he could swim in after dark. He shivered just thinking about that cold water. But cold or not, it was better than getting feathered by an overzealous guard.

He retreated and started a wide circle toward the ocean. The hike took him nearly an hour, but when he reached the edge of the woods, he found an empty, white-sand beach. The Vault City docks were visible a quarter mile away. The harbor passage was narrow and guarded by a pair of combination lighthouse guard towers. A chain was strung between them that could be raised or lowered to restrict entry.

From his current position to the docks had to be nearly a

mile of actual swimming when you factored in getting around the sea wall. There was no ice floating in the harbor, but it still had to be awfully cold. In the summer it would be an easy swim, but now he wasn't so sure.

As he stood thinking, a two-masted ship came sailing up from the east. Judging from the soot that covered every surface of the vessel, she was a whaler returning from a season of hunting. Lasil processed more whale oil than any other nation.

An evil idea popped into his head. Luca's orders were to secure the patch, no one said anything about not damaging the city. If he could get a flaming arrow into one of the oil warehouses, that would provide more than enough distraction to let him slip inside and do what he had to do. The trick was going to be finding a bow powerful enough to launch an arrow where he needed it.

He glanced back at the trees. Then again, maybe it wouldn't be that hard after all.

Luca spent the better part of a day and a half carving branches into bows, none of which worked worth a damn. His best effort launched a crude arrow all of forty feet. It was pathetic. How hard could it be to shape a piece of wood into a bow? Obviously a lot harder than he'd thought.

He tossed his most recent cracked, pathetic excuse for a weapon into a brush pile. He needed a new plan.

Luca walked back to the beach and stared at the harbor. It was the only weak point in the city's defenses and his only hope of getting inside. He paced as he discarded one plan after another.

Half an hour and five plans had passed when a voice said, "Are you from Garenland?"

Luca spun and ripped his sword from its sheath. A cloaked figure, his—at least Luca assumed it was a him—face hidden by a raised hood, lifted a hand. "Be at ease. My comrades have been expecting you."

Luca's blade never wavered. "No one knows I'm here. How could you be expecting me?"

"Your friend Oskar told us someone from Garenland would be coming and that you might be needing help getting into the city. When I couldn't find you on the opposite side of the city, I came to search here. I apologize if you've been waiting long."

Luca tried to process what he'd been told. Oskar had been assigned the Rolan infiltration, the second most difficult after Lasil, at least by Luca's estimate. He certainly shouldn't have been telling tales about his mission. If he had, Oskar must have found allies he trusted totally.

"Who are you exactly?"

"Forgive my lack of manners. My name is Christianson, I'm a wizard and a member of the underground. I've been assigned to help you complete your mission in any way I can."

Luca sheathed his sword. "I didn't know there was a wizard underground."

"It wouldn't be much of a secret organization if you did. We have members in every nation. Garenland has always been a haven for us. More than a few wizards facing the death penalty in one of the other nations has been ferried to safety in your country. Now that wizards have been given full rights as citizens, we are ready to embrace your cause and bring freedom to all our enslaved brothers and sisters."

Christianson sounded like a zealot, but having a wizard was too big an advantage to pass up. Completing the mission was all that mattered.

"Tell me, my friend, how do we go about getting into the city?"

"I saw you watching the harbor. You're right, that is the

only weakness in their defenses. But you don't want to go over the water, you want to go under it."

※

After a nearly two-mile hike from the southern side of Vault City to the northern side, Luca and Christianson stopped in front of a fallen log resting across a pile of boulders. They only had an hour before sunset and there was still no sign of a tunnel. He couldn't even imagine the time it would take to dig under the ocean from here into the city. Even with magic, it had to have been a titanic undertaking.

"Are you ready?" Christianson asked.

"I've been ready since I got here. Where's this tunnel?"

The wizard pointed and the stones and log vanished, revealing a stone passage deep into the earth. It wasn't even pointed toward the city. The tunnel mouth was aimed at the ocean.

"Quickly," Christianson said. "I have to reset the illusion."

With no other options, Luca started down the short, stone steps. He turned his foot sideways to fit them on each stair. It was like the tunnel had been made for children.

The passage went pitch black and he froze. A moment later a ball of white light appeared. Luca looked back and found his guide descending behind him. The entrance was invisible now, hopefully from both sides.

"We're not going the right way," Luca said.

"No, not yet. Don't worry, there's a nexus chamber about a quarter mile away. The city passage branches off from there."

The wizard assumed the lead and they set out again. Luca ran a hand along the wall. The rough stone was damp. He licked his finger and tasted salt.

"Are we under the ocean?" Luca asked.

"That's right. Don't worry, these tunnels were made by a far mightier hand than mine. Lord Karonin herself carved them centuries ago. They might leak a little, but we're in no danger of them collapsing."

That was reassuring, sort of. "Why did she make tunnels under the ocean?"

"Excellent question. We've been wondering exactly that since the tunnels were discovered fifteen years ago. So far, no one has come up with an answer that seemed reasonable. And it's not like we can ask a long-dead Arcane Lord. For our purposes, the tunnels serve as an excellent base, one that anyone without magic is unlikely to find and even if they did find it, these narrow passages would be easy to defend."

A quarter-mile underground in the dark seemed a lot further than it was. But finally Luca and his guide reached a large open cavern. Some tents had been set up along with a handful of more permanent-looking wooden buildings. Three other tunnels branched off from the central cavern. The only thing missing was people.

"Where is everybody?" Luca asked.

Christianson wouldn't meet his gaze as he said, "Please understand, it's not that they don't trust you, but if you don't know what anyone looks like you can't tell the guards if you have the misfortune to be captured."

Luca couldn't find fault with that reasoning and let the matter drop. If he had been running an underground organization and some crazy stranger showed up, he'd be reluctant to show everyone's faces as well.

"So which one leads to the city?"

Christianson pointed to a tunnel running ninety degrees to the one they exited. "It's quite late in the day. Perhaps you would like to eat and sleep somewhere safe before heading out early tomorrow?"

"How about we eat and go straight in? Arriving in the dark is liable to draw less attention anyway."

"In any other city, you would be right, but Vault City has a strict curfew. Anyone caught outside after dark faces arrest and a night in jail."

Seeing Luca's expression, he hastened to add, "They won't be harmed or punished beyond spending the night in a cell. King Kasimir is exceedingly paranoid about security in the city. Not without reason. After all, there's enough gold in the vaults to buy a small kingdom. All of Lasil's power comes from that wealth."

A curfew was going to make reaching the portal unseen incredibly hard, maybe even impossible. He needed to think and couldn't do it on an empty stomach.

"Fine, we'll spend the night here and move at first light." He frowned. "How will we know when first light is?"

"Don't worry," Christianson said. "I've spent enough days down here that I have an excellent sense of time. I'll know when we should go."

Telling Luca not to worry was like telling a fish not to swim. Still, for the moment at least, there was nothing he could do. Maybe a hot meal and a good night's sleep would inspire him. And if it didn't, he'd just have to make it up as he went along.

Luca blinked against the light as Christianson shook him awake. He felt like he hadn't been asleep for any time and now it was time to get going again. The food at least had been decent; after weeks of chewing on jerky and hardtack, even a stew made with dried vegetables was a welcome change.

He rolled out of his cot and stretched. His bones creaked and popped. The thin mattress of the cot had been only marginally better than sleeping on the stone floor. Luca rubbed his eyes and turned to Christianson. "Time to go?"

"The sun should be up. If you wish to break your fast, I prepared a pot of oatmeal. Not the most exciting breakfast I admit, but on the bright side there is honey."

Luca followed the wizard outside and a short distance away found a pot bubbling over a magical flame. After a quick breakfast they were on their way up another tunnel. There was nothing to distinguish this one from the one they followed down, beyond the slight rise in elevation with each stride. When he tried to wrap his mind around the amount of power it would've taken to carve these tunnels out of solid stone, he was reminded once again how good it was that the Arcane Lords were long gone, mostly anyway.

After ten minutes or so of marching, they stopped at the foot of another set of steps.

"We are under the city now," Christianson said. "You need to be quiet and do nothing to attract attention. If the guards get even the slightest inkling that we're up to something, they'll arrest us just to be safe. I assure you, you do not want to be questioned by the Vault City watch."

Luca didn't want to be questioned by anyone, but he just nodded and indicated Christianson should start climbing the steps. He followed the wizard up to a closed wooden door. Seconds passed in absolute silence until finally Christianson decided to open the door. They stepped out into a small, eight-by-eight room.

When the light vanished, the outline of a hidden door

became visible. Christianson listened at this one for a while as well before opening it. The more Luca saw of his partner's caution, the better he liked the man. They emerged into a dusty office that looked like it hadn't been used in years. Dust covered a lonely table and cobwebs hung in the corners.

"Where are we now?" Luca whispered.

"This is an unused office in a warehouse not far from the docks. The owner's daughter is a wizard and was taken as a slave. He has been helping us for the past five years. Don't worry, you will find no one more dedicated to the downfall of this kingdom than him."

The office had two doors, one to the right and one directly ahead. Christianson went to the one on the right. It opened into an alley beside the warehouse. The instant the door opened, the most horrific stench Luca had ever smelled washed over him. He coughed and fought to keep his oatmeal down.

"What, in heaven's name, is that?" Lucas asked.

"That would be the whale oil ships. The stench of rendering never really leaves them. Don't worry, once we get a little further inland the worst of the smell will fade. Try to keep your expression neutral as we walk, if you react strongly to the odor it will mark you as an outsider."

Luca did his best to smooth his face and followed Christianson to the end of the alley. The street was busy with people bustling here and there, some carrying packages, and others empty-handed. For a city renowned for its wealth, the people were largely dressed in plain, brown and black, and in some cases worn, clothing.

They merged with the flow of traffic and walked at a brisk pace toward the center of the city. Though the stink never truly went away, it did get tolerable about five blocks from the warehouse. The fact that the wind was currently blowing in their faces helped.

Some minutes of steady walking brought them into a large open plaza with the portal at its center. It looked pretty much the same as the Garenland portal. They stopped just outside of the plaza and Luca looked everything over. The first thing he noticed was the dozen guards stationed in groups of three all around the area. A pair of merchant wagons had already queued up for the first opening of the day. He wasn't sure which nation was first in the rotation, but it certainly wasn't Garenland.

Christianson tugged on his sleeve and said, "We can't linger here, the guards will get suspicious. There is a safe house nearby where we can discuss your plans."

Luca appreciated his optimism but having to approach in daylight with twelve men keeping watch really limited his options. He took one more long look and then allowed himself to be led away.

The safe house turned out to be a flat two blocks from the portal in a rundown apartment building across the street from a bar that smelled only slightly better than the docks. Lucas swore that once he finished this mission, he was going to request a transfer somewhere that smelled of roses and fresh-baked bread.

The flat had two rooms and a cast iron stove for cooking and heat. The chairs looked like they went to war with a pack of rats and came out on the losing side. Despite their appearance, Luca dropped into the nearest one and hung his head. How in the blackest hell was he going to get to the portal? He'd heard the king was paranoid, but this was ridiculous.

"Do you have any ideas?" Christianson asked.

Luca shot him a bleak look. "Do I look like I have any ideas?"

"Sorry, that was a foolish question."

"No, I'm sorry. I'm just feeling a little overwhelmed. Is there any time that the plaza is unguarded?" Luca asked.

Christianson took a ginger seat in the second chair. "Not as far as I know."

"We need some way to draw them off. How big a ruckus would I have to raise to get the guards to come investigate?"

"I doubt the plaza guards would leave their posts for anything less than a robbery at one of the gold depots."

Luca perked up at that, but Christianson shook his head at once. "Don't even think about it. The depots are fortresses. I doubt we could get into one if every member of the underground came to help."

"What about the whale oil storage buildings? Are they guarded?"

"Yes, though nothing like the vaults. I doubt a robbery there would get a reaction from the plaza guards."

"What about a fire?"

Christianson stared at him in horror. "You could burn down the city. The buildings in the dock neighborhood are nothing but dry wood."

"Wouldn't the wizards and every member of the watch do their best to put it out? Surely with all the city's resources the danger wouldn't be so great. Frankly, unless you have another suggestion, I see no other option. At least not one that two people could pull off."

Christianson's pained grimace told Luca all he needed to know. The wizard didn't have any other ideas. "Alright. I'll spark the fire and you do whatever you need to do. We'll meet back here then make for the tunnel."

"Agreed and try not to look so glum. It won't be that bad."

※

It didn't take Luca long to find a hidden spot in an alley with a view of the portal plaza. The guards were still right where he remembered. None of them looked especially nervous or even alert for that matter. He doubted they'd had to do anything other than stand around looking intimidating for a long time.

Well, that was about to change. Today they were going to earn their coin, though not in the way they expected.

Hopefully, Christianson wouldn't hold back too much. A small fire wouldn't be enough to get these guards to respond. The blaze needed to look like a threat to the whole city. While this sort of thing wasn't his preferred way to complete his mission, circumstances didn't allow for anything else. Luca was confident that the king would be forgiving about any damage as long as he got the patch in place.

The worst part of the job was waiting. It seemed like he stood in the shadows of the alley for hours before the first wisp of smoke appeared. It was another fifteen minutes before the first shouts. They were distant and didn't hold the tremor of terror he was looking for. Those came a few minutes later when the first explosion filled the air. The fire must've reached a cask of whale oil.

Men came running into the plaza shouting for help and waving their arms. One of the guards trotted over and while Luca couldn't overhear their conversation, he could easily imagine how it was going. It didn't take long before nine of the twelve guards went running off toward the docks. He'd hoped that all twelve would join in the rescue, but three distracted men would be a good deal easier to handle than twelve on the lookout for trouble.

As he'd expected, the remaining three guards were more focused on the thick black smoke filling the air above the southern part of the city than they were on protecting the portal. Luca slipped out of his hiding place and made his way north and east so he could approach the guards from behind. If he was lucky, maybe he'd be able to sneak up and attach the patch without them even knowing he was there.

Luca smiled to himself. Nothing had gone the way he'd hoped since leaving Garen. He had no doubt that the final task of his mission would be equally difficult.

At least there was no one in the streets to slow him down. Everyone appeared to either be inside or gone fighting the fire. When he reached the northern edge of the plaza, he found the guards facing away from the portal and muttering anxiously among themselves.

He dug the patch out of his pack and quietly drew his sword. Luca tiptoed toward the portal, his eyes never leaving the three guards. Step by step he got closer and they didn't seem to realize he was there.

Luca stopped directly under the portal. As soon as he was set, he threw the patch up towards the master rune. When the thin sheet of mithril was six inches from the target, white lines of energy shot out, grabbed it, and pulled it into position.

He was about to let out a silent cheer when one of the guards turned and shouted, "Hey! What do you think you're doing there?"

The flash must have drawn their attention.

Luca charged, hoping to take down at least one of them before they could pull their weapons.

His first thrust stabbed deeply into the central guard's

abdomen. It wasn't an instant kill, but he was definitely out of the fight.

Luca spun and slashed, but his target deflected the blow. The final guard counterattacked, forcing Luca back.

They came at him together. One attacked while the other held back, watching for an opening, ready to step in if his partner got into trouble.

It was a smart way to fight. Luca didn't dare attack too aggressively lest he leave himself open to a blow from the second guard. The two men had clearly fought together for a while.

His only chance of victory was to leave himself open and hope that the attacking guard took the bait. Hopefully they weren't any smarter than the wolflings. If he could lure the first guard a little way away from his partner, that would be all the opening he needed.

Steeling himself, Luca slashed at his opponent's head. The strike was blocked easily and when the counter came Luca staggered back, leaving his centerline open.

Just as he hoped, the guard lunged forward to run him through.

Luca spun away, evading the worst of the blow, but still taking a shallow cut across the ribs.

Ignoring the burning sting, he used his momentum and brought his sword down hard across the back of the guard's neck. The blow took his head halfway off and sent him crashing to the ground.

One on one now, Luca charged hard hoping to take out his final opponent quickly.

The remaining guard was having none of it. The man turned aside every blow and nearly took Luca's leg off at the knee with a hard uppercut slash.

Close wasn't good enough and the heavy blow put his opponent off balance. Before he could recover, Luca lunged and ran him through the heart. The guard slumped to the ground, the fight over.

The wounded guard was lying on his side ten feet away clutching his stomach. Having no desire to leave a witness behind, Luca cut his throat before cleaning his sword on the dead man's uniform.

His mission complete, Luca ran out of the plaza and hurried toward the safe house. Two blocks away he paused and ducked into a dark alley. He still had some basic medical supplies in his pack which he used to bind the shallow wound in his side. The last thing he needed to do was leave a blood trail to their hiding place.

With his injury tended to, Luca continued on his way. Hopefully by now they were getting the fire under control. Not that he cared all that much what happened to the city, but the king might be upset if his future holding was too badly damaged.

Luca was two blocks from the safe house when he caught his first glimpse of the flames rising above the roofs of the docks district. The acrid stench of smoke filled the air and soot-covered people stumbled by him as they rushed to get clear of the blazing fire.

He tried to figure out where the warehouse with the tunnel underneath was in relation to the fire, but he couldn't quite work it out. He was confident that Christianson wouldn't be dumb enough to set the fire anywhere near their exit.

Ten paces from the alley that led to their safe house, movement to his left caught his eye and he angled that way. A moment later blinding white light flashed out, filling his vision with spots.

When he could see again, Luca rushed down the alley and found Christianson surrounded by a group of five guards, all of them dead, their bodies smoking and charred.

Luca didn't know how strong a wizard Christianson was, but he was clearly not someone to take lightly.

"You okay?" Luca asked

"Yes." The wizard sounded out of breath but otherwise appeared uninjured. "I was almost to the safe house when they spotted me. I considered hiding, but feared they might locate our hideout."

"Speaking of watchmen, what do you say we skip the safe house and go straight for the tunnel? I think we've about pushed our luck as far as I dare."

"Agreed. The sooner we're out of the city the happier I'll be."

Christianson led the way through the smoke-filled streets. The block with their warehouse was virtually empty as everyone had already gone to fight the fire or fled for safer ground. They slipped into the tunnel and Christianson sealed the door behind him.

For the first time since they crossed the border, Luca felt safe. No matter what else happened he had completed his mission.

CHAPTER 15

Only five recruits remained in training at the range near Franken Manor. Enoch wasn't sure if there would be more coming now that the roads were clear of snow, but he doubted there would be many more. Anyone that was inclined to want to fight would have shown up already.

Young, eager, and itching to prove themselves, the recruits were full of life and hope. He envied them. If he'd been thirty years younger, he would have felt the same, but you couldn't just forget a lifetime of abuse and insult.

A volley of fireballs arched out from the students before exploding in bright blossoms of flame at the end of the range. All but one had hit home perfectly. Enoch walked over to a girl barely out of her teens and said, "You have to hold the targeting thread steady until impact."

"Yes, master." She stared down at her shoes. "I always flinch at the end."

"That's okay. We train now to correct those mistakes before they happen in battle. Are you all up for another round?"

He got a chorus of yes, sirs in response. He smiled at their enthusiasm and hoped it would last when the targets were living men instead of stone dummies.

"Master Enoch?"

He turned to find one of the house boys standing a few yards away, hands clasped behind his back. Enoch still wasn't used to regular people treating him with respect. He suspected most of it was reflected respect from Otto, but he couldn't deny enjoying the change.

"Excuse me a moment." Enoch joined the boy and asked, "Yes?"

"A new arrival, sir. The guards weren't sure if you'd want to talk to him before they let him come down to the range."

"Yes, I'll come interview him there. Just give me a moment."

The boy bowed and Enoch went back to his recruits. "Another straggler has arrived. You five take a break. Perhaps after lunch we'll have a sixth new recruit."

They all grinned, seeming pleased at the prospect of another wizard joining them. Enoch left them to rest and walked with the boy out to the front lawn. A man nearly Enoch's age dressed in a simple brown robe and heavy boots stood sandwiched between a pair of house guards.

Enoch waved them off and said, "Welcome. We're always glad to have a new recruit. Shall we walk while we talk?"

"Yes, Master." His voice was deep and gravelly, more like a drill sergeant than a wizard.

When they were out of earshot Enoch asked, "So how many threads can you wield?"

"I'm not actually here to join up. The wizard underground has decided it is time to reveal ourselves to your patron."

Enoch stopped dead in his tracks. He hadn't spoken to anyone in the underground since before he came to work for

Otto's father. He found he wasn't sure what to say. At last he settled on, "Why?"

"Two things have changed. Garenland granting wizards full citizenship rights is the biggest reason, but also the move they're making against the other nations has come to our attention." The underground wizard smiled at Enoch. "You didn't know?"

"No, but if they have, it's not a move Lord Shenk would want to make known far and wide. How, exactly, did you find out about it?"

"Our wizards have helped Garenland's agents complete their missions in Rolan and Lasil. Unless you judge it unwise, I would very much like to meet Lord Shenk and discuss how we might be of use and what we would expect in return."

"No, I'm sure if the underground wishes to be of help, Lord Shenk would welcome you all. Come with me. I believe he's in his office this morning. I'll introduce you. What is your name?"

"You can call me Cypher. I am the voice of the underground in Garenland."

⟡

Otto sat cross-legged on the floor of his workshop. His body nearly vibrated with the power of thirty-one threads' worth of ether. Every time he tried to draw in another one, he feared he might shake apart. Lord Karonin had said at their last meeting that at a certain point his growth would slow again and then it would be a matter of slow, patient work to advance.

Well, if there was one thing Otto didn't fear it was hard work. He'd do whatever it took to grow stronger. Still, his time for training was growing short. The Northern Army was on the march and he was due to rejoin them in a few days. It was just a quick check-in, but he felt better knowing what was happening. No one expected serious resistance until they reached the capital.

Everything was going to be settled at Marduke. If his spies succeeded, they'd probably win and if they failed, well, they still had a fair chance of winning, but the cost would be a great deal higher. And if there was anything Otto hated it was wasting resources.

He was about to try that thirty-second thread again when someone knocked on his door. Otto stood and grabbed a towel off the workbench. It was amazing how much strain channeling ether put on his body. He'd even noticed his weight had dropped despite eating more than usual. He'd have to be careful not to overwork himself lest he get sick. Being laid up in bed was the last thing he could afford.

At least the Bliss made it worthwhile. Each time his power increased, so too did his pleasure. Oddly, simpler magic no longer gave him the jolt it used to.

He shrugged and opened the door. Outside stood Master Enoch and a rough-looking wizard nearly as old. Otto frowned and said, "Master, who's your friend?"

"Lord Shenk, allow me to introduce Cypher, he's here as a representative of the wizard underground."

Otto couldn't get a read on Cypher's strength, but he assumed if he represented a magical organization, he must be fairly strong. "I wasn't aware of such an organization."

"We don't make a point of advertising," Cypher said.

Otto ignored the obvious comment and turned his focus on Enoch. "I assume you already knew about them. Is there any particular reason you didn't share that information with me?"

"I hadn't spoken with anyone in the underground for

twenty years. Frankly, my lord, it never occurred to me. They're a part of my past, not a bad part mind you, but a part I thought I'd left behind long ago."

Otto wasn't thrilled with his former master's explanation, but for now he'd let it go. He stepped out of the doorway to let them enter. "To what do I owe the pleasure of this meeting?"

"Full citizenship for wizards mostly," Cypher said. "But what pushed us over the edge was the agents you sent into the other nations to seize control of their portals."

Otto's heart skipped a beat. No one should know about that. He'd shared the information with only the spies and Wolfric.

"Don't worry, you don't have a blabber-mouth on your team. Our people in Rolan aided your man in completing his mission. The price was him telling us exactly what it was. Another underground wizard helped your man in Lasil."

He knew about Rolan and Lux, but Lasil was still beyond his control as of yesterday when he checked. Assuming Cypher was telling the truth and Otto could think of no reason for him to lie, then the secret mission was nearly complete.

"You have my thanks for your aid, but I assume it doesn't come free."

"On the contrary, seeing Garenland's law spread over the entire continent would suit the underground very well indeed. In fact, we wouldn't even need to be an underground if that happened. We could be a legitimate wizards guild. Especially if we had the king's approval."

Otto felt much better now that he knew what they wanted. A wizards guild wasn't even a terrible idea, assuming he could control it to his benefit. "And who would be the guild master?"

"Assuming we succeed," Cypher said. "You'll meet her when

the guild is officially chartered. I trust you'll want to be the first to join."

Otto nearly laughed. "I answer to one person and only one person and that is most assuredly not your guild master. I'll not make wizards slaves to a ruler. If you want to be recognized, membership must be voluntary. No blacklisting nonmembers, no coercion. And that is not negotiable."

Cypher smiled and held out his hand. "Fair enough. We accept your terms. Our people will be on the lookout for your man in Tharanault. Alas we have no agents in Straken."

"I would have been impressed if you did. I'll walk you out."

Otto led the way outside and upstairs. He avoided the main part of the house and exited from a side door. Cypher assured them that he could find his way from there and set out for the front gate.

When he'd gone Otto said, "You should have told me about them. Maybe not when you were my teacher, but last fall certainly."

"Forgive me, Lord Shenk. Truly I never thought they'd approach you. What little interaction I had with them led me to believe they had no interest in politics."

"Everyone has an interest in politics, Enoch, especially when it can benefit them. Freeing all the wizards is a pretty big benefit, especially if they join your guild."

Otto shook his head. Life never got easier, but at least the missions were progressing well. Hopefully soon the Tharanault portal would be his and they could move on Straken.

CHAPTER 16

Axel could hardly believe how easy the march north had been. He and the scouts had been riding a day ahead of the First Legion as they made their way through the central part of Straken. There was still snow covering everything, but it had melted enough to allow easy movement.

They rode past half a dozen towns and none of them showed any resistance. In fact, most of them were empty. He hadn't seen so much as a garden hoe raised in anger, no arrows arced in at them, nothing. It was beyond strange. He found himself all the more tense for the lack of fighting.

He'd spoken to his brother for a few minutes after he arrived the day before and Otto seemed to think they'd be fine until they reached Marduke where he expected to find enemy reinforcements waiting. Axel wasn't sure if he hoped Otto was right or not. Having to fight the entire Straken army and their reinforcements, including wizards, while climbing the massive city walls, wasn't an appealing prospect.

"Sir, rider coming in," one of the new guys said.

Axel recognized Colten at once. He wasn't riding hard, so Axel doubted it was anything serious. Though after days of boredom anything would be a welcome distraction.

Colten reached the column and saluted. "Enemy approaching, sir."

"That's a rather matter-of-fact tone. You don't sound terribly concerned."

"No, sir. They looked more like half-starved refugees than soldiers, but they are Straken citizens, so I assume they're the enemy despite the lack of visible weapons."

"Orders, my lord?" Cobb asked.

"Get everyone lined up and tell them to keep their eyes open. If this is some kind of ambush, I don't want to fall for it."

By the time the ragged band of men and women reached Axel's position, his group had formed a square and drawn their swords. Axel felt slightly foolish gripping a sword as people old enough to be his grandparents came shuffling towards them.

When they were twenty feet away he said, "That's close enough. What's your business with us?"

"We're surrendering," a toothless crone wearing a dark shawl and patched cloak said. "The winter finished what you lot started last fall. We haven't had a decent meal in weeks and with the war about to start up again, I can't imagine supplies from the capital getting through. It was a close vote, but we decided to try our luck with you rather than starve."

Axel couldn't help smiling. Even on death's doorstep the people of Straken kept their hatred fresh and strong. A pity such strong feelings were directed at the wrong group.

He sheathed his sword. "I'm afraid we can't feed you, Grandmother. We don't carry enough supplies for that. If you like, we'll be happy to escort you to the nearest town."

She spat at his feet. "Where do you think we came from, boy? There's no food in any of the towns. Everyone that could has fled to Marduke. Only the old and feeble are left."

"Your own people left you to starve?"

"This is Straken, boy. The strong flourish and the weak perish."

"Then why don't you go lie down somewhere and die quietly?" Cobb muttered.

"I'm not sure what you expect me to do," Axel said.

"You're Garenland filth. I figured you'd finish us off and maybe wear yourselves out a little in the process. It's all we have left to offer our people."

Axel stared at the woman. She was clearly insane. Cobb would no doubt argue that since she was from Straken that was a given. He was starting to think his second had a point about these people. Either way, there was nothing he could do for them.

"Wait here and the main body of the army will arrive in a day or so. They might be able to scrounge up some food for you."

"And if they can't maybe someone will put you out of your misery," Cobb said.

He really did hate people from Straken; even the elderly didn't draw an inch of pity from Cobb. Of course, he was raised in the northern province and had seen what Straken raiders did to his people firsthand for his entire life. Expecting kindness might be too much to hope for.

"Send a rider back to inform the legion commander and my brother that these people are waiting for them."

Cobb barked orders and a moment later one of the rookies was riding off to deliver the message. Turning them over to Otto might not be the best idea, but since he arrived Otto hadn't done any crazy experiments like that one last year. Maybe he really did just use those prisoners as a power source for his magic and took no pleasure in their deaths like he said.

Whatever his brother's thinking, Axel would never forget those poor mens' screams or Otto's utter indifference to their suffering.

"Let's move out," Axel ordered. "We're burning daylight."

○

After the abuse his backside suffered on previous wagon rides, Otto decided that he didn't care what anyone watching thought and brought a cushion with him this time. And a blanket. They were seventy-five miles into Straken and the temperature wasn't much above freezing. That was actually a good thing for travel as it meant hard ground and no mud. In the driver's seat beside him, Hans seemed untroubled by any discomfort. Otto envied the stoic sergeant his toughness.

Otto would have gladly remained behind in the capital and simply joined the army later by magic, but with the Northern Army separated into three legions, he thought it best to be present as much as possible in case they ran into trouble. The journey had been smooth sailing so far, but he didn't trust that to continue.

His real concern, however, was that there was still no sign that the agent they sent to Tharanault had completed his mission. Everyone else had put their patch in place within the expected timeframe, but the last was still dark. More than a month had passed and he was beginning to worry that the agent was dead or incapacitated. If the wizard underground had any information they hadn't shared with him. And he assumed they would have given their eagerness to ingratiate themselves with the Crown.

"Rider approaching, Lord Shenk," Hans said.

Otto shoved his thoughts aside and focused. The rider had to be one of Axel's men and if his brother had sent someone the news couldn't be good.

The scout fell in beside his wagon and said, "We encountered some starving refugees along the road. Commander Shenk wasn't certain what to do with them so he sent me to let you and the legion commander know that they were waiting."

"What sort of refugees?" Otto asked.

"Old men and women. They claimed that they had been left behind because they were too weak to keep up. That's cold, even for people from Straken."

Otto nodded and the scout rode off to find the legion commander. It was cold-blooded and while he had no good feelings toward the people of Straken they weren't known for abandoning their own people to die. There had to be something they were missing.

Twenty minutes later, the legion commander, a fancily dressed fop in gilded mail and silk tabard, rode up with his entourage. "My lord, what do you think we should do about these refugees? I suggest ignoring them."

"What else can we do? If there is a siege of Marduke we'll need every bit of food we have."

"My thoughts exactly." He sniffed in distaste. "We'll march on without stopping. It's a shame, but if the savages left their own people to die it's not our place to save them." The legion commander saluted and rode off.

"When you see them, Hans, pull out of line. I want to have a word with these people. I'm not sure what's going on, but something doesn't feel right."

"Aye, my lord." Hans made some hand signals to the rest of the squad riding on wagons behind them. Otto assumed it was to let them know they were stopping, but he hadn't bothered to learn all the gestures.

The sun was low in the sky when the main body of the legion reached the Straken refugees. They were sitting in the snow on the side of the road looking pathetic as only refugees can. Withered, worn, and gaunt, the small group looked like they'd had a terrible winter. Otto had seen healthier scarecrows.

Hans guided the wagon off to the side of the road and the others of the squad fell in behind them. Otto stood and looked down at the refugees. "Why did your families leave you behind? And don't give me that nonsense about the old and weak not deserving to live."

He didn't really care about their answers. In fact, he hardly listened as the old woman that seemed to be their spokesperson blathered on about the strong and the weak and all that other nonsense he'd just told her not to give him. As she talked, he sent threads of ether through their bodies.

The real reason they were left behind became immediately apparent. Their bodies were clogged with disease. He didn't recognize the specific illness, but they were clearly infected by something. They'd likely volunteered to stay behind in hopes of spreading it to some of the soldiers. Otto couldn't allow that.

"Are you even listening, boy?" the old woman asked.

"No, I'm not." Otto sent threads into each of the refugees' chests followed immediately by lightning that stopped their hearts. They all collapsed in a heap, instantly slain.

He rubbed his fingers together to gather heat and then sent a blast of flame to incinerate the bodies. They would be infecting no one now. When they made camp tonight, he'd have to speak to Axel and make sure none of his men got too close to the refugees.

The legion stopped to make camp not much over a mile from where they'd met the refugees. Otto left Hans and the rest of the squad to set up the tents while he sought out Axel. His pretend aide would join them later. For some reason, the man had rubbed Hans the wrong way and the two glared at each other so hard that Otto had finally ordered him to travel at the end of the line.

It didn't take long to find the scouts. They had their little tents halfway up and a fire already going to fix their evening meal. As was his way, despite being their commander, Axel was busy putting up his own shelter. Otto could only shake his head as he approached. The best part of being in charge was that you didn't have to do such tedious tasks yourself.

"Axel?"

His brother turned to face him. "Did you deal with the refugees?"

"Yes, they're all dead and their bodies burned. Did you or any of your men get close to them?"

Axel stared at him, a horrified expression on his face. "Are you mad? Why would you kill harmless old men and women?"

"Because they weren't harmless. They were diseased. A living trap meant to take advantage of anyone softhearted enough to get too close. I didn't recognize the illness, but from what it did to their bodies, I can assure you that you wouldn't want to catch it. Now, did you or any of your men get close to them?"

"Not too close, no. But I'll be sure to keep an eye on everyone. Should any of them show symptoms we'll have them isolated. I'm sorry, Otto. I should've known you wouldn't just kill them without a reason."

Otto waved off the apology and turned to rejoin his men. He no longer especially cared what anyone thought of him, including his brother. He'd do what he had to and anyone that got in his way would end up like the refugees.

CHAPTER 17

THE THARANAULT INFILTRATION

Holt's breath came in ragged gasps. He tried not to gag on the stench rising off the water around his knees. The tunnels under Thara City were both a blessing and a curse. A blessing because they gave him a dark place to hide after his mission went to hell. And a curse because all the city's water and waste ran through them. In all his life Holt never imagined being as filthy as he was now. He'd also never imagined his mission going so badly awry.

Things started off well enough. The journey from Garenland had gone smoothly. He traveled alone, avoiding people and settlements. Infiltrating Thara City had gone equally well. His claim of being from one of the outer villages come to the city for work had seemed to satisfy the gate guards. Once inside, it should have been a simple matter of applying the patch to the portal.

That's what it should have been, but of course it hadn't worked out that way. His first attempt had been aborted when a group of drunken caravan guards staggered through the plaza surrounding the portal. That shouldn't have been a big deal, but somehow the delay threw him off and when he tried again last night he caught the attention of a roving guard patrol. They'd ordered him to stop and he panicked.

Holt wasn't proud of that, but he couldn't deny the truth. That moment of panic was what caused him to fail. He'd drawn his sword and attacked even though he was outnumbered six to one. His training allowed him to defeat two of the guards, but a lucky thrust to his left shoulder left him hurt and bleeding. Somehow, he broke contact and fled to these tunnels.

Splashing in the distance indicated that his pursuers hadn't given up yet. Killing a couple of their friends had no doubt motivated them to keep up the pursuit despite the nastiness of the tunnel. He pushed away from the wall and started down the passage again. The few dull shafts of light that made their way through the tunnel ceiling didn't reveal much beyond muck and pocked stone.

His shoulder screamed at him, but he ignored the pain and kept moving as quickly and quietly as he could. Holt shuddered to think what was getting into his wound. Bleeding to death seemed unlikely, but fever and gangrene were distinct possibilities if he didn't get out of here soon.

"I thought I heard something," a voice shouted from behind him.

The orange glow of the guards' lantern was getting closer by the moment. He'd lost his sword during the fight and had only a dagger, the mithril patch, and the ruined contents of his pack. Fighting was clearly not an option. If they knew where he was, there was no reason not to pick up the pace.

Forcing aside the pain he sloshed along faster. There had to be a way out of here. He'd been following the water since he entered. The tunnel floor didn't slope much, but it was enough to create a weak current. Since the passage wasn't completely underwater, that meant there was an outlet. He just needed to find it before the guards caught up to him. And pray that it was big enough to allow him to escape.

A little bit further on a crack formed in the ceiling. It wasn't big, but it let in enough light that Holt could make out a few details of the wall. It was badly eroded, probably from spring storms over many years. It didn't look like anyone put any particular effort into shoring up this stretch of tunnel. In fact, he doubted it would take much to bring the ceiling down.

Now that was an idea. If he could seal off the tunnel, it would give him more time to find a way out. Not that he was going to do much with his little dagger. What he needed was...

There! A head-sized chunk of rock had fallen out of the wall. Okay, where would be the best place to strike? Assuming he could even lift the stone with one arm basically useless.

"Down here!" That was the closest shout yet.

No time to screw around. A little further down the tunnel he spotted a stone arch that looked important and well worn. He'd try there.

With a grunt more of pain than effort, Holt lifted the stone and staggered to the arch.

The voices were growing louder and closer by the second. He wasn't going to get more than a few blows to bring the ceiling down.

He roared and hammered the stone into the arch. It hit with a dull thud and some gravel shattered off.

Not exactly an auspicious start.

Two more strikes sent a long crack running along the wall.

The lantern light was getting closer and he could see shadows playing on the wall.

Come on, come on, he could do this. Just because his arm felt like it was going to fall off didn't mean it actually would.

Another hard blow sent fist-sized rocks falling out of the ceiling.

The guards hunting him appeared around a bend in the tunnel. "There he is! Hurry!"

One more strike. He could do it.

With the last of his strength, Holt sent the stone crashing into the crack that had started. The tunnel shook and he dove out of the way just as a rain of boulders came pouring down.

Quick as he landed, he dragged himself up and out of the water. He spat and coughed, trying to get the vile taste out of his mouth. When he turned back, he found the tunnel sealed and better yet a hole had opened in the ceiling. If he was careful, he should be able to climb up the stone pile and out of the tunnels. And not a moment too soon.

What he was going to do once he escaped was another matter, one he'd deal with if he didn't break his neck getting out of here.

After his efforts with the stone, his left arm was completely useless. He started up the pile, careful of his foot- and handholds on the slimy rock. Inch by miserable inch he climbed. Luck was with him for a change and the pile didn't shift while he was on it.

His head cleared the opening and he paused to look around. The area above the tunnel wasn't all that much of an improvement. The hole had opened in Thara's slum quarter. To his left was a fallen-over shack made of rough lumber and burlap and to his right an open stretch of road. About ten feet straight ahead was a two-story building that had lost half its second story. Holt didn't know much about the slums other than it was where the poor and the sick went to live out their last days.

Tharanault didn't have a reputation for kindness. Even

more than Straken, the nation was one of survival of the fittest. If you couldn't make it on your own, the state wasn't going to help you. In fact, if you didn't pay taxes, they viewed you as a liability and the sooner you died the better. Hence the reason they made no effort to improve the slum dwellers' lot.

He shook his head. Garen had some rough areas, but no one starved. This place was almost inhuman. At the very least, he wasn't likely to run into any guard patrols. This was a no-go area for them. Any law came from the residents themselves.

All things considered, he'd rather take his chances with people who hated the government than with people who loved it but had better healers. He was considerably less likely to get turned in here. Assuming he didn't die of infection.

Now that he knew where he was, it was time to pull himself out of his hole. Which was easier said than done.

He lunged forward, twisted and wrenched himself halfway out. With a final kick, he forced his legs out just before the stone his foot was resting on fell back into the water.

Lying on his back, staring into the night sky, he contemplated what had gone wrong with his life. Right now, volunteering for this mission would be the logical place to start. But that wasn't true. If he hadn't screwed up, the mission wouldn't have been an issue.

As he was gathering what remained of his strength and thinking how he might get to his feet, a filthy, bearded face appeared above him.

"Evening," Holt said.

"Yeah, I guess it is at that," the stranger said. "You a tunnel rat?"

Holt knew he looked bad, but he didn't think it was that bad. "I am today. Name's Holt."

"Everyone calls me Kringle." The man paused when a little

mouse popped out of his beard, looked around, and vanished back into the thick, matted hair. "You don't look too good."

"I feel considerably worse than that." Taking a chance that the locals hated the watch as much as he hoped they did Holt added, "I've got a watch patrol after me too. Stabbed me in the left shoulder."

Kringle spat to the side. "Bastards, every one of them. We ain't got much, but I'll take you to Momma Little. She's a fair hand at healing. Anybody around here can patch you up, it's her."

"I won't argue." With considerable groaning and straining, Holt forced himself up to his feet. "Lead on."

Kringle moved closer and slung Holt's good arm over his shoulder. "You're apt to fall down again 'fore we get there. Lean on me."

He hardly would have believed it possible, but Kringle stank almost as bad as the tunnels, though in a different way. It was probably mouse shit and accumulated grime. Not that Holt was in any position to complain.

Together they shuffled off to the west. Holt sent a silent prayer heavenward that Momma Little knew what she was doing. If she didn't, he doubted he'd see another day.

○

After what seemed like miles of painful trudging, Holt and Kringle paused outside a building that might have been a tavern once upon a time, but now had holes in its walls, a partially fallen-in roof, and a sign hung from a single chain that was squeaking in the breeze. There were no people around outside, but he thought he could hear faint voices inside.

"This is where your healer lives?" Holt asked.

"Hey man, beggars and choosers, right? You want to go inside, or you want to stand around out here and complain?"

"I wasn't complaining, just pointing out that a building with holes in the walls, especially in winter, might not be ideal for sick people."

As they shuffled toward the largest hole Kringle said, "Ain't nothing about this shithole that's ideal. At least the king hasn't ordered a purge in a few years. Probably on account of we killed half a dozen watchmen last time. Felt good too. Bastards."

Kringle spit to emphasize his point. "Anyway, it doesn't get that cold here most of the time and when it does, we can scrounge enough wood to keep the place warm. Watch the lip."

Holt barely got his foot over the remaining chunk of wall. Inside, ten crude cots filled three-quarters of the space. Three held shivering patients covered with thin blankets. At the far end, tending a glowing brazier, stood the fattest woman he'd ever seen. Her rear end looked at least four feet wide. Momma Little had to be a joke.

She left the heat of the fire, her stained white gown flowing around her as she approached. "What have you brought me, Kringle?"

"Some poor bugger got done dirty by the watch. He's hurt bad, Momma."

"Hmm." She looked him all over. "He's not a local. I know everybody."

"That's a long story," Holt said. "Maybe I could tell it after I sit down?"

"There." She pointed at the cot closest to the brazier. "Strip, I need to see what I'm dealing with."

With Kringle's help, Holt pulled his ruined tunic off and

tossed it on the floor beside his pack. His left arm sent waves of pain through him with each beat of his heart. That was nothing compared to the pain that struck him when Momma took a hot rag out of the pot on the brazier and used it to wipe the muck off his shoulder.

Holt nearly bit through his lip to keep from screaming. To say she didn't have a gentle bedside manner would be putting it mildly.

Finally she said, "I seen worse. You want me to stitch it up or burn it closed?"

What a choice. "Burn it. Do you have alcohol to clean the wound?"

"Some. Stuff's hard to come by."

"I can pay. Not much, but something."

She nodded and stuck a flat iron in the coals to heat. It looked like she was getting ready to torture him and having seen men get a wound seared shut, that wasn't far from what was going to happen. Momma Little waddled over to a broken cabinet against the far wall and returned with a bottle of clear liquid.

She pulled the cork. "This might hurt worse than the fire. Want a drink first?"

He really did, but he also didn't want to go blind. "I'll manage. Got something I can bite on? I'd prefer not to shatter my teeth."

"You got pretty good teeth. Just one more thing that tells me you're not from around here." She reached into the front pocket of her dress and tossed him a six-inch length of rope.

Holt took the rope, jammed it between his teeth, and nodded.

Momma poured the first slug onto his shoulder. He

groaned and clenched his fist. She hadn't been kidding. That was just like liquid fire.

"I gotta get some inside now."

Holt nodded again.

With her thumb and forefinger, she spread the wound open and poured more of the white lightning into it.

The first splash had been like a tickle compared to that. For a moment it felt like his entire body was burning. Holt nearly bit through the rope he clenched his jaws so hard.

"She's as clean as I can get her." Momma corked the bottle and put it back in the cabinet. Next she returned to the brazier and pulled the glowing iron out. "One more to go. Hanging in there?"

Holt grasped the sides of the cot to keep from bolting. Stray threads of hemp tickled the inside of his mouth. "Do it." The words came out garbled, but she seemed to understand.

Before he could think better of it, she slapped the glowing iron to his shoulder.

Holt's muffled scream hurt his throat and the smell of cooking flesh, his cooking flesh, filled his nose.

And then it was over.

He spat out the rope and panted, trying to let the pain wash over him the way his instructors had taught. It was easier said than done. He slumped down on the cot. It might have been worth going blind to take the edge off this pain.

Momma looked the burned patch of flesh over and muttered to herself. At last she said, "The outside looks good. But if you been in the tunnels, there's bound to be some nasty stuff inside. I'll fix you something to burn it out."

The last thing Holt wanted was more burning, but he knew she was right. He already felt off, like he'd picked up something.

When he struggled to sit up, Kringle gave him a gentle boost. "Easy now," the old man said. "You ain't in any shape to be moving around."

"My pack." Kringle grabbed it and handed it to him. "Thanks."

Holt opened it, tossed out a few ruined pieces of clothing, and finally came up with his money pouch. There was only a handful of silver coins in it, but hopefully that would be enough to secure a place for him, at least until he'd recovered.

"Here, some for you and some for Momma. It's all I have, but you're welcome to it. Thank you for everything."

"Anybody that's got the watchmen after him can't be all bad." Kringle looked like he wanted to spit again, but a hard look from Momma changed his mind. "What are you doing here anyway?"

"You can bother him tomorrow." Momma came trundling over with a steaming tin cup. "Drink this, quick like, it don't taste too good."

Holt took the cup and downed it in one go. She was right, it tasted horrible, like the bitterest greens you ever tried mixed with cheap whiskey.

"Good," she said. "You'll sleep a spell now. I'll take that pouch."

Holt handed it to her and she poured the meager collection of coins into her hand. He wished he could have done more. When Garenland took over he'd be sure to mention their help to the king. Assuming he could actually finish his mission.

His eyes were getting heavy. With a pained grunt he stretched out on the cot.

A moment later the world went dark.

"What do you think his story is?" Kringle asked when he was certain the stranger was unconscious.

Momma shrugged. "Nothing good you can be sure of that."

"Maybe I shouldn't have brought him here. We need more trouble like we need the plague. I just couldn't leave him knowing the watch was after him."

Momma patted him on the head and Kringle felt Wilbur, his pet mouse, shifting around in his beard. "Don't give it another thought. Anyone those bastards want can have my help anytime. He paid too, more than most of my patients can do. We'll get his story when he wakes up. If we don't like it, we can kick him out."

Kringle looked down at Holt. "Might be kinder if I just cut his—"

Momma raised a finger, cutting him off midword. "You hear that?"

He cocked his head. Outside the building people were moving around. The tread of heavy boots argued for outsiders, probably the watch. If they'd come here already, they must want Holt bad.

"Get him out of here," Momma said. "I'll buy as much time as I can."

"Don't do nothing crazy. We need you a sight more than we need him."

"I give my patients up for no one. Now move."

Arguing with Momma was a waste of time so Kringle slung Holt over his shoulder and headed for one of the holes in the back wall. One advantage to a well-ventilated building, it was easy to get out. He was three-quarters of the way through when he looked back and saw Holt's pack lying on the floor.

"Momma." When she looked his way, he pointed at the pack.

She hurried over and kicked it out of sight under one of the cots. Not feeling the least bit good about leaving, Kringle ducked outside and hurried across the street into a dark alley. He had a bolt-hole not far from here. He'd hide out there until the watchmen got sick of looking.

He didn't need to worry about Momma. She could take care of herself.

At least that's what he kept telling himself.

◊

Momma grumbled to herself as she worked her way over to the hole that served as entrance to her clinic. She really needed to drop a few pounds, her knees and ankles were killing her. But when you never knew where your next meal was coming from, turning down food seemed foolish. And often, food was all her patients had to pay her with.

Not today though. She patted the thin purse in her front pocket. Those few coins might not mean much for most, but she could use them to buy cheap alcohol, herbs, and coal to heat the brazier. All things she needed to keep the people stuck in his rathole alive another day.

Six armed watchmen forced their way in. Momma recognized the man in charge. Sergeant Smyth was better than most of the pigs that worked for the watch, if not by much. The men spread out, going from cot to cot.

"Looking for something in particular or just disturbing my patients for fun?" Momma asked.

"We're looking for a man with a stab wound. He killed two watchmen and fled into the tunnels. We found a hole not far from here where we assume he emerged. With a wound like he had, this would have been the first place he visited. You seen him?"

"Nope. I got three oldtimers fighting lung rot and that's it. Who is this man you're looking for?"

Smyth shrugged. "No idea. He ran before we could question him. All I know for sure is he's a killer."

"No one here, Sarge," one of the watchmen reported.

His men gathered around him and Smyth said, "I know you and the rest of the people here don't think much of us, but if you see him, please, let us know. He's a murderer and not the sort of person you want to take your chances with."

"Don't suppose there's a reward for information," Momma asked.

"Reporting criminals is your duty as a citizen of Tharanault," one of the younger watchmen said.

That was about what she figured. So far, their murderer had done more to help the people of the neighborhood than the watchmen ever had. And that was all that mattered to Momma.

"I'll keep my eyes peeled, Sergeant."

Smyth let out a long sigh. "Sure you will. Just take my warning to heart. You might not believe it but keeping you safe is part of my duty. Let's go, men. He couldn't have gotten far."

Smyth led his troop of happy assholes back the way they'd come. Maybe if he ever lifted a finger when they had real problems, she'd be more inclined to be helpful. As it was she'd be happy to see them all fall into the tunnels and stay there.

She shuffled over to where she hid the pack and opened it up. There was a glint of metal in the bottom. A quick tug revealed a hidden compartment with a square of shiny metal inside. It was marked with strange designs. Momma had no idea what it was, but she'd bet it was important.

○

Holt came to in a dark, smelly hole with Kringle sitting beside him. A thin shaft of light came through what he assumed was a partially open door. The last thing he remembered was drinking Momma's bitter potion. How had he ended up here rather than in the infirmary?

He was about to ask when muffled voices outside stopped him. While he couldn't make out exactly what they were saying, the tone indicated they weren't happy. Probably watchmen searching for him. He hoped nothing happened to Momma for helping him.

Time passed and his stomach started to rumble. That his appetite had returned despite the setting was a good sign. Hopefully they could get out of here soon and find some food, assuming he dared eat anything prepared in the slum.

"Wait here," Kringle whispered.

Holt gave him a thumbs-up though he wasn't sure if Kringle could even see it in the dark. The old man stood and eased his way forward, blocking the light. He stuck his head out then said, "Coast is clear. Let's get you back to Momma."

Kringle helped him stand and the two of them stepped out into a garbage-filled alley. From there it was a short walk to the infirmary. The neighborhood looked even worse in daylight which was saying something considering how bad it had looked last night. At least there were no watchmen around.

They ducked through one of the holes in the wall. The clinic hadn't picked up any more patients and Momma was sprawled out on one of the empty cots which sagged dangerously in the middle but didn't look too close to breaking.

While Kringle scratched his beard, Holt looked all over for his pack. If the watchmen had found it he'd have no hope of completing his mission. His shoulder screamed when he bent over to look under one of the cots. With a grimace he decided he'd wait and ask Momma what happened.

As if she could hear him thinking about her, Momma shifted and sat up. She rubbed her eyes, spotted them, and yawned. "They finally leave?"

"For the moment at least," Kringle said. "They didn't hurt you, did they?"

"Naw, just poked their noses into everything and asked questions like they always do. I said I hadn't seen you. Not sure Smyth believed me, but he couldn't prove otherwise so he left."

"Thank you for your discretion," Holt said. "My pack?"

"I bet this is what you're looking for." Momma reached behind her and came up with the mithril patch. Holt was at once relieved that the watch didn't find it and horrified that Momma had. "What is it anyway?"

He debated lying, but in the end if he wanted to complete his mission, he was going to need help. "It's magic. I was sent by Garenland to attach it to your portal so our head wizard can seize control of it. When the time is right, our army will march through and take over the city and then the entire country."

Momma and Kringle both stared at him.

"I'm not sure if that's a good thing or a bad thing," Momma said at last.

"It depends on whether you're happy with your current situation," Holt said. "I would think almost anyone else would be an improvement over the government you have now. At the very least, if you help me complete my mission, I promise you'll get all the supplies you need to run this clinic properly, even if I have to pay for them myself."

"What do we need to do?" Kringle asked.

"I need to get close enough to throw the patch at the portal's master rune. The magic will do the rest."

"Since they caught you near there once," Kringle said. "I bet they'll be keeping a close watch over the plaza. There are four roads that converge there. Maybe we could sneak you in amongst the merchants, but even that's iffy."

"What about the tunnels?" Holt asked. "Do they run under the plaza or at least nearby?"

Kringle looked at Momma who shrugged. "I don't think anyone's ever really mapped them. Heaven only knows where all they run. Though I doubt they'd run under the plaza. No one would be stupid enough to undermine something as huge as the portal."

Kringle had a point, but if they couldn't use the tunnels, he wasn't sure what he was going to do.

"Why not ask Digger?" Momma said.

Kringle grimaced. "Because he's crazy?"

"Nobody's perfect and nobody knows those passages better than him. If anyone can get you to the portal, it's Digger."

"Perhaps we could go talk to him," Holt said. "What could it hurt?"

"It could hurt your peace of mind, but Momma's right. The only way to know for sure is to ask him."

"Does he live far from here?" Holt asked.

"He lives in the tunnels, down a dead-end passage near the outer wall."

Holt frowned. Back into the tunnels, great.

Holt and Kringle decided that the safest way to travel to Digger's place was to take the tunnels. The watch would be unlikely to search for them there and even if they did, the passages were so twisting and turning that they'd have to have terrible luck to get spotted.

Before they set out, Momma had packed his wound in some rancid concoction and wrapped it in bandages smeared with thick, greasy fat. She warned him that if he got any water in the cut, she was out of the herbs she used to cure the infection. He promised to be careful and they set out.

That was half an hour ago and now, as they slogged through the water and filth by the light of a homemade torch, he was starting to question his decision. Maybe risking the watch and staying aboveground for a while would have been worth it.

"Are we getting close?" Holt asked.

"I think so," Kringle said. "We're moving in the right direction anyway."

"You think so?" What little confidence Holt had just went up in smoke.

"Hey, I haven't been this way in years. Just be patient and old Kringle'll get you there."

Holt contented himself with muttering under his breath. It wasn't like he had so many options for help that he could be picky. At least no one was chasing him this time and his arm, while still hurting, no longer made him wish he was dead. The smell had taken over that job.

They rounded yet another corner and Kringle said, "We're getting close now. That's Digger's mark on the far wall."

Holt squinted and could just make out the faint outline of a pickaxe carved into the stone. An appropriate design for someone named Digger.

"So what's he like?"

"He's... One of a kind. Eccentric, I believe, is the word you'd use."

"What would you use?"

"Nuttier than a shit-house rat."

"I heard that!" a gruff, harsh voice from the darkness said.

A hunched-over, gaunt stick figure of a man came shuffling out of the darkness ahead of them. For a moment Holt wasn't sure if he was alive or some sort of undead. He tapped along with a cane made from a chair leg and he wore cut-off pants and a tunic with more holes than cloth.

"Morning, Digger," Kringle said. "We were looking for you."

"Yeah, I heard you coming fifteen minutes ago. What do you want? No one comes to see me unless they want something."

"We had some questions about the tunnels," Holt said.

Digger turned a squinty eye on him. "And just who the bloody hell are you?"

"He's a friend," Kringle said. "We need to know if the tunnels run under the portal plaza."

"'Course not. They don't go anywhere near the city center."

"How close can we get?" Holt asked.

Digger picked something out of his nose and flicked it into the water. "I can get you within four blocks of the plaza."

"That might not be close enough," Holt muttered. "If we have to travel four blocks on the surface we're bound to run into watchmen."

"If we could draw their attention away for just a few minutes," Kringle said. "You could do what you had to and we could scram."

"Sure, but what kind of distraction?"

"Rats!" Digger said.

Holt turned to look at the old man. In truth he'd forgotten for a moment that Digger was there. "What do you mean?"

"I got a whole herd of them down here. In fact, they're getting a little thick. You scatter some bait where you want them and I'll get them to the nearest tunnel exit. When a few hundred rats come boiling out of the tunnels, you can bet the watchmen will be jumpin'. Either that or tucking their pants into their boots." Digger cackled like it was the funniest thing he'd ever heard.

Holt didn't think it was that funny, but it might just work.

It had taken most of two days for Digger to get his troops ready for battle. Holt shuddered just thinking about the little beasts. He stood in a shadowy alley while Kringle spread rat bait all around the plaza. He had offered to help, but Kringle just shook his head and told him to wait. There was no doubt every watchman in the city now had a description of Holt and his shoulder wound made him easy to spot.

Not that Kringle blended in. Even dressed in his best tunic, it was clear he didn't belong in this middle class neighborhood. Hopefully no one would stop him or ask questions.

Holt's smile was bitter. Given how things had gone so far on this mission, Kringle would probably end up getting an arrow through the gut. He shook his head and forced himself to think positive. Just because he'd had bad luck up until now, didn't mean things couldn't turn around.

Especially now that he wasn't acting on his own. Even though they weren't exactly the sort of troops he was used to, having allies made Holt feel better. He was used to being with a squad and being alone made him edgy. That was probably why he'd panicked when the guards approached him earlier. Maybe volunteering for a solo mission hadn't been the smartest move.

Across the plaza, a handful of wagons had gathered to travel to whatever nation was next on the rotation. Holt hadn't bothered to learn the local order and he only glanced at the collected merchants. His focus was on Kringle's ragged figure as he worked his way across the plaza. He paused every few yards and dark rat-bait pellets fell out his pant leg.

Two of the guards looked Kringle's way and he tensed, but they just shared a laugh before turning their attention back to the merchants. Holt let out a long breath.

That's right, you idiots. Mock the old man that was going to bring about your downfall. It'll serve you right if the rats eat your toes.

After a painful half hour, Kringle reached the opposite side of the plaza. With the bait spread, he would now make a circle back to Digger who was waiting to set his soldiers loose. Holt gripped the crude, homemade satchel Momma had sewed to hide the patch. If this didn't work, he didn't know what he was going to do.

Even covered, the sharp edges of the mithril square cut into his fingers, almost like it was reminding him to focus on the mission and not think about failure. That wasn't possible of course; even though it was magical, the square didn't have any awareness.

At least he was pretty sure it didn't.

He made a conscious effort to still his wandering thoughts and focus. It wouldn't be long now and he needed to be ready.

The first wave of squeaking vermin arrived a few minutes later. The carpet of rats came boiling down the eastern street and poured into the plaza. Shouts went up from the gathered merchants as the little beasts crawled over everything and everyone.

The watchmen stomped and kicked, trying to drive the rats back.

They weren't having much luck. Soon the watchmen were shouting and tearing rats off their backs and legs. Merchants were fleeing as fast as they could.

This was Holt's chance.

He lunged out from his hiding place and made straight for the portal. The watchmen nearest him were fully occupied with trying to avoid getting eaten alive. They didn't even notice as Holt hurried by them.

Thanks to the surprisingly fragrant repellent Digger had applied to his boots, the rats gave Holt a wide berth. He reached the portal, looked up, and spotted the master rune. With his target located, he took the patch out and got ready.

"Hey!" He turned to see a watchman looking his way. Somehow the woman had found a spot clear of rats. "Get away from there!"

Holt ignored her, drew back, and threw the patch straight up. Lightning sparked and pulled it into position.

The watchman was running his way, doing her best to avoid the rats as she came.

Though his mission was now complete, Holt had no desire to spend however long it was going to take Garenland's forces to arrive in the clutches of Tharanault's interrogators.

He ran. The plan was to escape via the tunnels, but he needed to cover the three blocks to the nearest entrance and he needed to do it faster than the speedy woman behind him.

Stride by stride his lead shrank. His injury had left him weak and slow.

Holt didn't need to look back.

He could hear the watchman's boots pounding right behind him.

Somehow he reached the alley where the tunnel entrance waited.

He ran between the two buildings and caught a glimpse of someone as he hurried by.

A moment later a loud crash brought him to a halt. He turned to see Kringle standing over the woman, a broken chunk of timber in his hand.

"Figured I'd wait and make sure you didn't need any help."

Between ragged breaths Holt said, "Thanks. Is she..."

"Still breathing, just out cold. Come on. Let's get out of here before her friends arrive."

That was the best idea Holt had heard in a while. He followed Kringle into the tunnel.

Looked like he was going to survive this mission after all. For a while there he'd had his doubts.

Now it was just a waiting game. Hopefully Garenland acted before the watch found him. But that was out of his control. Holt had done his part, now it was up to his comrades to do theirs.

CHAPTER 18

The Lady in Red was starting to feel like a beggar as she and her entourage emerged from the portal in Tharanault. The Garenland army was once again threatening Marduke and it was time to call in the alliance's aid. Rolan had already committed and was gathering troops. Now it was time to call on King Liatos.

She didn't labor under the illusion that they were helping Straken out of the goodness of their hearts. The other nations wanted to keep the fighting in Straken and away from their own precious capitals. Not that she blamed them. If Straken was able, they certainly would have done the same thing.

"Does it seem quiet here?" Mal, her head of security, asked.

She looked around. There wasn't a single merchant in the plaza. Usually there would be at least a wagon or two waiting for the portal to open. Under one of the shrubs lay a rat corpse.

"Something definitely happened," she said. "But whatever it was, we seem to have missed the excitement. Let's get to the palace. I'd prefer not to linger any longer than necessary."

"Yes, ma'am."

At Mal's command, the half dozen soldiers on her security team fell in around her. Since they were all Straken warriors, she could only see through the gaps between their broad backs. The Lady had gotten used to walking like this and soon enough they parted, revealing the dark, brooding exterior of Castle Tharanault.

A dozen men watched the front gate, twice as many as her last visit. Once again she was reminded that something had happened. The guards bowed and the lieutenant in charge said, "Welcome, Lady. His Majesty is always delighted by your company."

That was as bald-faced a lie as she'd heard in ages, but she didn't call the young man on it. "Thank you. Has something happened? Things seem a bit… off."

"I'll let His Majesty explain. He's waiting in his private parlor. I believe you know the way."

"I do, thank you." This time she led the way with her guards falling in behind her.

It wasn't that she especially trusted King Liatos, but she needed to pretend for appearance's sake. Walking around an ally's castle surrounded by armed men didn't paint the right image. And since she was counting on the king for his support, maintaining the correct illusions were essential.

It never ceased to amaze her how much some people with power, especially men, liked to be fawned over. Uther was better than most, but even he had his moments.

The halls of the castle were dark and brooding, with no hint of ostentation beyond the occasional battle trophy. It was very clear that the king, having lost his wife, had overseen the decorating himself.

At the parlor door, a pair of servants waited. They opened

the door and gestured for her to enter. The Lady turned to Mal. "Wait here. I'll be back soon."

"Yes, Lady." Mal bowed and moved to stand beside the far wall with his men.

Inside, King Liatos sat in an overstuffed leather chair with a full glass of wine in his hand. He wore deep red robes and his beard appeared freshly trimmed. Though she let nothing show, the Lady winced inside. The king had made it very clear on more than one occasion that she'd find a welcome place at his side should she wish to become a queen.

The role didn't interest her in the least. "Majesty." She offered a deep curtsy.

"Lady, always a pleasure to see you, even under such difficult circumstances. Please sit."

She selected a chair across from him but out of touching distance. "Since you mentioned circumstances, I couldn't help noticing that the city felt a bit tense. What happened?"

"Someone, we're not sure who, did something to the portal. Our wizards say everything appears to be working as it is supposed to. Since you're here and in one piece I assume it must be, but the merchants refuse to use it and I'm certainly not sending any of my soldiers through. I'm sorry, but you'll have to manage in Marduke without us."

After that pronouncement he could have knocked her over with a feather. How could someone even interfere with the portal? Its magic was powerful beyond anything she could imagine.

"As you observed, I came through with no difficulty. Does that not prove it's safe?"

"It only proves it's safe for the moment. Who knows when that might change?" He shook his head. "I am sorry, but as I said, I won't risk my soldiers."

"What shall I tell Uther and the other members of the alliance?"

"Tell them what I've told you. And tell them they might want to check their own portals just in case. Will you be joining me for dinner?"

So that was it. No help would be coming from Tharanault. Uther wouldn't be pleased, but she'd dealt with kings often enough to know that Liatos wouldn't be changing his mind, not until he was certain there was no danger to his soldiers.

"No, I fear I don't have much of an appetite. Plus, I need to return and let King Uther know what has happened."

And that he would have to make do with only half the reinforcements he expected.

CHAPTER 19

The massive stone walls of Marduke were in sight of the Northern Army once again. The three legions had reunited a week ago for the final march on Straken's capital. None of them had encountered much resistance on their marches. The sick old people Axel had found were the most dangerous things reported.

To Otto's left and right, the soldiers were deploying, setting up lines and digging defensive positions. No one believed they could take the city in one assault, even Otto, though he suspected the second attempt would meet with greater success. Yesterday when he returned to Garen, the portal showed Tharanault was now under his control. To say that Otto had been relieved would be a tremendous understatement. He had begun to fear that the agent they sent had been caught or killed.

Now that the other four nations had been compromised, all that remained was Straken's portal. That was going to be tricky, but with nearly a hundred wizards under his command instead of just twenty, Otto was confident they could hold off any barrage the enemy wizards could send their way. The hardest part was going to be getting his final spy inside and safely to the portal. He had a plan, but it wouldn't be easy.

"Lord Shenk." Otto turned to find General Varchi approaching. He was dressed in black-lacquered plate armor and had a full complement of his personal guard trailing him. "Could I trouble you to scout the city for me? I'd like to know what we're facing."

"As it happens, I was just about to do that. One moment." Otto closed his eyes and sent his sight flying toward the city.

This time he was careful to approach from the rear and high in hopes of avoiding enemy wizards. Soldiers were patrolling the walls in groups of four spaced about fifty yards apart. If their discipline held, it would make sneaking in trickier. Inside the city, the streets were packed with people, many of them fighters, but just as many regular citizens. Otto didn't dare get too close, but from a distance they looked thin and ill-used. Clearly Straken had a rough winter even with the help of their allies. Otto wished he could conjure up some sympathy, but he didn't have it in him.

He eased his way closer to the mustering ground near the main gate and quickly spotted Rolan's cavalry and their wizards, about forty of them. Thousands of huge Straken warriors milled around with little in the way of discipline. They'd get that ironed out when the fighting started. While Otto thought little of them as people, he would never make the mistake of underestimating their skill as fighters.

He frowned and made another sweep of the area. There was no sign of Tharanault's heavy infantry. Surely they would have arrived by now if they were coming. Could they have gotten lucky enough that the alliance had broken already? That would be a boon beyond belief.

Satisfied with his scouting, Otto returned his sight to his body. General Varchi was still waiting when he opened his eyes. "We've had a bit of good luck. Tharanault didn't send any fighters or wizards. We'll have the advantage with magic this time, rather than an even fight as I feared."

"Where do you suppose they are?" the general asked.

Otto shook his head. "No idea. But I suggest we prepare to attack as soon as possible lest they change their minds."

"Sound advice. We'll finish preparing our defensive position today and attack at first light tomorrow. Will your wizards be ready?"

"We're ready now, just give the word."

The general smiled faintly before turning back toward the command area. Otto headed for his camp. As he made his way through the army, he received plenty of salutes and even more quick glances that just as quickly looked away. He made them nervous, all the wizards did. He'd hoped after fighting together last year that the soldiers would look more favorably on his war wizards, but perhaps it was too soon for that.

He found Korgin, his final infiltrator, setting up his tent like a good pretend assistant. As soon as Otto stepped inside Korgin straightened and bowed. "News, my lord?"

"I just finished scouting the city. It's overflowing with refugees."

"We expected that, did we not?"

"Indeed we did, but not this many. They're spilling out onto the streets. I wouldn't be surprised if every healthy citizen of Straken was holed up in there. That should make it easier for you to go unnoticed, assuming you wear the correct disguise."

Korgin nodded. "Looking like a refugee shouldn't be hard. When do I move?"

"Tomorrow during the first assault. The guards patrol in

groups of four. Assuming they don't break for the attack, I'll make an opening for you."

"I won't let you and the king down."

"You'd better not, your fellows would never let you live it down if you were the only one to fail his mission."

○

Otto found he was too anxious to sleep and at the first sign of dawn threw off his blanket and went outside. The morning was clear and cold, not a cloud marred the sky. Somehow he imagined it should have been darker given how many people were going to die today. Just went to show you how indifferent the world was to the doings of its meaningless inhabitants.

A noise from near the wagons caught his attention and Otto walked over to find Hans polishing his giant suit of armor. "Couldn't sleep?"

"No, my lord. Even after all these years, I still get worked up before a big battle. It's going to go differently this time. We'll show them."

"Yes, we will. It helps that they only have half as many wizards on their side. How has your training with the armor gone?"

"Good. We can all use them like they were an extension of our own bodies. I never imagined I'd have a chance to use such a thing." Hans shook his head in wonder.

Otto knew just how he felt. Every time he learned a new spell or technique, he got the same jolt of excitement. Did Lord Karonin still feel that way after she'd been an Arcane Lord for centuries? Otto hoped so. He didn't want to lose that sense of wonder when he became one.

"Korgin should have breakfast ready before long."

Hans's lip curled in distaste.

"Why do you dislike him so? You're both servants of the Crown."

"He's different," Hans said.

When he didn't elaborate Otto asked, "How? If there's something I need to know, speak now. His mission will begin in hours and if I can't trust him to do what he needs to..."

"You can trust him to do his duty," Hans said. He blew out a long sigh. "All he and his friends ever volunteer for are the flashy jobs liable to get them a promotion, never the grunt work. They didn't win many friends in the palace guard with that attitude. And they didn't care, which pissed everyone off even more."

"Brownnoser then?"

Hans nodded. "Exactly."

"Father had a few of those in the garrison. He hated them. There was one guy, I can't remember his name, anyway, he would always hang out near Father, eager to jump in whenever he needed something. Eventually Father got fed up with him and assigned him apple patrol."

"Apple patrol?"

"Yeah. Every year there are apples left on the ground after the harvest. We turn the pigs loose to eat them. Sometimes wolves get the idea that they're easy pickings, so guards are assigned to keep them away. It's cold, smelly, muddy work and only people that get on Father's bad side end up doing it. He did it for the rest of his career and everyone else learned not to brownnose my father."

Hans chuckled. "I think I might like the baron."

"No, you wouldn't. No one likes him and he likes no one.

Except Mother. Everyone loves her. Speaking of pigs, I smell bacon. Brownnose or not, Korgin can cook."

Three hours later the army was finally assembled and ready to attack the city. The only things missing this time were siege weapons. The wizards would be filling that role. Not that Otto would be leading them. He'd selected one of his best sub-commanders for that task.

He and Korgin stood off to one side waiting for the first wave to march. Once they did, he needed to get Korgin into the city then return to Garen to wait for the signal that indicated the Straken portal was under his control. When that happened, would he ever have a surprise for Uther and his army.

"This may be the foulest get up I've ever worn," Korgin said.

He was dressed in the most ragged, filthy tunic and trousers they could find. Otto was pretty sure Hans had taken extra pains to really mess it up. At the very least he certainly looked like a refugee. As long as you didn't look too close and see the weapons strapped underneath the frayed cloth. He also held a length of rope attached to a grappling hook

"You'll survive. Don't forget you need to move aside as soon as the patch is attached. I plan to activate it as soon as I can."

"I remember, Lord Shenk. My tabard is hidden in my pack as well, so the army won't mistake me for the enemy."

"Good." The ether stirred as his wizards prepared their first spells. "Get ready to move. The battle begins soon."

Soon turned out to be only moments later when the first fireballs arced out toward the walls. The spells shattered on the enemy's defensive barriers and the enemy's counterattacks were smashed apart by the Garenland wizards.

Satisfied that everything was going as it was supposed to, Otto and Korgin hurried north to circle the city. They kept to the tree line even though Otto seriously doubted anyone was looking their way given the explosions coming from the front gate area. But being cautious never hurt anyone.

It did slow them down and a little over five minutes later they were far enough away that Otto stopped. He studied the wall and scowled when he spotted the patrols still on guard. At least they had frozen in place. Taking out two of them should be enough to get Korgin in unseen.

Otto gathered ether and formed eight targeting threads. They snaked out, invisible vipers waiting to strike. Each pierced one of the guards' chests. When all eight were ready, Otto sent ten threads' worth of lightning coursing through them. All eight men dropped without a sound.

"Lord Shenk."

Otto looked where Korgin pointed and spotted one of the patrols running toward the fallen men. They hadn't raised the alarm yet at least. Another quartet of threads killed the investigators.

They waited a full minute before running over to the base of the wall. Korgin began to swing the hook but Otto said, "Save that for getting down the other side. Hold on."

An ethereal platform appeared under Korgin's feet and lifted him up to the top of the wall. The instant he was clear Otto let the construct fade. He'd done his part, now it was up to Korgin to do his.

Otto became one with the ether and raced toward Garenland. With any luck, by the end of the day, Marduke would be theirs.

CHAPTER 20

Korgin gave the corpses on either side of him a quick glance, shuddered, and looked for a place to hook the grapple. He'd never seen Lord Shenk in action before though he'd heard the rumors. The reality was considerably worse. It shouldn't be possible to kill someone that easily. Not that he felt much sympathy for the enemy, but he felt certain that if he got on the young nobleman's bad side it was just as likely to be him lying on the ground with a smoking hole in his chest. Best if he didn't do anything to give Lord Shenk a reason to kill him.

He found a crack, drove one of the hooks into it, and tossed his rope over the side.

Korgin climbed down the rope and landed at the foot of the wall. There was nothing visible in either direction. From the center of the city, the portal stuck into the sky, the shining metal a stark contrast to the dark wood and stone of the surrounding buildings. Sounds of battle still came from the front gate. The army wouldn't be able to sustain an assault for too long. He needed to move.

Hunching over like a tired, sick man, Korgin hurried at a fast walk toward the portal. He hadn't gone far when he reached the first collection of refugees. In fact, he smelled them before he saw them. If they stank this bad now, what would the city be like in the summer? Hopefully he'd be long gone by then.

The gaunt, bearded faces of the refugees followed him as he made his way through the gathering. It looked like mostly old men, women, and kids. The younger men were probably at the wall fighting. Korgin nodded in passing but didn't speak or slow. No one troubled him and before he knew he was clear of the first group.

He crossed one of the main streets and darted between two buildings. There were probably more sensible ways to get to the portal, but he was only interested in going straight ahead. There were no maps of Marduke so his knowledge was limited to what he could see.

Another group of refugees appeared directly in front of him. This one looked like mostly women and kids. He nodded to them as well and tried to hurry past.

A strong arm grabbed his and spun him around. A woman in rags nearly as tall as he was glared at him. "Why the hell aren't you on the wall? My husband had to fight and he's got a broken hand. You look healthy enough."

Korgin grimaced. He didn't have time for this. "I have a message to deliver. Stand aside."

"You ain't no messenger," the belligerent woman said. "We seen them running here and there. They wear a special uniform not rags. You're a shirker, that's what you are."

There were some mutters now among the other refugees.

Korgin drew a dagger and put it to the woman's throat. "I'm a messenger. And if you don't want me to deliver a message to you, then you'd best let go and forget you ever saw me."

She glared at him with such anger he feared he'd have to cut her throat, but finally she let go and backed away.

"You'll get yours after we deal with the pigs from Garenland. I never forget a face."

Korgin shook his head and hurried on. She could remember his face forever if she wanted to, he didn't care. All that mattered was getting the patch attached to the portal. Once that was done, he suspected she'd have more to worry about than him.

After leaving the most recent group of refugees behind, he hurried down another alley and emerged directly across from the plaza that surrounded Straken's portal.

He grinned. There were a few evergreen shrubs, a quartet of stone benches, and not a soldier in sight. Perfect.

Korgin pulled the patch out of its hiding place and darted across the open space. A little ways from the portal, a squad of ten armed and armored soldiers leapt out from behind the various shrubs. They surrounded him with swords drawn.

One of the soldiers, Korgin assumed he was the squad's leader, said, "So the Lady was right. She said something happened to the Tharanault portal and that we needed to be careful of our own. Can't say I was pleased to miss out on killing Garenlanders, but it seems my reassignment was for the best. What is it you have there?"

Korgin waved the mithril patch back and forth. "This? It's magic. Watch."

He sent the patch sailing up toward the portal. The magic grabbed it and pulled it into place. "Ta-da."

"What did you do?"

Before Korgin could think up a good answer, the portal flared to life.

CHAPTER 21

Otto paced in front of the Garenland portal. It didn't do a bit of good for his frame of mind, but he found he couldn't stand still. A full legion of soldiers filled the mustering area to bursting. They'd been brought into the city quietly, a company at a time, just in case there were any Straken spies remaining in the countryside.

He slapped the control rod against his palm. With his master's guidance, Otto had altered the rod so that it actually did something rather than just being a ceremonial device. He also figured out its original purpose. Much like when someone struck one of his runes, when Edwyn had struck a portal rune, Valtan must have sensed it and activated the portal. The rest of the time it opened and closed on a set schedule and the touching was just ceremonial. It was an interesting system; one Otto was soon to break.

Now the rod could do far more than just send a signal. He could control all the compromised portals, or at least he'd be able to once the final patch was in place.

The only bad thing he'd found about near-instant transportation was that he had to constantly wait for those slower than him to catch up.

Ten minutes after lifting Korgin over the wall of Marduke, a faint vibration ran through the control rod. The ether shifted around the portal as the Straken portal came under his control.

It was time.

"Prepare to advance!" Otto shouted.

The soldiers that had been lounging around hopped to their feet, settling their shields on their arms, and drawing razor-sharp blades. Otto charged the rod with ether and struck the Garenland rune.

Lightning ran through the portal and the runes shifted, melting and reforming as the magic was rewritten. Anyone in the other kingdoms watching at that moment would be getting quite a display. When the magic calmed, Otto touched the Straken rune. The portal glittered to life.

Like a well-oiled machine, the legion marched forward, vanishing rank after rank into the swirling, silver ether. When the last of them had vanished, Otto followed.

He emerged an instant later in a now-crowded plaza in Marduke. A quick glance around revealed a badly outnumbered squad of Straken soldiers holding Korgin hostage. The legionnaires didn't seem quite sure what to do.

Lucky for everyone, especially Korgin, Otto knew exactly what to do. He rubbed his iron ring and ten threads of ether bound the soldiers.

"Don't just stand there," Otto said. "Legion commander, take your men and seize the gate so the Northern Army can enter."

"As you command, Lord Shenk." The commander, a man easily three times Otto's age, gave a quick fist to heart salute and said, "Legion forward!"

Nine thousand men marched off toward the gate. Since he couldn't hear sounds of battle, the Northern Army must have fallen back after the first assault. Which reminded Otto…

He summoned a ball of ether and threw it into the air where it burst in a brilliant display visible only to his wizards. That was the signal to attack again.

With his part of the immediate battle finished and feeling a bit worn out, Otto walked over to Korgin and the bound soldiers. "Congratulations on completing your mission."

Once Otto had pulled the hand holding the dagger to his throat safely away Korgin said, "Thank you, Lord Shenk."

"I see you ran into some trouble."

"They set an ambush. It seems Holt was spotted in Tharanault and they sent a warning that we might make a run at their portal."

Otto frowned as Korgin disentangled himself from his captor. If Tharanault knew they had interfered with the portal, that would make the eventual subjugation of the nation more difficult. His main worry was whether or not they warned Rolan and the others. Given that Rolan's cavalry had shown up he judged it unlikely.

"What should we do with this lot?" Korgin jerked a thumb at the bound soldiers.

Otto drew his mithril sword and with a handful of powerful swings left the soldiers headless. He released his magic and the bodies collapsed in a heap.

Korgin swallowed audibly. "That's one way to go I suppose. What now?"

"Now we find a secure location to wait for the Northern Army. I don't know about you, but I have no desire to be run over by retreating enemy soldiers."

They settled on a flat-topped roof not far from the portal

that afforded them a clear view of the main avenue through Marduke. Now it was simply a matter of waiting.

○

Axel stood beside General Varchi as the pair eyed the fire-scarred walls of the city. All around them soldiers bound injuries or mended weapons. The first attack had been a draw. The wizards basically negated each other, leaving it up to the fighters to settle things.

Otto's giant suits of armor had done the most damage. The massive steel suits hurled boulders and tree trunks at the archers lining the battlements. Each throw had crushed a handful of men. But even with the magic armor on their side, the soldiers never managed to get their ladders in place. Not that anyone was overly concerned. The main purpose of the first assault was to draw attention away from the portal so Otto's agent could do what he needed to. They'd held out as long as they could, but eventually retreat was unavoidable.

"What do you think, Commander? Will your brother's mad plan succeed or will we need to spill the blood of thousands of our men to take that miserable wall?"

"Having seen what Otto can do, I'd be a fool to dismiss him. If I was a gambling man, I'd wager a year's pay that we're inside the wall by dark."

The general shook his head. "You're that confident? While I will admit that the wizards have been an amazing asset to our army, I can't believe anyone is capable of taking control of the portals."

"We'll know soon enough, sir."

Axel was about to say something else in his brother's defense when a young wizard, her face smudged with soot, came running up. "General, Lord Shenk just sent his signal. Our forces have entered the city."

"Ready the First and Second Legions," General Varchi said. "I'll lead the Third myself as a reserve. If this works the way it's supposed to, they'll open the gates for us. Order all wizards to engage. We need to draw the magic users' attention away from the men inside."

"Understood, sir." The wizard saluted and ran back the way she'd come.

Other messengers were speeding off to carry his orders to the legion commanders. It wouldn't take long to get everyone moving.

"What about my scouts?" Axel asked.

"You'll stay in the reserve with me. You and your men are too valuable to risk catching a stray arrow." The general must have read Axel's disappointment in his expression. "You've all done your part. None of you have anything to prove, either to me or your legion commander."

Axel nodded. It wasn't that he was eager to risk the lives of his people, it was just that they'd been fighting Straken for so long, he wanted to be a part of the final blow. Hiding in the back while others rushed the walls wasn't his style.

"Yes, sir. If you'll excuse me, I need to gather my men."

The general dismissed him with a wave of his hand.

Axel hurried away. The scouts had set up not far from the command area, so it didn't take him long to join them. All around, the First and Second were forming squares and preparing to advance. There was no grumbling and malingering. Everyone hoisted their shields and stood shoulder to shoulder with his brother.

Everyone but Axel and his scouts. Like it or not, he had his orders.

He found Cobb and the rest checking the straps on their armor and the archers filling their quivers. Cobb looked up at his approach and said, "We're not marching."

"No. General Varchi has ordered us to remain in reserve. It seems scouts are of little use in a siege."

Cobb kicked the dirt. "I thought we were finally going to see some action."

Some of the others muttered a little as well, but most of them seemed happy enough to avoid assaulting the walls. Axel didn't blame them. Even if the attack went exactly as planned, they were going to leave a lot of bodies behind.

"Don't look so glum," Axel said. "You can take an arrow some other time. For now, we need to join the general."

Axel led his force back to the command area. It might not be what they preferred, but in the army, you seldom got what you preferred.

⚬

Hans and his squad weren't attached, officially, to any of the legions. They served Lord Shenk and that was all, but with him gone doing wizard stuff, they'd been joining the First on their attacks. It seemed the best use of the magical armor and so far, they'd done a ton of damage, probably more than any other unit, including the wizards, though that was mainly because the war wizards were constantly countered by the enemy spellcasters.

The five of them had plenty of operation time left on their armor, so when he saw the rest of the army, Hans ordered his guys into the armor. They had barely straightened when one of the wizards came running up to them.

"What is it?" Hans asked.

"Lord Shenk has arrived in the city. Our forces inside will be attacking the enemy from behind. Please refrain from launching any missiles that might sail over the walls and injure them."

Hans grinned. So his gambit to seize control of the portals had worked. Not that Hans had doubted that he would succeed, but still, it was an amazing accomplishment. Lord Shenk would be in a good mood when they joined up with him.

"Understood," Hans said. "We'll attack in a more direct fashion. Be sure to cover us from the enemy wizards."

She touched her fist to her heart in salute before running off to rejoin her unit.

That salute had been pretty good. They'd make soldiers out of those wizards yet.

Hans led his squad towards the front of the rapidly forming battle line. The infantry looked up at them as they clanked by. Even after half a year, the regular soldiers weren't used to the giant armor. Not that Hans blamed them. Even the biggest of the men only came up to his waist. A solid blow, armor or not, and you were dead. Of course they had nothing to worry about.

It was the Straken forces that needed to worry.

It took less than half an hour for all of the legionnaires to gather and prepare to march. When the order came, Hans was careful to match his longer stride to those of the regular soldiers. He wanted to get to the wall first, but not too far ahead. He needed the archers as well as the wizards to cover them if what he had planned was going to work.

The first arrows started clattering off his chest plate about a hundred and fifty yards from the wall. Inside the armor, it sounded like a heavy rain was falling and the arrows did about as much damage as drops of water. The armor's steel plate was easily ten times thicker than what you would find on a typical suit of armor. More importantly, no fireballs exploded around them and no lightning crackled through their bodies. It seemed the wizards were doing the job.

The front line stopped and held their position fifty yards from the base of the wall. They were counting on the legion already inside to open the gates for them.

The archers drew and fired, trying to keep the enemy's head down. They'd all hoped that their comrades inside, with the advantage of surprise, would've had the gate open by the time they reached the wall. Unfortunately, it appeared that things weren't going as smoothly as planned.

Maybe Hans and his men could do something to help. "Keep pressing forward! We're going to climb that wall."

The armored warriors reached the base of the wall in ten long strides. With no hesitation, he slammed his fingertips into the stone as high up as he could reach.

The force of the armor drove them three inches into the stone. He pulled himself up then slammed his toes in, securing his perch. Hand over hand they climbed toward the top of the wall. The enemy archers must have decided they were a grave enough threat to risk taking an arrow and soon they were once again under a hail of shafts.

Even at close range the bows were useless. Most of the shots bounced off their massive helmets and careened around in every direction. Hans ignored it all and kept climbing.

When he reached the top of the wall, a handful of spearmen rushed over and tried to push him off.

They'd have had better luck trying to push over a mountain. The tips of their spears scraped against his armor accomplishing nothing beyond filling the air with a horrid screech.

Hans reached over and, using the battlements for leverage, hoisted himself up. A few sharp kicks cleared the immediate area of archers. When the rest of his squad had joined him, he left them to deal with the soldiers still on the wall and turned his focus downward.

The legion that came through the portal was a few hundred yards away from the main gate but were held up by Rolan's cavalry. They weren't being pushed back, but they weren't advancing either. It was a stalemate. If they were going to get the rest of the soldiers inside, he'd have to break that stalemate.

The way to do that was both obvious and simple. Hans drew the massive sword strapped to his back. "We're going down there."

The guys didn't offer a word of objection, instead drawing their own weapons and leaping after him.

The armor's fall was broken by a pair of stunned Straken soldiers. Blood flew in every direction when he crushed them to pulp.

Hans didn't give the rest a chance to recover from their surprise.

He swung his weapon in broad strokes, slicing through six or eight soldiers with each pass.

The main gate was only ten steps away. He managed one before his body started to spasm.

Muscles clenched and his teeth rattled as lightning poured through the steel armor. The wizards must not have been able to protect him now that he was out of sight.

An explosion staggered him and seared his skin. Suddenly jumping in to break the stalemate didn't seem like such a great idea.

He tried to turn his head to see where the wizards were hiding, but the muscles of his neck were locked.

"What do we do?" one of his men managed to ask.

Hans wished he had a good answer. Focusing with all his might, he managed to turn a fraction, just enough to see a collection of wizards with their hands raised and pointing at them. They had to be the source of the spells assaulting him and his men. Pity he wasn't free to do anything about it.

The pain grew worse by the moment and just about the time he thought his body was going to give out, a massive fireball exploded in the wizards' midst.

Their bodies flew everywhere, most of them in several pieces.

The pain vanished and he was free to move again.

A flash of light from one of the rooftops not far off caught his eye. Though the distance was too great to make out any details, he was certain that was Lord Shenk up there. Hans doubted he was going to be pleased that the armor had been put at risk, but if they got the gates open, hopefully he wouldn't be too upset.

Hans had seen Lord Shenk upset and wasn't eager to have his ire pointed at him.

"Cord, with me. The rest of you deal with the cavalry." Hans turned toward the gate, his sword carving a deadly path before him.

It took only seconds for the enemy force to break. Getting harvested like wheat was too much for even the bravest soldier. Soon enough they had a clear shot to the gate.

Hans strode through it, reared back, and kicked the heavy wood. The armor's power overwhelmed the gate and after only five strikes, the legions had a clear path through. He stepped aside and thousands of angry Garenland soldiers poured in.

Around the gate chaos reigned. Men screamed and fought

and died. Hans hardly dared move for fear that he'd hit one of his men along with one of the enemy.

Anyway, they'd done their part. No sense hogging the glory.

It didn't take long for the enemy to surrender. The soldiers were rounded up, disarmed, and placed under heavy guard. The surviving wizards were separated and placed under the watchful eye of Garenland's war wizards augmented by two hundred archers. Better safe than sorry where wizards were concerned.

Hans and his squad left the sorting to the legions and went to retrieve Lord Shenk. He was still standing on the rooftop where Hans had spotted him earlier. At least he'd sheathed his sword, which hopefully meant he wasn't thinking about punishing them.

Hans reached up with his heavy, open gauntlet and Lord Shenk jumped into it. Korgin followed with considerably less enthusiasm. Hans set them down then climbed out of the armor. He bowed and said, "Congratulations, my lord, your plan worked. Marduke is ours."

"Hardly ours, but we've taken a major step forward. There's still the castle to seize, but hopefully that won't be too big a job, especially since they're all out of wizards." Lord Shenk narrowed his eyes. "Quite a bold move, leaping into the city with no wizards to protect you."

Hans cleared his throat. "Frankly, my lord, I didn't consider that line of sight would be a problem for our wizards. I assumed they'd have some magical way to keep track of what was happening. It was good fortune that you were here to help us out."

"Yes, and better fortune for you that the armor wasn't

damaged. In the future, try to be more careful with your decisions."

Was that it? Just a stern lecture about being careful? Hans forced himself not to wipe the sweat from his brow in relief. "Yes, my lord."

Lord Shenk had turned to face Castle Marduke. It was an imposing structure with its dark stone walls and many guard towers. "With any luck we'll deliver Uther's head to Wolfric by the end of the day. Hopefully still attached to his body since I'm sure the king would enjoy seeing the beheading firsthand."

Hans shivered at Lord Shenk's offhand tone. As if the beheading of a king was no big deal. And to him it probably wasn't. Just one more obstacle out of his way. Hans dearly hoped he never found himself as an obstacle to the young lord.

CHAPTER 22

Arcane Lord Valtan sat cross-legged in his meditation chamber and let the ether swirl around and wash over him. Sometimes Markane felt like another world, disconnected as the island nation was from the rest of the continent, but what happened there affected them whether they liked it or not.

The colors of the ether were endless and ever changing as he studied them. Little of the Bliss remained to him now. After centuries of channeling massive amounts of ether, he no longer felt the rush from the meager forty threads he could call on now.

Sometimes he regretted his decision to bind the bulk of his power to the portal network. But regret or not, he'd felt compelled to do it as penance for the evil he and his fellows had committed both here and on the other worlds they'd visited.

That binding had been the second most difficult decision he'd ever made. The first was to betray and destroy his fellow lords. They'd trusted him like a brother and he cast them into the netherworld, the one place from which they could never return.

Now he was immortal, alone, and constantly bored. Some days, when the humans' squabbling was especially petty, he wished he'd cast himself into the void along with his comrades.

A jagged line ran through the smooth swirls of the ether, cutting short his maudlin thoughts. He hadn't seen a reaction like that in years. With a thought he became one with the ether and followed the echo of the line straight to the portal. All around the mithril ring the ether was roaring and agitated. Someone had tampered with his spell.

No one living should have the knowledge or power to do something like this. He waved a hand, attempting to smooth the ether. It did calm, but not completely. Still, it was enough to allow him to see what had been done. Someone had seized control of the continental portals. He could no longer activate them or access them from here. The Garenland portal was also working again despite him cutting off its activation rune.

Any wizard capable of this was a threat. Not to him, but to the order he had so patiently built. Valtan needed more information.

He shifted from the portal to the royal palace. King Eddred was in his throne room holding court with the various nobles and merchants that advised him. The king appeared especially weak today, scrunched down in his throne and practically buried under his royal robes. Two portly nobles were haranguing him about something while the rest nodded in agreement. Greedy fools the lot of them, but no worse than any other mortal he'd met.

Valtan appeared in an empty spot to one side of the throne. Every gaze in the room turned toward him. Valtan was well used to being stared at and ignored them.

"Court is finished for today," he said.

No one spoke as they hurried to make themselves scarce.

Valtan turned his attention to the guards. "Out."

These were good men and loyal to their sad excuse for a king, but when Valtan gave an order, loyal or not, they obeyed. Soon it was only him and the king.

Eddred shrugged out of his robes and sighed. "Many thanks for the rescue. Though if you're here, I'm sure the news is grim."

"Indeed. Someone has seized control of the portal network, cutting us off from the continent."

Eddred's eyes went wide and his mouth opened. "How is that possible?"

"It isn't. No one living has the knowledge to do what has been done. That said, clearly someone has found the knowledge. I need to know what's happening on the mainland."

"War is going on. Garenland is fighting Straken while Rolan nips at their southern flank. All the nations have imposed tariffs on Garenland's goods. Lastly King Von Garen the Elder has been murdered and his son has taken the throne."

"How did I not know about this?" Valtan demanded.

Eddred raised an eyebrow. "You never cared about the goings on of the wider world. I invited you to my daily briefing, but you never bothered to show up. I assumed you had other matters that required your attention."

Valtan had no recollection of that conversation, but to be fair, so much of what the mortals said was tedious and of no great value. Perhaps he should have paid more attention.

"How goes the war?"

"Details are few given that we trade very little with Straken and not at all now with Garenland. The argument you interrupted just now was between one group that wants to take advantage of the war to sell weapons to Straken and the other that thinks we should stay out of it. I'm not sure why they felt the need to have the argument in front of me given how little anyone pays attention to my commands."

"I need more details," Valtan said. "Side with the group that wants to sell to Straken. Send someone to ask questions in port. Not just in Straken, but in all the ports we visit."

"We don't really visit any ports beyond Crystal City in Lux. Everything else is done by portal."

"That's not an option now. I suggest the merchants get their ships ready to sail. We may be facing the greatest threat since the fall of my fellow Arcane Lords. I must not be blind to what is happening. I require you to serve as my eyes since I can't leave the city."

Eddred blanched. Clearly that was a bigger task than he was looking for. "Are you sure you want me to do it? I believe there's an admiral around here somewhere that would be happy for a project."

"No, you will do it. I have guaranteed your family's rule for a thousand years. I'm calling one of my markers. You're a king, it is time to start acting like one."

Valtan vanished into the ether. Eddred was a poor tool, but he was trustworthy despite his weakness and he had just enough wizard potential that he could see the ether if he concentrated. That skill would be vital in his mission. If what Valtan feared was coming actually arrived, he needed to get Eddred in some sort of shape to face it.

CHAPTER 23

The First and Third Legions had Castle Marduke surrounded. Otto stood behind the front ranks and considered the odd situation he faced. Eighteen thousand men should have no trouble taking the castle, especially since the battlements were empty and so far, not so much as a single arrow had arced out at them. Where were the defenders? Surely Uther hadn't sent them all to the outer wall.

Otto closed his eyes and sent his sight flying toward the keep. He passed through the stone walls and found the gloomy halls beyond empty of soldiers and servants. If Otto had been the suspicious type, he might have feared a trap, but unless the plan was to bring the entire castle down on their heads, he saw no danger of that.

After searching the place top to bottom, he headed for the throne room. At last he found someone. Uther himself sat on his throne in the empty chamber, only a blazing fire for company. It was like he was waiting to be taken into custody. While Uther was known to be a brave man, he couldn't possibly think he could fight off an army alone.

Otto returned his sight to his body and opened his eyes. Beside him, General Varchi asked, "What did you find?"

"Not much. Uther seems to be alone in his throne room waiting for us. I didn't find a single other person."

"Strange. What could he be thinking?"

"He must be up to something, but what I can't say. Maybe he's just resigned. Either way, we need to get in there. With your permission, I'll take Axel and his scouts. They're better at this sort of thing than regular infantry. The rest of you should maintain a defensive perimeter just in case."

General Varchi nodded. "Easily done, Lord Shenk. We'll await your report."

Otto nodded and a runner was dispatched to fetch the scouts. Since Wolfric sent a message this winter explaining to the good general how the new chain of command worked, he'd been much more agreeable. That suited Otto very well as having to constantly argue every decision got tiresome quickly.

Axel and a hundred men arrived a few minutes later. There were more scouts, but that was plenty to search the castle. They moved a short distance away and Axel looked from Otto to the raised portcullis and back.

"What's the plan?" Axel asked.

"We're going inside. Divide your men however you see fit to search the keep. You and I, along with, say ten others, will greet our host."

"Uther's in there?" Axel said.

"Indeed, alone it seems, just waiting for company. It's rude to keep a king waiting."

"I don't like it," said Axel's crabby second-in-command. Otto couldn't recall his name, but he always reminded him of Sergeant Hans.

"Your objection is noted, Cobb," Axel said. "Split your force, half upstairs and half down. I'll take first squad with me."

"Yes, my lord." Cobb barked orders as they marched toward the castle.

Otto let the scouts take the lead, after all walking into danger was their job, not that he believed they were actually in much danger. He and Axel walked silently at the rear. If his brother had questions, he kept them to himself. The group passed under the portcullis without incident.

When they reached the castle entrance Cobb shoved on the heavy double doors and they opened inward without a squeak. The interior was dim, but every once in a while, a Lux crystal broke the gloom. The entry hall was empty of both decorations and people.

At the far end a staircase led to the second floor. Forty men broke off and ran up the stairs.

"Which way?" Cobb asked.

"The throne room is straight ahead through that door." Otto pointed at an oak door with iron bands blocking their way. "If you take the right-hand hall then the first left, you'll find the stairs to the basement."

Cobb looked at Axel who said, "You heard him, get a move on."

After a few wordless grumbles, he complied, leading another forty men out of sight, leaving them alone with the final twenty. Otto led the way to the throne room door. It opened as easily as all the rest of the doors.

"This feels so wrong," Axel said.

Otto agreed but what could they do? "We'll have answers soon enough."

The throne room was almost uncomfortably hot. A huge fire burned in a massive hearth that looked like it could hold an entire tree. Slouched in the throne sat King Uther. His massive frame appeared sunken and weak, like the loss of the war had drained his strength. His beard had gone fully gray and his long, wild hair flowed unbound by his crown.

"Took you bastards long enough." Uther's words slurred and he took a long drink from the goblet on the table beside him.

"We would have been here sooner, but we ran into an army," Otto said.

Uther barked a laugh. "Fat lot of good that did. I thought for sure I had you weak merchants. I was going to have your king on his knees begging me to spare his life. Instead, look at me. A king with no country, my people starving, my army destroyed. I'll go down as the king who lost Straken to a bunch of gold-grubbing Garenlanders."

"If you're looking for sympathy, you'll find none here," Otto said. "Garenland didn't want this war. But you just had to keep pushing. Well, you got what you wanted. We'll see what King Wolfric wants to do with you, but I suspect you have an appointment with the axeman in your future."

"If that's what you think," Uther said. "You're in for a surprise."

Otto was about to ask what he meant by that when Axel asked, "Where is your crown?"

"Looks like one of you is paying attention. The Lady is taking it to my son. I may be remembered as the king that lost Straken, but he will be remembered as the king that took her back." Uther coughed and Otto caught a glimpse of blood on his lips.

Otto reached out through the ether. The dregs of Uther's wine were mixed with poison. The miserable coward didn't want to face execution.

A rumble shook the castle and Uther smiled in triumph. "They made it out. Your doom is sealed. My death has bought them time to escape."

"No." Otto gathered ether and poured it into Uther's body. No way was he going to take the easy way out.

Neutralizing the poison still in his stomach was easy enough, but plenty had gotten into his blood as well. That would be harder. Otto forged a filter around Uther's heart and used it to remove as much poison as he could.

Sweat poured down Otto's face as he fought to keep a man he hated alive.

It was difficult work, nearly as complex as forging the patches and he didn't have Lord Karonin to guide him. Nevertheless, he strove with all his might and soon all the poison had been destroyed. Uther's breathing was labored, but he was alive and would likely stay that way.

The thunder of approaching steps dragged Otto's attention away from the now-unconscious Uther. Cobb and his men came rushing into the throne room.

"What happened?" Axel asked.

"We found a tunnel, but it collapsed before we could explore."

"Lucky for you," Axel said. He turned to Otto. "What should we do with Uther?"

"Take him to the portal. We'll bring him to Wolfric. If anyone deserves to see the man die, it's him."

Dust from the collapsed tunnel choked the air. When it cleared, the Lady in Red nodded to herself. The mechanism had worked exactly how the engineers said it would.

There was no way anyone would be following them through the debris choking the passage. She'd hoped they'd never have to use it, but in her wildest dreams the idea that she would escape without Uther never crossed her mind. And yet here she was, carrying the heaviest burden of her life.

She patted the pouch at her side. The simple gold circlet inside felt like it weighed a ton. Uther's son, Uther the Younger, hated her. What he would do when she showed up at his camp alone and carrying his father's crown hardly bore thinking about. But bring it she would. The Lady owed Uther that at a minimum. If she survived the encounter with his son, that would be a bonus.

"Lady. We should go before the Garenlanders come looking for us." Mal's face was pale and pinched with worry.

She didn't blame him. In fact, he looked better than many of the guards and servants that had fled with her at King Uther's command. They had plenty of supplies, but it was going to be a long climb into the mountains to find Prince Uther's camp.

There was nothing she could do about that. Surrender was hardly an option. Wolfric hated her nearly as much as he hated the king. The only fate awaiting her if she got captured was a slow death. If she had to die, better if it was at the hands of her new lord.

"Lead the way, Mal," she said.

Her head of security took point and they set off toward the distant mountains. For now, the walking would be easy, but as they gained elevation, the snow would increase as would the difficulty.

She shook her head. Whatever it took, the Lady would fulfill her king's last request.

Axel's men had fully cleared the castle and found nothing of interest beyond the collapsed tunnel. Otto was satisfied that the city was now fully under their control and he said as much to General Varchi. The conversation had been brief, Otto basically told him that for the moment he was in charge of an entire country. The general had simply nodded as if this was an ordinary thing for him.

Otto admired his confidence if nothing else. He'd borrowed Axel, two squads of his men, and set out for the portal.

Three-quarters of the way there, Otto paused and turned to Axel. "There's one more thing I need to do. I'll meet you at the plaza."

"Sure, take your time. It's not like we can leave without you."

There was that. Otto turned toward the gathered prisoners. He wanted to have a word with the captured wizards before he left. They needed to know that Garenland didn't consider them the enemy, but rather unfortunate victims. At least that's how Otto felt. Of course, if they decided to become enemies, he'd happily kill them all. But that would be a terrible waste and he hoped to avoid it.

He wove his way around groups of disarmed soldiers, all of them surly looking. The more he saw the less Otto believed ruling these people was going to be worth the effort. None of them would make good, loyal citizens. Better if they were used as free labor in the mines while Garenland settlers worked the land. Assuming anyone from Garenland wanted to move to Straken. It wasn't like land was in short supply at home.

Otto shrugged as he spotted the wizards. What happened here wasn't really his concern. The only things he wanted from the miserable nation were peace and mithril. He'd kill as many people as it took to get them.

One of his sub-commanders, a young woman with a mithril ring on her right hand, spotted him approaching and offered a salute. "Lord Shenk, is all well?"

"Perfectly. We've captured the king, though some of his servants escaped. Have the prisoners given you any trouble?"

"None, my lord. They've been as peaceful as lambs."

"Good. Have any of them said they were in charge? Never mind, I'll ask." Otto walked past her and over to the Rolan wizards sitting in the dirt, heads hanging. "I know fighting us wasn't your idea. Please understand I don't hold you responsible for what you had to do."

As he spoke, the prisoners looked up one after another. When he was sure he had their attention, Otto went on. "I understand that your families have been taken hostage. If we can free them, will you swear allegiance to Garenland? You'll be granted full rights as citizens as well as the responsibility to protect your new homeland."

"If you can free our families," one of the men said. "You will have our loyalty until our dying day."

The others all murmured their agreement. Their eyes shone with hope. Now that he'd given them that hope, Otto couldn't take it away. If he failed to free their kin, he'd have no choice but to kill them all. The risk of them lashing out was too great.

"Do you know where they're held?"

"In the capital somewhere," the spokesman said. "They never let us visit them there, but sometimes they're brought to our barracks. Please, my lord, my mother is nearing seventy. I don't wish for her to spend the last of her days in a prison."

Otto held out his hand. "I swear on my honor as a wizard

and nobleman of Garenland, I will see them free. You understand that I have to keep you in custody until I have."

"We understand." The man took Otto's hand. "May all the angels in heaven watch over you, and good luck."

"I won't turn down heaven's help, but there's something I need from you."

"Anything."

"I need some blood. I can use the connection between you and your family to track them down."

The spokesman let go and turned up his left wrist. "Take all you need."

Otto turned back to his sub-commander. "Your dagger."

She drew the weapon and offered it to him hilt first. He scoured it with ether to make sure the wizard didn't get an infection then made a short, shallow slice. Blood coated the edge of the blade.

Otto sent ether through the blood and then outward. His thread was drawn strongly to the man he cut. Good, he should be able to use it to find his mother. That was a close enough link to track.

"See that his wound is bound. I'll be keeping your weapon. If you need one, the quartermaster should have a replacement."

She saluted and Otto turned back toward the portal. As he walked, he got different looks this time. Probably carrying a bloody blade made him look like some sort of executioner.

When he reached the portal, Axel was waiting along with the gathered Fourth Legion. They would be returning to Garenland to help with the conquest of the other nations.

"What, did you have to murder someone before we left?" Axel asked.

"Funny." Otto drew the control rod with his other hand and touched the portal. "Let's go home."

CHAPTER 24

Wolfric stared down at Uther, the man who, at least indirectly, was responsible for the death of his father. He didn't look nearly as imposing on his knees in a cell. That he had chosen to try and take his life with poison came as a shock. Wolfric had always assumed the great warrior king would want to die with a sword in his hand. Just went to show you that sometimes the myth was more impressive than the person behind it.

Otto stood off to one side, hands clasped behind his back, waiting for Wolfric to come to grips with what had happened. That was what Wolfric liked best about his dear friend. He knew when to speak and when to stay silent. Some moments needed to be savored. This was one of them. There were so many ways he'd like to kill this man. Pity he could only do it once.

"So much for conquering Garenland," Wolfric said at last.

Uther coughed and said, "I might not be conquering it, but my son or his son or some other member of my family years from now will. The people of Straken are strong. They'll weather whatever you do to them and come back to strike you or your heirs down. Just wait."

"Brave words from a man in a cell waiting to be executed." Wolfric paced a few times then paused. "Perhaps I'll let you live. Once we capture your son, you can hang together. Yes, that would be fitting. What do you think, Otto?"

"I think Uther is irrelevant save for how we might use him as bait to draw out the prince. If you wish him to live, may I suggest putting him to work in the mines with his troops? He's still got a few good years of labor in his half-dead body."

Wolfric laughed. "Brilliant! Tell me, Your Majesty, when was the last time you did a real job? Probably never. It should be educational."

"We can keep him here under guard until the mines are secure." Captain Borden was so quiet Wolfric had almost forgotten he was there as well.

"Yes, that's fine." Wolfric yawned, bored with the prisoner already.

"If I may," Otto said. "There's another urgent matter we need to discuss."

"Of course. But let's do so somewhere more pleasant." Wolfric turned to Borden. "He's in your charge. Should anything happen to my prize prisoner, I'll hold you accountable."

"I'll see to it, Majesty." Borden saluted.

Wolfric led the way out of the dungeon and up to the royal library. The chairs were comfortable there and the smell of leather and parchment soothed his nerves.

When they arrived, servants had set out a bottle of wine and two goblets. Otto used a bit of magic to open and pour the wine. Wolfric smiled. He never tired of those tricks.

"Very well, my friend," Wolfric said. "What's so important?

With Straken mostly under control, I thought you might want to take a few days, see your wife and daughter, rest for heaven's sake."

A faint grimace flitted across Otto's face, there and gone so quick Wolfric wondered if he'd imagined it. "Pleasant as a few days of rest might be, we dare not delay in seizing the other portals. What I have done, Lord Valtan can undo. Making those patches was six months of arduous work for me, but for an Arcane Lord, making them would be the work of days. We must take physical control of the portals so no spy can get close enough to put a new patch in place."

Wolfric frowned. He hadn't considered the possibility that they might lose control of the portals as easily as they seized that control. Otto was right, they needed to act fast. "What's your plan?"

"I want to take control of the legion we pulled together to invade Marduke through the portal and turn them into a force to control access to the portals, including ours. Fifteen hundred soldiers at each location, wizards as well. We'll build fortifications around them and search every person and wagon that wishes to pass through. It will slow the process, but as long as it's secure, nothing else matters."

"You've given this a great deal of thought. When do you plan to strike?"

"I'll divide the legion today and assign commanders to each unit as well as wizards. Rolan needs to fall first. If I can secure the families of the wizards they sent to Straken, they've promised to join our cause. Thirty-plus extra wizards is no small gain. They also know the country and will be a great help bringing the nation to heel." Otto paused in his headlong rush. "Assuming you grant me permission, of course."

Wolfric laughed. "I have no doubt everything you suggest

will work out for the best. However, I do have one condition. When you move on Lux, I want to come with you. I want to see the look on our former allies' faces when they find out their new situation."

"That's another thing," Otto said. "How do you want to structure the empire? Traditionally you'd have a governor overseeing each of the new territories. Would you trust the current rulers even if they swore allegiance to you?"

"I wouldn't trust Liatos or Villares beyond the reach of my sword. Kasimir doesn't care about anything but gold so if we let him continue to rake in wealth, he'll toe the line. I'm inclined to remove Philippa on principle after she betrayed my father, but she knows her people and lacks the means to strike at us anyway. That leaves Straken."

"May I suggest leaving General Varchi and the Northern Army to run the country? There's bound to be trouble and they're used to dealing with Straken fighters."

"Good idea. I doubt pacifying Rolan or Tharanault will be quick or simple, so we may need to take back some of his men."

"I recommend the Third. They took the fewest casualties in the Straken campaign and should be fresh to keep fighting." Otto stood. "If you'll excuse me, I need to get back to work."

Wolfric waved a hand in dismissal. Otto hurried out, leaving him alone to think. So far, the plan was proceeding well, but there still remained a great deal to do. He didn't know what he'd do without Otto. His friend was a font of wisdom and energy. Wolfric felt more and more tired the more they accomplished while Otto was exactly the opposite.

Once he was emperor of the entire continent, Wolfric could finally relax. He smiled to himself. If only it would work that way.

CHAPTER 25

Otto spent the rest of the day arranging the troops and assigning wizards to serve as portal guards. Luckily Enoch had completed training some of the new recruits, so he didn't have to pull very many from the Northern Army. The first unit of fifteen hundred were already on duty protecting Garenland's portal. The second unit would come through to seize the Rolan portal at his command.

After a decent night's sleep in his own bed, Otto had risen, eaten a quick breakfast while avoiding his family, and set out for the portal. Just as ordered, the second unit was in place and waiting.

Otto strode up to the commander, a middle-aged veteran chosen for his attention to detail rather than any tactical brilliance. He saluted and said, "Lord Shenk, my men are gathered and ready to move at your command."

"Excellent, Commander. As soon as I open the portal you'll need to enter quickly."

"Understood. We packed some basic prebuilt fortifications

we can use to restrict access until something more permanent can be constructed."

Otto smiled. That was exactly why he'd chosen this commander. "I hope to be less than an hour, but there can be no guarantees with this sort of mission. See you on the other side."

He drew the dagger he'd used to collect a blood sample and became one with the ether. Surrounded by the swirl and flash of the ether, Otto connected a thread to the dried blood and willed it towards Rolan. The streamer shot out like a hunting hound and Otto followed right behind.

The trip took only an instant in real time though it felt longer to him. Soon enough he found himself inside a long wooden building lit by the orange glow of an iron stove. Scores of people lay in crude beds or sat at rough tables eating thin gruel. It was as miserable a prison as Otto had ever seen. If this was how Rolan treated the families of wizards, it was no wonder they were eager to make a deal with him.

His tracking spell stopped in front of an old woman who stood near the stove shivering. Her stole was ragged and thin, hardly enough protection for this time of year. He ended the spell and looked around for guards. There didn't appear to be any inside, so he pulled back for a wider view.

The prison sat in the middle of a walled compound. Four towers manned by archers dotted the corners of the wall. Three squads of four men armed with truncheons patrolled the grounds. Two smaller buildings probably served as barracks for the troops or maybe storage for food and supplies. He didn't know and didn't care. Having seen how they treated people guilty of no crime beyond being related to a wizard, Otto would feel no shame when he slaughtered them all.

The roof of the prison was flat, so he appeared there.

Before the guards could react, threads shot out, piercing all the archers. Lightning followed a moment later.

Once all the ranged fighters were down, he drew his mithril blade, strengthened his body with ether, and leapt to the ground.

One of the guard patrols shouted for him to stay where he was.

Otto obliged and a moment later four brawny men armed with blunt iron truncheons came running.

He sprinted to meet them.

Impossibly sharp mithril combined with magical enhancements to his speed and strength ended the fight before it really began. His sword sheared through their weapons like they were made of paper. Flesh and bone yielded even easier.

Seconds after they shouted, the guards lay in many pieces on the ground, their blood soaking the dirt.

The remaining patrols rounded the corner and saw what had happened to their comrades.

Foolishly they chose to attack.

Eight men only lasted a few moments longer than four. When Otto finished, he flicked the blood off his sword and sheathed it. With a sigh of relief, he released his physical enhancements. They always took more out of him than attack spells. Still, it had been worth the extra energy to kill these cowards with his own hands.

People needed to learn that you couldn't target the families of wizards, not anymore and not if you wanted to live a long, healthy life. These men had learned that the hard way. Otto would teach as many people as he had to until they learned not to mess with his people.

With the compound secure, he walked over to the prison door and unlocked it with a flick of ether. He pulled the door open and smiled to hopefully look less threatening. "My name is Otto Shenk and you are free now. If you'll follow me, I'll take you to your family members."

Pale, gaunt figures shuffled toward him. The old woman he'd first observed huddled by the stove led the way. "Are they okay?" she asked. "Is my boy okay?"

"He is as are many of the others. Not all, I'm afraid. They were forced to fight by Rolan soldiers and our wizards killed some of them when we counterattacked. I am sorry about that. But rest assured now that you're free, you and your loved ones will be safe."

There were murmurs from the gathered prisoners, many of them hopeful and some anxious that their relative was one of those killed. There was little more Otto could tell them.

"If you're strong enough, we need to get to the portal. From there I can take you to Garenland where you'll be reunited with your relatives. Follow me."

The former prisoners fell in behind Otto. The gate in the prison wall opened easily after he sliced the lock off. Outside, the city was quiet, at least the area around the prison was quiet. They'd built the compound near the outer wall in the northeast corner of the city. In the distance the portal jutted up like a beacon of freedom.

At least to them it was. To the people of Rolan, it was about to be a source of trouble.

Otto kept his senses, both magical and mundane, peeled for trouble. The escape had gone smoothly so far, but it was only a matter of time before someone spotted the group of escapees trudging through the streets. The people might not know what was going on, but at least a few of them would be sure to warn the nearest watchman. And once that happened, all bets were off.

"Young man." The woman in her ragged shawl hurried to walk beside him. "Why are you doing this for us? The people of Garenland have never been friends of those from Rolan."

"We're still not," Otto said. "But we are friends of any wizard that wishes to be free. Your son and the other survivors have pledged their aid in bringing Rolan and the other nations under our control if I can get you to safety."

She nodded. "So you want to use my boy just like everyone else."

"No, ma'am. You and your son are both free to make your own choices. When Garenland has conquered the continent, our law will govern all nations. And under that law, wizards will have the same rights and duties as any other citizen. That's my goal. I'll happily accept the help of anyone that wants to make that dream a reality. And I'll destroy anyone that tries to stop me."

She looked at him with wide eyes.

"Sorry, was that a little too intense?"

"No, I—"

He stepped in front of her and smashed an incoming spell apart.

Otto traced it through the ether and found a wizard trying to hide between a pair of buildings. The man was a weakling, but apparently loyal to Rolan. Pity.

A ten-thread tentacle of ether lashed out, smashing through the enemy wizard's protective barrier and reducing his head to pulp.

"Everyone stay close. They'll be coming soon."

Sometimes Otto hated to be right. At the next corner a squad of ten watchmen waited. Half carried crossbows and the other half drawn swords.

One of the watchmen, probably a sergeant though Otto

didn't recognize the markings on his brown uniform, said, "Throw down your weapon and surrender. We're not going to let you kidnap these citizens."

Otto threw back his head and laughed. Kidnap, was that what they were calling this jailbreak?

"Here's my counteroffer. Stand aside and make no effort to stop us and I won't kill you all where you stand. How dare you accuse me of kidnapping when you're the ones who kept these innocent people in a prison just so you could use them to control their sons and daughters." Otto grew angrier by the moment. "In fact, I rescind my offer."

Two dozen threads shot out and lightning quickly followed. The watchmen collapsed and twitched as the electricity caused their muscles to clench.

When Otto ended the spell, some of them were still breathing, but none of them was going anywhere soon. He would have happily cut the survivors' throats, but he didn't want to waste the time or energy.

They set out again. Perhaps that squad was the only one nearby. Luckily for them and luckier for any watchmen that might have shown up, the group reached the portal without encountering any further opposition.

The reason for that was obvious the moment they reached the edge of the plaza. He counted a hundred watchmen and a handful of wizards standing in ranks waiting for them. That was a lot even for Otto. If he attacked, it would take most of his strength to defeat them and even then, he wasn't sure he had enough power left to finish the job.

If he didn't, they were dead.

Otto gathered his power, but before he could attack, a fireball slammed into the gathered watchmen from the left and a second later from the right. The enemy formation was devastated in an instant.

Lightning crackled, arcing into the survivors.

Otto didn't know who was helping, but he wasn't about to complain.

"Lord Shenk!"

He turned to see Oskar running toward them, a young, skinny girl with him. The infiltrator was dressed in a simple tunic and trousers, no sign that he served an enemy nation visible.

"Friends of yours?" Otto asked when Oskar had stopped and saluted.

"Members of the wizard underground. I never would have completed my mission without their help. I expected more than just you when the invasion began."

"More are coming, but I needed to free the families of those wizards forced into combat by Rolan. It looks like the path is clear. Let's move out, everyone."

Otto led the way to the portal. He ignored the dead and dying watchmen. Distasteful as it was, he'd harbored no illusions about this being a bloodless process. A trio of wizards fell in beside them as they walked. Two of the younger ones looked to an older man with a salt-and-pepper beard for orders.

"This is Miguel," Oskar said. "I owe him a great deal."

Otto held out his hand and the older man shook. "I've met some of your fellows in Garenland. It's a pleasure and thank you for your help. Rest assured we won't forget all you've done."

Miguel nodded. "All we want is freedom and a chance to make our own way. Give us that and we'll call it even."

"That and a wizards guild."

Miguel started. "They told you?"

"Of course. No need for secrets among allies." Not for them at least. Otto had plenty he'd keep to himself.

He drew the control rod from a hidden pocket inside his cloak, charged the tip with ether, and touched the rune for Garenland.

"Everyone stay clear," Otto said.

The portal came to life and a moment later the first rank of the portal guard stepped out. In less than a minute, all fifteen hundred were through.

The commander saluted. "We'll take care of things here, my lord, rest assured."

"I have every confidence, Commander. Should anyone of importance come by, tell them someone will be coming to discuss terms in a few days. These three wizards—" Otto indicated Miguel and his companions with a sweep of his hand "—are local allies and should be treated accordingly."

With that introduction out of the way, Otto led the prisoners through the portal.

CHAPTER 26

Otto and Wolfric, along with a hundred members of the palace guard and fifteen hundred legionnaires, had gathered at the Garenland portal. They were preparing to march on Lux. Otto would have been just as happy to save the easy target for last, but the king was determined to confront Queen Philippa after her betrayal at the compact meeting. Some things just weren't worth the argument.

The day before, Otto had reunited the Rolan wizards and their families. It had been a tear-filled moment and one of the best things he'd done in a long time. As soon as he explained their options, fifteen wizards had immediately volunteered to join the army and serve the Rolan portal garrison. He'd teamed them up with five Garenland wizards and that should be enough to secure that portal. And if it wasn't, Otto wasn't sure what they were going to do.

"Are you sure you want to do this?" Otto asked for the third time. It wasn't that he was afraid of what Lux might try, but why risk the new emperor?

Wolfric nodded. "I want to see the look in her eyes when she realizes she backed the wrong side. I want to break her spirit the way her betrayal broke my father's."

Well, Otto had tried and no one could say he didn't. "Okay. Let's do it."

He charged the control rod with ether and touched the Lux rune. The portal crackled to life and the legionnaires marched through first followed by Otto and Wolfric surrounded by the palace guard.

When they emerged on the other side, Wolfric staggered a step. Otto put an arm on his shoulder. "Are you okay?"

"Yes, going through on foot feels different than going through in a carriage. The light is more intense. I'm fine now."

Otto nodded and let go. The portal plaza was empty but in the distance a group of watchmen was staring at the small army appearing in their city unannounced. After a few seconds of stupid staring, one of them ran off toward the Crystal Palace.

The legionnaires, meanwhile, quickly went to work erecting crude wooden barricades that would help control access to the portal. The bulk of the soldiers formed a defensive perimeter with Otto, Wolfric, the palace guards, and ten wizards at the center. There should be an agent here somewhere. What was the man's name? Henry, that's right. Perhaps word hadn't reached him that they'd arrived.

"Should we approach the palace or wait here?" one of the guards asked.

"Wait here," Otto said only to be contradicted a moment later by Wolfric.

"We'll go to her. I want to meet Philippa on her own ground and show her who's master now."

If it was any other nation, Otto would have argued harder

against it, but they were in Lux. He was fairly certain he could destroy what passed for their army on his own if it became necessary.

"We leave the portal in your hands, Commander," Otto said. "Let no one approach."

The commander saluted. "As you command, my lord."

Otto and Wolfric set out surrounded by the palace guards. The walk to the Crystal Palace wasn't far, but as they passed shop after shop, everyone inside came to the door and stared. Otto ignored the looks and focused on potential threats. There wasn't much from these pampered weaklings. Maybe they could find someone worth worrying about on the docks, but here, not so much.

About halfway to the docks someone shouted, "Lord Shenk! Your Majesty!"

A man dressed in the uniform of the Lux watch came jogging toward them.

The palace guard immediately leveled their spears.

Otto squinted as the watchman grew closer. "Henry? What in heaven's name are you doing in that getup?"

"I took a position with the Lux watch while waiting for your arrival. It's a long story. How can I be of assistance?"

"It's alright," Otto said to the palace guards. "He's one of ours. Make a path."

The spears snapped up and the guards parted just enough to let Henry through. The group set out again and as they walked Otto asked, "Did you encounter the wizard underground?"

Henry blinked. "I wasn't aware such a thing existed. In fact, I'm not certain I encountered a single wizard during my mission or after."

Otto nodded and scratched his chin. Either the underground had no agents in Lux or they had decided not to get involved. The local wizards must have been kept under tight watch if Henry hadn't run into a single one in the weeks he'd been here. That would need to change and quickly.

The group didn't encounter anyone else and soon found themselves facing the Crystal Palace. The white stone structure was beautiful. Clearly no one had ever expected it to have to withstand a siege. It was all graceful lines with crystal highlights glinting in the sun. The tall, slim towers didn't look like they'd survive a single strike from a catapult stone.

The drawbridge was down and a party of twenty soldiers in blue and white tabards stood waiting. They carried lances from which blue pennants bearing the Lux crystal fluttered. They didn't look like they had any intentions of fighting and no archers appeared on the battlements. What was the queen's game?

"King Wolfric," one of the guards said when the group had stopped. "Her Majesty, Queen Philippa, extends a warm welcome to our Garenland friends and invites you and your party to join her inside."

She was going to pretend this was just another state visit rather than an invasion. That made sense. It wasn't like she had much choice in the matter. Otto glanced at Wolfric. The king's jaw bunched and relaxed as he chewed over the invitation. He'd clearly been hoping for a more aggressive confrontation.

"We accept her generous offer," Wolfric said after a long moment. "Please, lead the way."

The Lux guards turned as one and marched into the courtyard. Otto's group followed, everyone tense and looking for a trap. The chances of there being one were vanishingly small. Lux's only chance was for Philippa to charm a good deal out of

Wolfric and he suspected the clever queen knew it. He equally suspected his friend wasn't in any mood to be charmed.

Across the perfectly groomed grounds, another group, this one smaller and consisting of a woman, four guards, and... Otto blinked a couple times and shook his head.

"Is that King Eddred beside Philippa?" Otto asked. He'd only seen the king of Markane once and at the time Otto had had other things on his mind.

"I believe it is." Wolfric scowled. "What's he doing here? I can't remember the last time Eddred left his precious island."

"How much do you want to bet he's investigating for Lord Valtan? He couldn't have come through the portal, but it's only a few days' sailing distance. Valtan would need someone reliable to see what was happening since he can't leave the capital."

"If he needed someone reliable, why would he send Eddred?" Wolfric asked. "How much do you think Valtan already knows?"

"About what I did to the portals? Everything. But knowing and being able to do anything about it are two different things."

When they reached Philippa and her delegation, the palace guards parted and Wolfric strode toward her with Otto a step behind and to his right.

"Wolfric." Philippa opened her arms as if to embrace him. Despite her age, the queen retained her beauty. Her pale skin remained largely smooth, and her low-cut white gown emphasized her ample chest. Her hair was pulled back in a simple but elegant style, probably all her servants had time for given their sudden appearance. "You should have sent word; I would have prepared a proper greeting."

"Spare me the court talk, I'm not in the mood." Wolfric

crossed his arms. "I'm sure you've noticed that the portal no longer functions as it used to."

Eddred perked up at that. Otto kept half his attention on the Markane king. Maybe he could get some clue as to Valtan's intentions.

"I did," Philippa said, trying to maintain her smile. "I assume you have an explanation for that."

"Garenland now controls all the portals." Wolfric nodded toward Eddred. "Except Markane's. If you wish to resume using it, you'll have to accept some new rules."

"Such as?" Philippa's smile was wholly absent now. It seemed she'd come to realize her charm offensive wasn't going to work.

"One, Lux will become a province of Garenland. You will be allowed to remain as ruler under our laws. Your title will go from queen to governor. Two, all wizards will be freed and given full rights as citizens. And last you will pay a gold royal per head to use the portal. Our soldiers will maintain access to it and your merchants will be searched before being allowed to approach."

As Wolfric spoke, all the blood drained from Philippa's face.

"You can't be serious," she said. "Leaving aside the insult of forcing me to swear fealty and serve as your steward, how will we survive without the wizards to produce our crystals?"

Wolfric glanced at Otto who stepped forward. "Your wizards will be free to continue creating crystals, but you'll have to pay them just like any other artisan. The new arrangement might reduce your profit margins, but that's a small price to pay for giving them their freedom and dignity, right?"

"What if I refuse?" Philippa asked.

Wolfric smiled. "If you refuse, I'll replace you with a governor of my choosing. I'm sure there are plenty of Garenland nobles that would be happy for the job. Either way, our soldiers are staying here and guarding the portal."

"What have the other rulers said about this offer?"

"You're the first I've spoken to. Well, not counting Uther. He's in my dungeon at the moment. I've appointed General Varchi to oversee Straken in my name. I'm certain a similar arrangement can be made for Lux if you prefer."

Philippa slumped, all signs of pride melting away. "I could have been your stepmother if only things had worked out differently. How can you do this to me?"

"Do you really need to ask? After you betrayed Father at the council meeting? It broke his heart and I think his mind. You couldn't have hurt him worse if you'd run a dagger through his guts. Be grateful I'm giving you this chance and not throwing you in a cell beside Uther. Now what's your answer?"

"I accept your terms. Lux will become a province of Garenland and all shall live under your laws."

"Good. Rest assured that should you betray me or fail to fulfill your duties, I will have you removed. Permanently."

Wolfric turned to leave but Otto said, "I'll join you by the portal. I need to have a word with King Eddred."

Upon hearing his name Eddred flinched as if struck. Otto crooked his finger and beckoned the so-called monarch a safe distance away from Philippa and her guards.

"You really shouldn't order a king around like this, it's bad manners," Eddred said even as he followed Otto away from his companions.

"You're no more a king than Philippa is now a queen. Valtan is the real power in Markane and we both know it. Let's stop pretending. I assume he sent you to find out what was happening with the portals."

Eddred couldn't meet Otto's gaze. "Something like that.

While I'm not a wizard, I have just enough connection to the ether to allow me to see its flow. And I can speak to the other rulers as an equal."

Otto smirked. None of the other kings saw Eddred as an equal, but they would all treat him as one out of fear of Valtan. "And what will your report be?"

"I'll tell him what I saw." Eddred shrugged. "What he makes of it he may or may not share with me. Is there anything else? I need to get back."

"Just one more thing. I don't know what Markane's intentions are. You've always professed neutrality, though more out of convenience than anything I assume. I'll warn you just once. Stay neutral. We have no desire to go to war with you, but if you interfere in our new empire, all bets are off. Am I clear?"

"Perfectly. I will relay your message to Lord Valtan. Since you were kind enough to share a warning with me, allow me to share one with you. Lord Valtan is no one you want as an enemy. Think hard about that before you make any more decisions."

Otto nodded, turned on his heel, and set out for the portal. He hardly needed a warning about Valtan, but the Arcane Lord had bound himself to the portal in Markane and as long as Garenland didn't stray too close, they had little to fear.

That was Otto's theory, anyway.

CHAPTER 27

Marching through the snow and trees had reduced the Lady in Red's once-fine dress to rags, her toes were numb, and her fingers were little better. The group had lost three servants to the cold and left them frozen on the side of a mountain. The journey had not been easy to say the least.

But at last Mal had found signs that people had come and gone. There was even a trail, assuming you could call a path barely wider than her waist a trail. At least her feet weren't buried in the snow.

Directly ahead of her, Mal's broad form blocked the worst of a chill breeze. He looked back at her, a concerned frown creasing his craggy features. "We're getting close, my lady. If you wish to turn back, this is our last chance."

She wouldn't turn back now. Whatever Prince Uther might do to her, she would complete the final task given to her by the king. Besides, no one would survive the trip back down the mountain. They had supplies for another two days at most and everyone was exhausted.

"Press on, Mal. We need to get the others to shelter."

He nodded and trudged forward.

Five minutes later he stopped again. If Mal was going to ask her if she wanted to change her mind every hundred yards, it was going to take forever to reach the prince's camp.

He looked back again. "We have company."

The Lady shuffled around beside him. Twenty figures dressed in white and gray camouflage stood blocking their path. The rangers carried crossbows and had their signature curved swords at their belt.

"I must speak with the prince," she said.

"We know you, Lady," one of them said. "His Highness will not be best pleased to see you or the many mouths you've brought."

"I merely carry out my king's final command. Once I have delivered my message, I'm at Uther's service."

"Let it be on your head then." The rangers fell into line. "Follow us. Our camp is right over this ridge."

The camp wasn't terribly impressive: a collection of tents pitched around a central fire pit. More rangers in white and gray moved around silently attending to whatever task they'd been set. A few glanced their way, but most ignored the Lady and her party entirely.

How long had Prince Uther been living wild like this? She couldn't remember exactly when he left, but it felt like months. She shook her head. He was certainly tougher than most nobles she'd met in her travels.

Their guides led them to a tent that looked no different than any other. Mal took a step toward the flap, but one of the rangers stopped him. "Only her."

"It's okay," the Lady said when it appeared he was going to argue. "Whatever comes, I'm prepared to face it."

Mal grunted and stepped out of her way.

The Lady in Red brushed through the flap. Inside a single man waited. Prince Uther sat on a simple folding camp chair, his broad back to her. He was dressed the same as the rangers, only a collar of fur distinguishing him from his men.

"Your Majesty," she said. "Your father—"

"Do you not remember what I said would happen if I ever saw you again?" Uther's voice was rough and not as deep as his father's.

"I remember."

"And yet here you stand, knowing I will most likely kill you. Why?"

"Your father's last command was that I bring you the crown and do my best to serve you as I did him. His wish was that we work together to make Garenland pay for what they've done to Straken." She took the crown from the pouch at her side. "Those were his final words to me."

Uther rose and turned to face her. A scar ran down his left cheek to his chin and his hair had turned white in the center. Three days' worth of stubble covered his face. But his eyes were what drew her gaze. Narrow and shot with red, she'd never seen such angry eyes. As far as she knew, the Lady had never done him any harm, yet his hatred was as strong today as when she first met him years ago.

"You keep saying 'last' and 'final.' Did you see my father die?"

"No, Majesty, but he was drinking poisoned wine when I left and if the poison didn't kill him, surely the Garenlanders would."

"No, until I see his body or hear news of his death from someone I trust, I must assume he's alive." Uther snatched the crown from her hands. "I will hold onto this for him and serve as regent in his absence. As for you..."

He trailed off as though trying to think of the worst death he could imagine. The Lady remained silent. Her words would have no influence on him and begging would only make it worse.

"I'll spare you for now. You must have some value if Father kept you around. No doubt letting you live will please him when he's back safe. Your soldiers and servants are another matter. None of them are trained to survive out here and we lack the supplies to keep them fed. They'll have to go back."

"Most won't live through a return trip," she said. "It would be kinder to cut their throats now."

"I will not murder my own people. The rangers will get them safely back to civilization. From there it will be up to them to find somewhere to hide or to surrender to the enemy."

The Lady kept her expression neutral but inside she cheered. Perhaps the prince wasn't the mad monster she'd feared. At the very least she'd earned a reprieve. But for how long she couldn't say.

CHAPTER 28

Otto could hardly describe his relief when Wolfric agreed to allow him to handle contacting the other kings. If anything happened to the new emperor, it would throw things into chaos at a vital moment and Otto had to believe their enemies would know that.

The moment they returned from Lux, the palace guard had hustled him back to the safety of the castle, leaving Otto standing beside the portal with the next group of portal guards. The wizard contingent was grinning to themselves. Probably figured after fighting a war in Straken, portal duty would be easy.

He hoped they were right. Despite everything, all Otto really wanted was peace so he could focus on his studies. Anything and anyone that got in the way of that would be removed. The next target was Lasil. They should be the easiest to deal with after Lux, or so he hoped.

"Are your men ready, Commander?" Otto asked.

"Ready, Lord Shenk," the man said. Otto hadn't even bothered to learn his name. As long as he did his job, nothing else mattered. "I'll need a hundred men to escort me to the castle for a meeting with King Kasimir."

"Understood. First and second squads, you're with Lord Shenk. Is there anything else, my lord?"

Otto took out the control rod and said, "No, that's it."

He opened the portal and the soldiers marched through. Before he followed, Otto had a momentary thought about how this irregular opening and closing of the portals was affecting Lord Valtan, but then he shrugged. Surely an immortal wizard could handle it with no trouble.

On the other side of the portal, the soldiers had set up a perimeter and were already erecting their rough fortifications. Enemy soldiers were watching them from all four corners of the plaza. Clearly someone had anticipated their arrival. Otto sniffed. A pall of smoke hung over the city.

Otto's guards formed up around him and they went over to the closest group of soldiers. "I would speak to your king."

"His Majesty has been expecting someone since the portal ceased to function," the unit commander said. "Follow us and we will escort you to the castle."

Otto waved the man on. "After you. What's with the smoke?"

"There was a fire in the docks district. A renegade wizard set one of the whale oil warehouses ablaze and it spread. Luckily loss of life was minimal."

Otto nodded and followed the soldier toward the castle. He suspected, strongly, that the fire had been set by one of the underground wizards, probably to help his agent get access to the portal. It pleased him to hear that they were willing to go that far for the cause. An ally that balked when the time for action arrived was of little use.

No one troubled them as they walked through the streets

and soon enough the group arrived at Lasil Castle. Much like Vault City itself, the castle was blocky and tough looking, the sort of place only a crazy person would consider attacking. A crazy person or someone with a large force of wizards anyway.

The portcullis clanked up as they approached. Otto glanced up when they passed through and saw the gleaming of armor in the murder holes above them. No one tried anything though, so he ignored the implied threat.

The courtyard was empty and their guide led them into the main keep. The halls were even more stark than Castle Marduke. No decoration of any sort broke the endless expanse of dark stone. There weren't even any tapestries to help ward off the chill. King Kasimir's reputation for austerity hadn't been overstated.

Finally, the group reached another door that opened into the throne room. Otto left his guards near the door and walked toward the throne on his own. There were a few guards in Lasil's gray and silver livery standing behind the throne, but he ignored them. All his focus was on the man seated before him. King Kasimir's thin, sunken face glowered at Otto.

"I assume you have demands," the king said. "We require the use of our portal so get on with it."

Otto did so, giving him the exact list Wolfric had given Philippa.

When he finished Kasimir said, "The toll is acceptable, but freeing our wizards won't do. They're too valuable a resource to give up. As for being governor instead of king and implementing Garenland's law, that won't do either. Here's my counteroffer. You can control access to the portal and we'll agree to your toll. I and my sons after me will remain king. We will implement the laws we see fit and retain control of our wizards."

Otto frowned. "I fear you misunderstand. This isn't a negotiation. If you wish to remain in any position of authority, you will accept all our terms. Otherwise we'll remove you and put a governor in your place."

"Everything's a negotiation, boy. I doubt your king wants another war right after fighting Straken for a year. Why don't you take him my offer and see what he says?"

"I don't care to waste his time. As for a war, I'm not worried. The question is, how would you like the rest of your city burned to the ground and your precious banks emptied of all their gold? I have enough men and wizards with me to destroy this city. The only other thing your miserable nation has to offer is the gold mines and we'll be happy to seize those as well. So you tell me, Kasimir, how do you want to handle this?"

One of the guards went for his sword.

Otto hit him with enough lightning to cook his flesh in his armor. The unlucky man collapsed, sizzling like a freshly roasted steak.

"Anyone else reaches for their weapon and I'll consider that a declaration of war."

"Calm down," Kasimir said. The guards beside him relaxed a fraction. "It seems you leave me with little choice. However, I will continue to call myself a king."

Otto shrugged. "If it makes you feel better, you can call yourself a dancing monkey. As long as Garenland's laws are obeyed and your wizards set free, I don't really care about the title you claim. You have one week to implement the changes I've outlined. An inspector will be coming to make sure you have fully complied. If you haven't, then I will be coming back. And I assure you, you don't want that. Clear?"

"Perfectly."

"Good." Otto turned on his heel and marched back the way he'd come, his escort falling in around him as he passed. He strongly suspected Kasimir was going to be trouble. Still, he'd give the man a chance to prove his loyalty to his new master. If Otto turned out to be wrong, so much the better.

The walk back to the portal proved every bit as uneventful as the walk to the castle. When they reached the plaza, the soldiers that had been watching them when they arrived were gone. As they got closer, the portal guard commander waved him over.

Otto angled his way. The legionnaires had a man in soot-stained clothes surrounded, their swords drawn and ready to strike. He wasn't a wizard, that was clear from a glance.

"This fellow claims to be an agent of the Crown, my lord," the commander said.

Otto racked his brain. "Luca, yes?"

"Yes, Lord Shenk. I've been keeping watch for your arrival per my orders."

"It alright, Commander, he's with us."

"Can't be too careful. Sheathe swords and release the prisoner."

Once Luca was free Otto led him a little way from the soldiers. "Report."

"The infiltration was difficult but successful thanks to the help of a friendly group of wizards. Are you familiar with the wizard underground?"

"We've met and they aided several of your fellow infiltrators. Well done on completing your mission. The fire was your doing I suppose?"

Luca winced. "Yes, my lord. It was my idea anyway. One of the wizards carried out the task. Things got a little out of control."

Otto shrugged, not terribly concerned. "Anything else of note?"

"The wizards are operating out of a sprawling tunnel complex that extends under the harbor. I only explored a fraction of it given that it wasn't part of my mission and the wizards didn't seem keen on me poking around."

All the more reason for Otto to eventually take a look himself. "That's fine. For now, I want you to remain here, advise the portal guard commander, and keep an eye on what's happening at the castle. I have my doubts about Kasimir. I'll be expecting a report on his actions when I return next week."

"Understood. Hopefully I can get a clean uniform. These clothes have seen better days."

Otto pulled a small pouch out of an inside pocket and tossed it to Luca. "Buy some civilian clothes. I don't want you to draw attention."

Luca hefted the pouch and nodded. "As you wish, my lord."

There was no reason to activate the portal for just himself, so Otto became one with the ether and returned to Garenland. Matters were progressing nicely, but now the real hard work began: bringing Rolan and Tharanault to heel.

CHAPTER 29

"This is where they came out sure enough," Cobb said.

He was standing beside Axel, staring at a heap of broken stone that filled a hole in the ground. It was the exit to the escape tunnel the Lady in Red along with the servants and guards had used to get out of Castle Marduke. A clear trail of tromped-down snow led away from the collapsed tunnel and toward the distant mountains. They had lucked out in that there hadn't been a snowstorm since the assault on the castle.

Axel squinted at the snowcapped peaks. There was only one reason she'd be headed that way: the prince. Uther the Younger had to be hiding in those mountains somewhere. He took some solace in the knowledge that the escapees were headed northeast and most of Straken's mines were to the northwest. Securing those were the biggest priority. At least that was Otto's biggest priority and Axel assumed the king's as well.

He smiled to himself. They had to get something of value out of this miserable war after all, something beyond peace in the northern province at least. A cheap source of valuable minerals would be an excellent start.

"What do we do?" Cobb asked. The other guys were looking to him for orders.

Axel shook off his thoughts and focused on the matter at hand. "We'll follow them for now. I don't want to get too far away on our own."

"Still worried about those rangers?" Cobb spat to one side. If there was one thing he hated most, it was Straken rangers. Axel knew just how he felt.

"We haven't seen, much less fought, a single ranger since the assassin last year. They've got to be somewhere and my guess is they're protecting the prince. I don't know how many rangers they have, but I suspect it's more than we have scouts. Plus they know the terrain. We'll play it safe for now. Colten, you're on point."

The youthful scout and his team took off after the tracks. If there was anyone Axel trusted not to walk them into a trap, it was Colten. After a five-minute head start, Axel and the rest of his men set out.

The hike started out easy enough, but around midafternoon they reached the foothills and started going up. The snow was soon up to their knees. Walking in the trail helped and all his men were in excellent physical condition, so no one complained. What he couldn't imagine was a line of palace servants trudging up this mountain.

An hour later they found Colten and his group waiting. They were standing around a frozen corpse in Straken livery. It was a woman, probably in her midfifties. Axel guessed a kitchen maid but had no real idea. His worry about the servants hadn't been misplaced after all.

"I assume you didn't just stop for a body," Axel said.

"No, sir. A little way up a second trail intersects this one and continues southeast away from the capital. It was a large group with scouts in front, at the sides, and following behind. I'd say they're not more than a few hours ahead of us. Who should we follow?"

Axel frowned. Why would the prince split his already small group of rangers? He had to have a reason.

"Could you tell anything from the main body of tracks?"

"Like what?" Colten asked.

"Like whether they wore servants' shoes or soldiers' boots."

"I didn't actually look that close." Colten hung his head. "Sorry, sir."

"Forget it and let's take a look now."

They made the short walk to the second trail and Colten crouched. "Definitely not soldiers, no tread on a lot of the tracks."

"What are you thinking, my lord?" Cobb asked.

"I think they sent the noncombatants out of danger along with a small force of rangers to guide them. I further think that if we follow this trail, we'll find a nice, little contingent of rangers just waiting to get picked off. I don't know about you, but I prefer hunting a target to walking into an ambush."

"Sounds good to me." Cobb grinned and tested the edge of his sword.

○

It was nearing dark when Axel smelled smoke. The scouts had been trailing what they assumed was a small group of rangers and civilians since cutting their trail earlier in the day. The wilderness north of Marduke was almost devoid of settlements, so the smoke had to be the targets setting up camp for the night. He doubted the rangers would surrender, but hopefully the servants wouldn't do anything foolish.

A hundred yards after he smelled the smoke, they caught up to Colten's advance team. They were crouched in the snow, nearly invisible in the fading light.

Colten touched his fingers to his lips and Axel nodded. The enemy was close.

Axel pointed at his eyes. The response to his silent query came at once. Colten pointed south then held up three fingers, three more to the east, and two to the north. Finally, he made a fist and held up all ten fingers. Eight on guard and ten watching over the servants. Less than they'd hoped for but still a worthwhile target.

Axel nodded again then pointed at Colten followed by south and east. Next he tapped Cobb on the shoulder and pointed north. Axel would lead the main force himself against the camp. Finally he held up five fingers and made a fist.

Colten and his team vanished at once. Cobb grabbed a squad of his own and slipped silently into the growing darkness. Axel would give them five minutes then move in with the main force.

He grimaced as he counted in his head. He hated waiting. While he considered himself a fair leader, he'd never move to the highest ranks given his inability to send others into battle while awaiting the outcome. It was a character flaw; he wouldn't deny that. It was one everyone in his family shared, even his father liked to wade into a fight, hacking and fighting beside his men. There had to be something wrong with the Shenk men.

When five minutes had passed without a sound, Axel motioned his scouts forward. It pleased him that they made hardly a whisper across the snow. Even the newer guys maintained stealth as they eased closer.

Soon enough the enemy camp came into view. Thirty men and women huddled around a small campfire over which an iron pot bubbled. Rangers in white and gray cloaks watched over them. Though their faces were covered, from their body language, Axel doubted they were happy with the assignment they'd received.

They were about to be considerably less happy. He made the sign for archers then designated everyone's target. When they were at full draw Axel pointed at the camp.

The bows twanged as one and down went the rangers, each pierced by two arrows.

The servants screamed and leapt to their feet.

Before anyone could take a step to escape, the scouts surged into the clearing and surrounded them. Axel glanced at Cobb's men as well as Colten's. No one appeared injured. That was a relief.

"Keep calm and don't resist," Axel said. "We have no interest in hurting you. Raise your hands above your heads."

When the servants had complied Axel said, "Third squad, check them for weapons."

The scouts moved in and quickly patted everyone down. A few small utility knives were found and confiscated.

Axel was proud to see that not a single one of his men took advantage of his order to touch the female servants inappropriately. That showed good discipline. He wouldn't say anything of course. Good discipline was the minimum he expected from anyone under his command.

When the search was completed Axel motioned Cobb and Colten over. "No trouble?"

"Nah," Cobb said. "This lot wasn't expecting trouble. They weren't asleep or anything, but you can tell the difference."

Axel knew what he meant. When you were expecting an attack there was a certain tension in your mind and body. And why would they expect trouble? They were in the mountains in the middle of nowhere.

"Set a guard," Axel said. "We'll camp here tonight and take them back to the city tomorrow."

One of the prisoners groaned.

"Relax, you won't be harmed. Once the city is secure, noncombatants will be released to return to their farms and villages. I assume you all have family. When the time comes, leave with them. There will be no work at the palace. Who's in charge?"

They all looked at each other and finally an older, bald man dressed in black stepped forward. "I'm the chief steward. That makes me the highest ranking among the servants. Not that anyone actually listens to us."

"I'll listen to you," Axel said. "You're going to tell me everything about Prince Uther's camp, his soldiers, and what he and the Lady in Red are planning."

The steward shook his head. "I fear you have captured the wrong people. None of us were privy to their discussions. The camp is two days from here, higher in the mountains, but they were packing up to leave at the same time we were. There were many rangers there, but I didn't count them."

Axel frowned. He didn't seem like he was lying. Certainly if they were leading the servants to safety, Prince Uther wouldn't want them to know anything they might reveal, either accidentally or on purpose. And the Lady in Red had a reputation for secrecy.

"Well enough. Someone in Marduke will want to talk to

you when we arrive, but for now I'm content. The stew looks ready. Eat and sleep. We leave at dawn."

Axel moved away from the group and Cobb joined him.

"Pretty useless catch," Cobb said.

Axel shrugged. "We killed two squads of rangers, that's no bad thing. We also know the prince is on the move."

"Yeah, but to where?"

That was indeed the question.

CHAPTER 30

After a good night's sleep, Otto set out for the portal. He wanted to wrap up matters in Rolan early so he could focus on Tharanault. They already controlled the Rolan portal and now it was time to make an offer to King Villares. Given his antagonism, Otto held out little hope that an agreement could be reached.

Still, he had to try. Assuming the king refused a demotion to governor, Otto would have the perfect excuse to remove him.

If he was being honest, he expected an easier time dealing with Rolan than Tharanault, who clearly knew something had been done to their portal. His forces would certainly be marching into a trap there. How serious a trap he wouldn't know until they arrived.

Otto barely made it downstairs when Edwyn called from the dining room, "Otto, my boy. Do you have a moment?"

He grimaced but turned from the front door to the dining room. Edwyn's rotund figure was seated at the huge table, not a morsel of food in sight. The cooks were probably still preparing the massive meal, it was early after all.

"Edwyn, is all well?"

"Yes, indeed. The capital's been quiet, the first caravans of spring have departed and as far as I know encountered no bandits. The other merchants were wondering when they might expect to resume using the portal."

What he was really asking was when could he resume the highly lucrative auctions that had made the family so rich. "I assume you've noticed the fortifications being constructed around the portal."

"Yes, such ugly things in the heart of Gold Ward."

"Ugly but necessary. Similar construction is proceeding in Lux, Lasil, Straken, and Rolan. Regular operation of the portal will resume once they're all complete. All shipments will be searched coming or going, including ones from Garenland. We've had enough trouble with infiltrators to not take any chances."

"Of course, of course, better safe than sorry. So, weeks, months?"

"By summer I would say for Lux and Lasil. The rest will be determined by the situation on the ground. I'm sorry I can't give you a more certain answer."

Edwyn waved off his apology. "Think nothing of it. Even a wizard can't control everything. By the way, have you seen your daughter lately? She's getting bigger by the day."

"I've been busy. Speaking of which, I need to get going. Good morning, Edwyn."

"Be careful, Otto. We'd hate to have anything happen to you."

Otto sincerely doubted Annamaria would care a lick if he

dropped dead tomorrow. In fact, she'd probably celebrate. Pity for her he had no intention of getting himself killed.

He left the dining room just as the servants were emerging from the kitchen laden with steaming platters. The delightful smells nearly made him turn around, but he shook it off. He'd grab something at a tavern on his way.

Half an hour later, Otto strode into the portal plaza. Two of the guard towers were nearly complete and a section of wall connecting them would be going up shortly. A dozen wagons laden with building supplies were lined up facing the portal.

Otto stopped beside the first wagon. "Are you bound for Rolan?"

"Yes, my lord," the driver said. "We arrived a few minutes ago so as not to keep you waiting."

"Splendid. I'll open the portal."

A moment later the ether swirled through the massive mithril construct. Otto leapt onto the bench beside the lead driver and they passed through. The streaks of ether were absolutely beautiful no matter how many times he saw them.

All too soon they emerged on the other side. The portal guards on duty motioned the wagons off to the left. The sun was well into the sky above Rolan and the guards were busy hammering boards onto the side of the first tower. If they kept up the pace, they should have the fort built in six or eight weeks. That would be a relief to Otto. While it wouldn't guarantee the portal's safety, a physical barrier along with guards would certainly help.

He hopped down from the wagon and went looking for Oskar. He'd left the spy in town to keep an eye on Rolan's response to them seizing the city center. The lack of any sign of fighting not to mention no one even watching what they were doing was strange. Otto expected to find the plaza surrounded by soldiers just waiting for a chance to strike.

He grabbed a passing soldier and asked, "Where's Oskar?"

"No idea, my lord. He left early this morning and hasn't returned."

Otto grumbled to himself then asked, "The unit commander?"

"Overseeing construction of the tower."

Otto nodded his thanks and let the man go. He strode over to the work crew and quickly spotted the commander standing a safe distance away, hands on hips, watching them nail the second-story platform into place.

"Commander," Otto said. "How do you fare?"

"We're progressing nicely as you can see. The locals haven't given us a moment of trouble. Strange I admit, but I'm not complaining. Building is far more difficult if you have to watch out for enemy archers."

It certainly was which was why Otto expected there to be a few on the nearby rooftops. "Did Oskar give you any indication of his intentions when he went out this morning?"

"No, my lord. I'm not entirely certain where he falls within the chain of command, so I didn't demand an explanation. While we're on the subject, is he under my command or is he simply sharing our post?"

"He's not directly under your command, but I expect you both to share information and work together for the good of Garenland."

"Of course. Everything I do is for the glory of our homeland. Rest assured, you'll have no cause to complain on my end."

Otto clapped him on the shoulder and left the men to their task. Finding Oskar would be difficult since he had no way to track the man magically. Just sending his sight over the city looking would be a frightful waste of time and energy. In the end, he decided to simply wait. Oskar would return when he finished whatever he was doing.

There was nothing pressing back home and he wasn't planning to visit Tharanault until tomorrow. He found a camp chair and settled in.

Otto had barely gotten comfortable when a shout from one of the soldiers on guard duty brought him straight to his feet. He hurried to where the shout had come from and found Oskar running toward the partially built tower. He had a scroll clutched in his hand.

The spy spotted Otto and angled his way. He stopped directly in front of Otto panting for breath. "Found this... nailed to the... castle gate."

Otto took the scroll and unrolled it. The short note said that while they may control Rolan City and the portal, the rest of the kingdom would resist to the death any attempt by Garenland to seize control. It was signed by King Villares. This explained why there were no soldiers watching. Everyone able to fight had probably already left the city.

"There was nothing else?" Otto asked.

"No." Oskar had caught his breath and straightened up. "They must have all snuck out during the night. I know at least a few guards were on duty when I walked by the castle last night and the watch patrols were out. I swung by watch headquarters on my way to the castle; everyone was gone."

"So the capital at least is really ours. What about the people?"

"I saw a few out and about, just women and children."

"Trusting souls," Otto muttered. "Leaving their families

behind to our tender mercy. Lucky for them we're the honorable sort."

"What are we going to do?" the unit commander asked.

"You're going to do the job assigned to you. I'll arrange a garrison to patrol the city and secure the walls. I doubt Villares will try anything too drastic given the thousands of his people we have in here with us. I need to go back and make arrangements. Keep your wits until reinforcements arrive."

Oskar and the unit commander both saluted.

Otto headed for the portal. He knew Rolan wouldn't go down without a fight. Apparently the king meant to prove him right. It was a pity and a waste of life but what could you do? If they didn't surrender, Otto had to defeat them.

CHAPTER 31

Having made his report to Wolfric and recommended that the Southern Army be alerted to Rolan's potential increase in aggression, Otto retreated to Franken Manor. The sun hung low in the sky and there was no time left to make a move on Tharanault even had he intended to. That would wait until morning.

He yawned and closed his workshop door behind him. Just because he had to wait to invade, didn't mean he couldn't at least take a look at what awaited him. He walked past his workbench to a bare section of wall and waved his hand in front of it, brushing the ether as he did. The illusion he'd created to hide a shallow niche vanished revealing the crystal ball he took from Lord Karonin's armory.

The cool, smooth crystal felt good in his hand. He'd found the device to be of use only in limited circumstances. The lack of detail in the image was a problem, but the range was excellent. Settling the crystal in a tripod he'd had made for it and himself in a hard, wooden chair, he focused on the ether, forcing it into the ball to awaken the magic then compelling it to show the Tharanault portal.

He'd never been there himself so at first it tried to show him the Rolan portal. Willing the view to shift southwest he eventually coaxed it to the right place. As usual the image looked warped in the crystal, the portal appeared as an oval rather than a perfect circle and the plaza around a blurry mess.

Sweat poured down his face as he tried to hone in. Bit by bit the resolution improved. When it did, he swallowed a sudden lump. The portal was surrounded by crude fortifications. Hundreds of soldiers kept watch as though expecting an attack at any moment. He couldn't tell if there were any wizards among them but had to assume so. Taking the city was going to be every bit as hard as he'd feared. Collecting reinforcements and wizards would be his first task tomorrow.

Wiping the sweat from his brow, Otto released the ether. It never ceased to amaze him how a seemingly simple task could exhaust him more than launching half a dozen fireballs. Lord Karonin said it was because sustained effort drained a wizard more than a quick gather and release. Which made sense but didn't really help.

Otto returned the crystal ball to its hiding place and restored the illusion. What he really needed was a good night's sleep. Tomorrow's problems would be dealt with then.

The trudge from the basement to the second floor felt like miles. He considered a light dinner and immediately dismissed the idea. He felt too tired to even consider food. As he turned toward his room, a shrill wail filled the air. Clenching his teeth, Otto turned toward Annamaria's suite.

In the hall outside, Mimi was holding the baby and pacing, trying to silence her. She spotted Otto approaching and winced.

"Apologies, Lord Shenk. The little one is fussy tonight."

"Why is the child not with her mother?"

"She's a bit under the weather and didn't want Abby to catch her cold."

"Abby, that's the name she settled on?"

"Do you like it?" Mimi asked, a bright smile lighting her face.

Otto couldn't have cared less what Annamaria named her brat. Abby was as good a name as any. "It's fine. Why don't you take her into one of the guest rooms? That would muffle the sound some."

"I don't think Miss would—"

"It wasn't really a question, more of an order."

"Ah, right you are, my lord." Mimi made a face at the baby. "Come on, we're going for a walk."

"One moment." Otto walked closer and looked down at the small round face peeking out of the mass of blankets wrapping her.

He conjured invisible ethereal lights right in front of the baby. No reaction. Probably still too young to be able to see anything, assuming the baby had wizard potential. Otto had been five before he ever caught a glimpse of the ether. It was unreasonable of him to assume Abby would be different.

"Take her away."

Otto turned back to his room. Yet another disappointment. He shouldn't be surprised. Nothing to do with Annamaria had failed to disappoint him since he met her.

Otto emerged from the Straken portal along with three wagons of building materials. While they had plenty of timber in Straken, it was easier to process it at mills in Garenland and bring the planks back finished. Otto didn't really care. All that mattered was the fortifications surrounding the portal were coming together quickly. Three watchtowers were up and a fourth was proceeding quickly. Walls should be rising in a few days.

Nodding to himself, he went looking for Sergeant Hans. The magical armor would be key to quickly breaking through Tharanault's defenses. As he strode through the quiet streets, he got an occasional nod from the legionnaires going about their business or an angry glare from the locals. He ignored both. As soon as the weather turned warmer, the locals would be driven out and Marduke would become a garrison city inhabited only by people from Garenland.

At least locating the enchanted armor was simple. After the portal, they were the most powerful magical items in the area. They practically glowed in the ether. Hans and the guys sat around a fire cooking breakfast, the armor kneeling behind them. As soon as they spotted Otto approaching, they leapt to their feet and saluted.

Hans said, "Lord Shenk. Is all well?"

"No. You all will be coming with me. Tharanault knows we're coming and has set up an ambush. You'll be breaking through it."

The men looked at each other and smiled.

"Not to complain, my lord, but we've gotten plenty sick of carrying and lifting eight hours a day." Hans scowled as he glanced back at his armor. "I don't figure war machines were meant to be used to speed labor."

"That's as good a use for them as any. But right now I need them for their primary purpose, killing people and smashing fortifications. Once I collect the rest of the forces I need, we'll be marching on Tharanault directly. Finish your breakfast and get ready. I shouldn't be over an hour."

"Don't forget to show him, Sergeant," one of the men said.

"Show me what?" Otto asked.

"You're going to love this." Hans grinned. "The warehouse isn't far if you have time."

Otto wasn't on an especially tight timetable and Hans wasn't the sort to waste his time. "Lead on."

Three blocks later Hans pulled open the heavy front door of a warehouse marked with the dragon emblem of Straken. Inside it was dark, but Otto could make out the shapes of half a dozen wagons loaded with gray stone.

He frowned. Maybe Hans would waste his time.

"Do you know what this is?" Hans asked.

"Stone?"

"Ore. Six full wagonloads of unrefined mithril ore. They've been saving it up rather than trade with Garenland."

Otto's eyes widened. That was more mithril than he'd ever seen in one place outside of a portal. "How long have they been storing it?"

"Years. Just think what you could do with this much wealth."

Otto was already doing exactly that and he forced himself to stop. It was a rich find, but they had other priorities right now. "We'll be claiming this for the Crown. Did you find it?"

"No, my lord. The general ordered teams to canvas the city and see what we had for materials. One of them found it."

"They did well whoever it was." Otto put the image of heaps

of silvery bars out of his mind. "Let's get back. I still have soldiers to collect."

They stepped back outside and Hans closed the door. They hadn't taken a step when a voice from behind called out, "Lord Shenk. I got word that you had arrived with another load of building supplies. Excellent timing. We were getting low."

Otto turned to find General Varchi and twenty of his personal guards approaching from the direction of Castle Marduke. The general looked fit and well rested, his uniform crisp and freshly laundered.

"General. You were my next stop," Otto said. "I'll be taking Hans and his squad, forty wizards, and the Third Legion to pacify Thara City. If you could have them meet me at the portal, that would speed things up considerably."

"No, I'm afraid that won't do at all. I can't spare the men or the magical armor. It would slow the repairs and construction too much."

Otto cocked his head. He'd thought they had the chain of command sorted out. Maybe being promoted to provincial governor had gone to the general's head.

He'd straighten that out presently. "Ah, I see you've misunderstood. I'm not asking your permission. I'm informing you that I'm taking them. Your assistance would be helpful, but your consent is not required. I assumed you understood which of us is in charge, but clearly it's slipped your mind. You can speak to your men and explain what's going on or I can, but either way, we're marching in an hour."

Otto turned and walked away with Hans at his heels.

"I don't think you made a friend," Hans said.

"That wasn't my goal. The good general needs to remember those men don't serve him, they serve Garenland. If I need a legion of the Northern Army in Tharanault, then by heaven that's where they're going."

CHAPTER 32

Despite his protests, General Varchi had the Third Legion ready to march with time to spare. Nine thousand men were gathered in the plaza, forcing construction on the fort to halt. Otto had spoken to the wizards himself and they were eager to fight. Or more likely they were like Hans and eager to do anything besides construction work. If their luck held, they wouldn't regret that.

The plan was simple enough and hopefully it would be effective. Hans and his squad would take the lead position in their magical armor with the wizards directly behind protecting them from incoming magic. The rest of the soldiers would follow after a brief delay.

Otto took out the control rod and activated the portal. The armor clanked through. Otto and the wizards slipped in right behind them.

The lights and streaks of ether filled his vision for a moment and then he was through.

Screams and explosions filled the air.

Otto didn't even think.

He jumped behind Hans and formed a bubble of ether around his armor.

An instant later an enemy spell shattered on the barrier. On either side, the other wizards were defending as best they could.

Once in a while, one of them would fling a counter spell that exploded amidst the enemy forces.

Arrows clattered off Hans's armor, doing no more damage than the wind.

A lightning bolt hammered into his barrier. Otto traced it back to the caster and fried him with a blast of his own.

When the enchanted armor struck a section of crude fortification, in this case what appeared to be a pair of wagons nailed together, the crash of breaking wood was thunderous. Their massive gauntlets grabbed the wagons and hurled them at fleeing soldiers.

The enemy wizards soon stopped their bombardment as well. Otto couldn't see much from behind Hans's leg, but at least a few wizards appeared to be surrendering. Hopefully all of them would. He hated killing wizards. They should be on the same side after all.

Behind him, the rhythmic stomping of thousands of boots heralded the arrival of the Third Legion. They faced little resistance now that the initial assault had broken the enemy position.

Per their orders, the wizards fell back and joined up with the legion which was quickly breaking up into smaller groups suitable for fighting in the tight confines of the city. The whole process took only minutes and then they were fanning out, leaving Otto and the enchanted armor alone in the plaza.

"What now, my lord?" Hans asked.

"Now I switch the portal target to Garenland and bring the

portal guard through to consolidate control of the plaza. Then the six of us will head to the castle to say hello to King Liatos."

"Do you think he'll be there?"

Otto shrugged. He'd only met the king once, briefly, at the gathering last summer and they hadn't even spoken directly. If the king was brave, he'd certainly be waiting. If he was smart, he would have abandoned the city as soon as he realized Garenland's forces were likely to show up. Though where he would abandon it in favor of was an open question. Unlike Rolan, the people here weren't horsemen and didn't have a history as nomads. Living off the land in rough country wouldn't be easy.

Otto used the control rod to adjust the portal and a moment later the first members of the portal guard appeared. When all fifteen hundred soldiers had arrived, he switched the portal off.

"You know what to do, Commander," Otto said.

The unit commander saluted, started barking commands, and getting his men into position. Out in the city, fires had flared. The legion had orders not to search house to house. Instead they were to torch any building from which an enemy attack originated. It was a brutal tactic that would be a death sentence to any civilians hiding inside, but that was the enemy's fault not theirs.

Putting everything else out of his mind, Otto lifted himself on Hans's shoulder with an ether platform. His defensive spells settled into place, protecting both himself and the armor.

He tapped Hans's helmet. "Let's go."

They set out at a quick, bone-rattling walk. The armor's long strides ate up the distance despite the relatively slow pace. Otto would remind himself of this if he ever felt like complaining about a wagon ride.

His gaze flicked from side to side, seeking any potential threat. An arrow skipped off his shield and Otto traced it back to an archer on a nearby rooftop.

A lightning bolt ended the threat.

Aside from that one attacker, the journey to the castle went off without a hitch. Just outside of arrow range Hans stopped and asked, "What now?"

Otto studied the outer wall. Archers scrambled around, hurrying to gather above the main gate. More soldiers on foot, most of them armed with spears, formed up beyond the main gate. There were no wizards visible which didn't surprise him. You wouldn't want anyone compelled to fight guarding your final fortress.

"I'll handle the archers," Otto said. "You break down the gate and wipe out the guards. Set me down."

He rode to the ground in Hans's gauntlet and gathered the ether to him. There were twenty archers visible. Otto sent a thread to each of them, wrapping it around their bows before touching their chests. An instant later, white-hot flames streaked out, destroying their weapons and setting their uniforms on fire.

The archers dropped their ruined weapons and flailed around, trying to put out the flames.

Hans didn't need an order. The five suits of magical armor stomped straight toward the main gate. A few hard kicks smashed the portcullis. Unstoppable gauntlets crushed the guard house to pieces sending chunks of stone flying at the gathered soldiers. Using the magical armor sometimes seemed unfair, but in war the only rule was to win.

Some broke and ran, but most held fast, the tips of their spears trembling.

Hans and the others drew their swords and quickly swept

aside those foolish enough to stand and fight. Otto picked his way through the rubble to join them in the courtyard. No further threats presented themselves.

"I'm going to have a look around," Otto said. "Be on your guard."

The men shifted to form a circle around him. Otto closed his eyes and sent his vision into the castle. Just as he feared, guards were already gathering just beyond the closed door. He flew down the halls and past scrambling servants and running soldiers.

A few minutes of searching brought Otto to a war room, complete with a map of Thara City and miniature figures representing the defenders and attackers. The king and what Otto assumed were his generals stood around it. He added another thread for his hearing and listened in.

"Our spotters say they already broke through the first defensive line," one of the generals said. "That giant armor smashed our barricades in seconds."

"They refuse to enter any buildings and engage our fighters," another said. "Instead, their wizards simply burn the building down with everyone in it."

"And what of our wizards?" the king asked.

"Dead or surrendered," the first man said. "We knew they weren't going to hold if this became a real fight. Threats might have gotten them to show up, but when their minders broke and ran, they gave up."

The king grumbled something Otto couldn't quite make out.

A messenger burst into the room. "Majesty, the front gate has fallen."

King Liatos leapt to his feet. "What!?"

"The giant armor broke through and slaughtered the defenders. We're preparing to defend the keep, but..."

The king's fierce expression sagged. He looked from one general to the other. "Is there anything we can do to stop them?"

Otto added a third thread and said, "You can surrender."

Everyone looked around for the source of his voice.

"I'm speaking to you via magic. I have no desire for further loss of life. Order your soldiers here and throughout the country to turn in their weapons and no one else needs to die. Tharanault can continue on largely as you always have just under Garenland law. A governor will be appointed to oversee the affairs of the kingdom."

"And where does that leave me?" the king snarled.

"Still alive to enjoy a quiet retirement. You have five minutes to decide. Failure to surrender will result in the destruction of the castle with you and everyone else inside."

Otto released the thread for his voice so they wouldn't hear any sounds he might accidentally make. He really hoped the king would make the correct choice. While killing didn't bother Otto, he was getting thoroughly tired of it.

"You heard the wizard," King Liatos said. "What do you think?"

Both generals hesitated before answering. Otto didn't blame them. There was really no good option for them and he doubted either of them wanted to die today. Most generals he'd met preferred younger, more expendable men do that for them.

"I think you should accept the wizard's offer," the right-hand general said. "This isn't a battle we can win and don't forget your daughter is upstairs."

The king winced and nodded before turning to the second man. "Do you agree?"

"Reluctantly, Majesty. Garenland has overreached badly. In time they will fall and we can resume our rightful place as one of the leading nations. We can't do that if your bloodline dies here."

"So be it. Wizard, if you're there, I accept your terms."

Otto restored his voice. "Excellent. Have everyone come outside without weapons. And I mean not even a dagger. If I see a single weapon you all die. Once that's done, you will send orders to your soldiers still fighting in the city to surrender."

"Understood. We'll be out shortly."

Otto returned to silence but kept watching. He had no intention of being taken by surprise. Liatos did exactly as he was told, ordering everyone to disarm and head for the front gate. When they were nearly ready to come outside, Otto let all his threads fade.

"They're coming out, Hans, be on your guard but don't attack."

"As you command, my lord."

Otto shifted so he was standing in front of the armor.

A moment later the main gate opened and a line of people emerged with the king in the lead, a girl around Otto's age at his side. Liatos looked much less intimidating than when Otto saw him in Markane. Losing your kingdom could do that to a man.

Otto stepped forward. "You made the wise decision. Rest assured your people will not suffer under Garenland's rule. We desire only the best for all those living under our laws."

"Yes, of course you do. I've dispatched runners to those still resisting. When can my daughter and I leave for our country estate?"

"I fear you've misunderstood," Otto said. "When I said you could retire, I didn't mean in Tharanault. Having you here would do nothing but undermine the authority of the new governor. You and your lovely daughter will be coming to Garenland. There's a perfectly nice villa in Garen where you can settle down in comfort. Of course, how much comfort you'll receive is directly related to how well behaved your former subjects are."

"I see. You might be young, but you're not stupid. Wolfric chose his first councilor wisely. My most trusted generals will do all they can to help your governor."

Both generals saluted.

Otto smiled and nodded. The job wasn't finished, but unlike Rolan, he felt confident that Tharanault would soon be properly under Garenland's rule. Now he needed to get back and speak to Wolfric. The first stage was complete. It was time to move on to tying up loose ends.

CHAPTER 33

After nearly a week tromping around in the snow, Axel and his scouts descended from the northern mountains and turned toward Marduke. They'd found the prince's camp exactly where the steward said they would and also like he said, the camp was empty. A trail led east, but they lost it after a day of tracking. If he was being honest, Axel wasn't too disappointed. Getting ambushed by a few hundred rangers in unfamiliar territory was a good way to end up dead.

As they approached the city walls Cobb asked, "What do you think he's up to?"

"The prince? He was traveling dead east. The only thing of any interest, at least that we know of, are the mines. I assume General Varchi has sent a force to secure them. I doubt Prince Uther has enough men to drive them out, but he might lay siege, try and starve them out."

Cobb snorted. "I doubt he has that kind of supplies, not after the winter Straken had."

Axel nodded. Cobb made a good point. Whatever the

prince had planned, there was nothing Axel could do about it now. He needed to let General Varchi know what they found. After that it would be up to him to decide their next move.

"Looks like work has slowed on the main gate," Axel said. "I don't see the enchanted armor either."

A few of the soldiers inside nodded as he passed and turned toward Castle Marduke. The general had wasted no time moving in. He might have been better than most leaders, but he still liked his comforts.

The streets seemed quieter than usual. Where was everyone? The silence was unnerving.

At the castle gate, the guards on duty waved them through. Inside Axel headed for the former throne room. The general was using it as a command center and that was where Axel found him, scowling at a map and muttering to himself.

"Sir?"

General Varchi looked up. "Commander Shenk. Your prisoners arrived two days ago but had limited information to share. Did you locate the prince?"

"No, sir. We lost their trail and deemed it prudent to return rather than risk an ambush. As best I can tell they were headed toward the mines."

"Of course they are. There's nothing else worth a damn in this heaven-forsaken country. If they show up, my garrison will deal with them. I sent a thousand men plus wizards to secure the area."

"The city seems quiet, sir."

"Yes, thanks to you brother. He took my magical armor, half the wizards, and the Third Legion. How does he expect me to complete my work without the resources I need?"

Axel had no answer and doubted Otto cared. If his little brother decided he had more need of the men and material, he wouldn't hesitate to take them. He was much like Father in that respect. And since he had the king's ear, there was nothing the general could do about it.

"Orders, sir?"

"Take a couple days to rest. Eventually I'll want you to check out the mines and see what else we need to do to secure them. I doubt much will happen until the ground thaws and mud season is over."

Axel saluted and led his scouts out of the room. A rest would be welcome, but he doubted the peace would hold, not until Prince Uther was dead or in a cell beside his father.

※

After his meeting with Queen Philippa and the encounter with King Wolfric and his advisor, Eddred departed for home. The winds were against them and the trip took nearly a week. He spent those days pacing and thinking in his cabin. What he'd learned combined with Otto Shenk's comment before he left put him in a difficult position. While Eddred hated seeing what was happening to the other kingdoms, it really wasn't Markane's problem. They had always tried to remain neutral.

Granted he had never considered that when Garenland was kicked out of the Portal Compact, matters would end up like this. And even if he had, what could they have done about it? Lord Valtan could have refused to deactivate Garenland's portal, but that would make the idea that the nations ruled themselves a lie. The vote had been held and everyone agreed on the course of action. That the results hadn't been what anyone expected was hardly Markane's fault.

"Approaching port, Majesty!" the lookout called.

Eddred sighed. In the end he would do what he always did, let Valtan decide and carry out his wishes. Thoughts and talking to the contrary, the Arcane Lord ruled Markane in all but name. Eddred understood that and accepted it, just as his forbearers had. When confronted with overwhelming might, there was no other option really. As Queen Philippa learned the hard way.

Up on deck, Eddred watched the ship sail smoothly into the harbor and tie off at the royal berth. The docks had gotten busier over the past few weeks as without the portal, they were forced to transport goods by ship. This was less of a hardship for the skilled sailors of the island than it would have been for a landlocked country like Garenland.

When the final rope was tied off, Eddred hurried down the gangplank. He didn't bother with guards or a carriage. From the docks, it was only a ten-minute walk to Castle Markane. No doubt Lord Valtan was in his tower doing whatever immortal wizards did in their spare time.

The guards saluted as he passed through the entrance. Just inside, one of the palace runners, a boy of about twelve, stood waiting. He bowed and said, "Lord Valtan requests you join him as soon as possible in the library."

Eddred frowned. Valtan never spent time in the palace library. It was so vastly inferior to the one in his tower there was no point. He must have simply chosen the place to wait for Eddred's return. And if he was waiting, that meant trouble.

"Thank you," Eddred said and immediately turned toward the library. It was in the rear of the castle, away from the hustle and bustle of court. Not that the Markane court was all that busy, but it used to be. Eddred hated that part of his job. He just sat on his throne and listened to everyone argue while they ignored him.

He reached the library door and pushed it open. Inside it was dark despite the bright sunlight outside. Valtan must have done something to the windows to dim everything. Eddred found the Arcane Lord seated in one of the overstuffed leather chairs, his head in his hands.

Valtan looked up as Eddred approached. His face was pale and his eyes bloodshot. Eddred had never seen him in such poor shape.

"What news?" Valtan asked.

"Garenland is seizing control of the other nations. In exchange for returning the use of their portals, they're making the rulers into governors and imposing Garenland's laws, including full citizenship of wizards. They're also building fortifications around the portals themselves."

Valtan nodded. "Smart. Their wizard knows we need direct access to the portals to restore my control over them."

"Forgive me for asking this, Lord Valtan, but are you well?"

"No. Activating the portals takes a lot out of me; that's why I designed a specific pattern of activation and rest. Two days ago, someone activated the Straken portal, connected it to Tharanault, then a few minutes later switched the connection to Garenland. When the portals were finally shut down, I nearly fainted."

"Is your life in danger?"

"Of course not. I'm immortal. But immortal doesn't mean free from pain and weakness. It's hard to function when you never know if someone's going to drain a large portion of your energy. I need to regain control of the portals."

"I spoke with Otto Shenk, Wolfric's chief advisor and a wizard of considerable power. I suspect he is the architect of your difficulties. He said that as long as Markane remained neutral, Garenland wouldn't trouble us. Perhaps we might negotiate an agreement with regards to a schedule for the portals."

"No. Garenland must be stopped and control restored to me. We will help their enemies defeat them. Neutrality may have served us in the past, but it will not serve here. Tell the merchants they can sell to Garenland's enemies: food, weapons, whatever they need. If they can't afford to pay, give them the supplies."

"And our soldiers?" Eddred asked. "We have few enough as it is."

"Our land forces are too small to be of use, but we can offer sea transportation if they need it. This war must be won, no matter what."

Eddred kept his face calm, but inside his mind raced. Everything about what Valtan suggested struck him as a bad idea. But even so, what choice did he have but to obey?

"As you wish, Lord Valtan. I will begin making arrangements at once."

Otto and Wolfric sat alone in the king's—make that the emperor's—private dining room. The servants had just finished clearing away the dishes and setting out glasses of fine port wine. Otto took a sip and sighed. How long had it been since he took the time to relax and enjoy a meal? He couldn't say, but it felt good to do so now.

The other nations, now little more than Garenland provinces, were largely calm. That wouldn't last of course, especially in Straken and Rolan.

But for now, Otto was content to take a few days to

recover. He'd used so much magic over the past few weeks, his body ached nearly as badly as his head.

Wolfric raised his glass and said, "To your success, my friend. None of this would have happened without your tireless efforts."

Otto smiled, raised his own glass, and took another sip. "Many people played a part, but I appreciate your words. A great deal remains to be done, but I can see it now. The empire we dreamed of seems like a reality. A few fires remain to be stomped out of course, but the heavy lifting is done. You now rule the entire continent of Etheria."

Wolfric drained his glass. "Etheria, that's a name you seldom hear anymore. Did you ever wonder why?"

"I assumed it was because most people think of their own country as being a distinct thing rather than a small part of something bigger. Besides, Lord Karonin isn't the most beloved figure in the world and she was the one that named the continent and her empire that. Do you think we should change it?"

"I thought the Garenland Empire had a nice ring to it."

Otto laughed. "It does indeed. In time we can hope that the rest of the people develop similarly warm feelings."

Wolfric leaned forward. "Do you think they ever will? One day, will a child born in Straken think of his or herself not as a citizen of Straken but as a citizen of the empire?"

"Maybe not in Straken."

They both laughed again.

"So what's next for you?" Wolfric asked.

"That depends on what happens out in the empire. My biggest priority is hunting down Villares in Rolan. As long as he's out there causing trouble, we won't know real peace on the southern border. Once I've fully recovered, I mean to lead the search. Hopefully Axel can deal with Prince Uther and General Varchi can get the mines producing. Then we need to figure out the new system of trade.

Wolfric raised his hands in surrender. "And here I thought you said the heavy lifting was done. If I didn't know better, I'd say it was only beginning."

Wolfric didn't know how right he was. Establishing the empire was only the first step up the mountain that was becoming an Arcane Lord. Difficult as the climb was, Otto had no intention of stopping until he reached the top.

AUTHOR NOTE

Hello everyone and thank you so much for checking out The Portal Thieves. This was a fun book for me since I got to spend a little time with some different characters. My favorite was Holt. I really gave the poor guy a tough assignment.

But now the war is over and the loose ends need to be snipped. That's what book 4, The Master of Magic is all about. I hope you'll join me.

Thanks for reading,

James

ALSO BY JAMES E WISHER

The Portal Wars Saga
The Hidden Tower
The Great Northern War
The Portal Thieves
The Master of Magic

The Dragonspire Chronicles
The Black Egg
The Mysterious Coin
The Dragons' Graveyard
The Slave War
The Sunken Tower
The Dragon Empress
The Dragonspire Chronicles Omnibus Vol. 1
The Dragonspire Chronicles Omnibus Vol. 2
The Complete Dragonspire Chronicles Omnibus

Soul Force Saga
Disciples of the Horned One Trilogy:
Darkness Rising
Raging Sea and Trembling Earth
Harvest of Souls
Disciples of the Horned One Omnibus

Chains of the Fallen Arc:
Dreaming in the Dark
On Blackened Wings
Chains of the Fallen Omnibus

The Aegis of Merlin:
The Impossible Wizard
The Awakening
The Chimera Jar
The Raven's Shadow
Escape From the Dragon Czar
Wrath of the Dragon Czar
The Four Nations Tournament
Death Incarnate
Aegis of Merlin Omnibus Vol 1.
Aegis of Merlin Omnibus Vol 2.

Other Fantasy Novels:
The Squire
Death and Honor Omnibus

The Rogue Star Series:
Children of Darkness
Children of the Void
Children of Junk
Rogue Star Omnibus Vol. 1
Children of the Black Ship

ABOUT THE AUTHOR

James E. Wisher is a writer of science fiction and fantasy novels. He's been writing since high school and reading everything he could get his hands on for as long as he can remember.

To learn more:
www.jamesewisher.com
james@jamesewisher.com

CPSIA information can be obtained
at www.ICGtesting.com
Printed in the USA
BVHW032307181221
624452BV00016B/212

9 781945 763779